DEATH OF A NEIGHBORHOOD SCROOGE

"I almost forgot," Missy said, as I headed for the door, "Scotty mentioned something at breakfast about wanting to talk to you about the script. Would you mind popping in his office on your way out?"

I couldn't think of anything worse, except staying one more minute watching Prozac's lovefest with Missy.

I headed downstairs, prepared to tell Scotty I was not about to do a stitch of work. Not today. Not on Christmas.

As it turned out, I would not have to work with Scotty that day. Or any other day for that matter. Because when I stepped in his office the first thing I saw was Scotty Parker slumped over his desk, bashed in the head with Aunt Harriet's frozen Yule log . . .

Books by Laura Levine

THIS PEN FOR HIRE

LAST WRITES

KILLER BLONDE

SHOES TO DIE FOR

THE PMS MURDER

DEATH BY PANTYHOSE

CANDY CANE MURDER

KILLING BRIDEZILLA

KILLER CRUISE

DEATH OF A TROPHY WIFE

GINGERBREAD COOKIE MURDER

PAMPERED TO DEATH

DEATH OF A NEIGHBORHOOD WITCH

KILLING CUPID

DEATH BY TIARA

MURDER HAS NINE LIVES

DEATH OF A BACHELORETTE

DEATH OF A NEIGHBORHOOD SCROOGE

Published by Kensington Publishing Corporation

A Jaine Austen Mystery

DEATH OF A NEIGHBORHOOD SCROOGE

LAURA LEVINE

KENSINGTON BOOKS
www.kensingtonbooks.com

KENSINGTON BOOKS are published by

Kensington Publishing Corp.
119 West 40th Street
New York, NY 10018

All Kensington titles, imprints, and distributed lines are available at special quantity discounts for bulk purchases for sales promotion, premiums, fund-raising, educational, or institutional use. Special book excerpts or customized printings can also be created to fit specific needs. For details, write or phone the office of the Kensington Special Sales Manager: Attn. Special Sales Department. Kensington Publishing Corp., 119 West 40th Street, New York, NY 10018. Phone: 1-800-221-2647.

Kensington and the K logo Reg. U.S. Pat. & TM Off.

ISBN-13: 978-1-4967-0850-2
ISBN-10: 1-4967-0850-4
First Kensington Hardcover Edition: October 2018
First Kensington Mass Market Edition: October 2019

ISBN-13: 978-1-4967-0851-9 (ebook)
ISBN-10: 1-4967-0851-2 (ebook)

10 9 8 7 6 5 4 3 2 1

Printed in the United States of America

For my readers,
XOXO

ACKNOWLEDGMENTS

As always, a big shout out to my editor extraordinaire, John Scognamiglio, for his unwavering faith in me and Jaine—and for his never-ending supply of terrific story ideas.

And kudos to my rock of an agent, Evan Marshall, for always being there for me with his guidance and support.

Thanks to Hiro Kimura, who so brilliantly brings Prozac to life on my book covers each year. To Lou Malcangi for another super dust jacket design. And to the rest of the gang at Kensington who keep Jaine and Prozac coming back for murder and minced mackerel guts.

Special thanks to comedy maven Frank Mula, for his treasured friendship, jokes, pretzels, and Dewar's on the rocks. To Mara and Lisa Lideks, authors of the very funny Forrest Sisters mysteries. And to Vic at Big Security for his words of wisdom about video security systems.

To Joanne Fluke, author of the bestselling Hannah Swensen mysteries, for her many kindnesses (not to mention a cover blurb to die for). To John Fluke, product placement guru at Placed for Success. And to the resilient Mark Baker, who's been there from the beginning.

Major hugs to my family and friends—both old and new—for your much-appreciated love and encouragement.

And finally, a heartfelt thank you to all my readers and Facebook friends. You're the best!

Prologue

I blame Connie Van Hooten for everything. If she hadn't packed up her staff and gone yachting in the Mediterranean, I would've never spent that cursed Christmas as a murder suspect.

At first, it had all seemed like a dream come true.

I remember the exact moment my neighbor, Lance Venable, came rushing into my apartment with the good news.

"Guess what we're going to be doing this holiday season?" he said, excitement oozing from every pore.

"Binge watching *30 Rock*? That was my plan."

"No! We're going to be spending two glorious weeks in Bel Air. One of my customers at Neiman's has hired us to house-sit her fabulous home over the holidays!"

The Neiman's to which Lance was referring was, of course, the famed department store, where

Lance works as a shoe salesman, fondling the toot-sies of the rich and famous.

"Not only that," Lance was babbling, "Connie's paying us each a thousand bucks!"

Good news indeed. Not only would we get to stay at a ritzy estate in Bel Air, we'd be getting paid for the privilege—money that would come in espe-cially handy during the holiday season when my writing assignments usually dry up like a snow cone in the Sahara.

"Lance, that's wonderful!"

"You should see the place. It's got so many valu-ables, it's practically a museum!"

Lance went on to explain that because of the museum-quality trinkets in her mansion, Connie Van Hooten had a strict No Pets policy. Instead, that generous woman had offered to put up my cat, Prozac, along with Lance's adorable pooch, Mamie, at the Fur Seasons Pet Hotel, a five-star getaway for L.A.'s most pampered furballs.

Like I said, it all seemed like a dream come true.

Except for one furry fly in the ointment.

My cat, Prozac.

She knew something was afoot the minute she saw me start to pack.

In spite of the gobs of praise I'd been heaping on the Fur Seasons, yakking about their luxurious accommodations, I could tell Prozac was not happy about her upcoming stay. Tiny little clues. Like the way she hissed whenever I went near my suitcase. Or the damp surprises I was finding in my slippers in the morning. But I kept telling myself that once she got settled in her new digs, she'd be fine.

Then came the day of our departure.

Lance had already dropped off Mamie at the pet hotel and was en route to Casa Van Hooten. I, however, was running late, due to a tiny temper tantrum from my beloved kitty as I tried to get her into her cat carrier.

Trust me. Daniel had an easier time in the lions' den.

At last I'd managed to get her in the carrier and set off for the hotel, Prozac wailing nonstop every minute of the way.

Once inside the Fur Seasons—a bubblegum pink building in one of the trendier sections of West Hollywood—Prozac grudgingly settled down in my arms, glaring at Kathy, the perky concierge who was showing us around the joint.

"Here's our pet spa," Kathy said, as we passed a lavender-scented retreat filled with pampered pets on grooming tables, paying more for their haircuts than I do.

"And our media center," she said, leading us into a room with a theater-sized screen and a showroom's worth of overstuffed armchairs.

Pets were sprawled on the chairs, some snoozing, some playing with squeaky toys, others gazing at a nature video on the screen, no doubt dreaming of their future directorial debuts.

"And finally," Kathy said, leading us down a pristine hallway, "here's Prozac's bedroom."

She pointed to a cute little haven of a room, its

twin bed covered in a downy duvet, with matching drapes and sixty-inch flat-screen TV.

"So what do you think?" Kathy asked.

"I think I want that TV," I said.

Nestled in my arms, Prozac gave a disdainful sniff.

Smells like Cat Chow and Mr. Clean to me.

"I'm sure your darling Prozac will adore it here," Kathy gushed. "Won't you, Pwozie-Wozie?"

A menacing hiss from Prozac.

You call me Pwozie-Wozie one more time, lady, and your pinkie is history.

Well, this was it. Time to say good-bye.

Giving her one last hug, I plopped Prozac on her downy bed.

And suddenly I felt a stab of remorse. Was I doing the right thing? After all, this would be our first Christmas apart. I tried to tell myself Prozac wouldn't know Christmas from any other day in the year, but that cat can sniff out any holiday that involves presents or drumsticks.

No, I assured myself, Prozac would be fine. Just fine. This place was the epitome of deluxe. Heck, I'd be happy to stay there if they had Chinese food and Chunky Monkey.

"Bye, darling. I promise I'll stop by on Christmas Day and bring you a great big present."

She shot me one of her pitiful Little Orphan Annie looks.

Go ahead. Leave me all alone in the hands of perfect strangers. Break my heart. Desert me in my hour of need— Hey, do I smell salmon?

Indeed, she did.

For at that moment a Fur Seasons attendant came bustling into the room with a bowl of char-broiled salmon.

"Bye, Pro!" I called out, as she swan dived into the stuff.

She glanced up at me vacantly.

Yeah, right. Whatever.

So much for broken hearts.

Chapter 1

"What a palace!" I said, surveying Connie Van Hooten's hangar-sized living room, with its limestone fireplace, triple crown moldings, and cathedral-quality stained glass windows.

"Isn't it fab?" Lance gushed. "And check this out!"

He gestured to a wall-length étagère filled with Lalique crystal, Fabergé eggs, and other priceless doodads.

"Good Lord. It's like I'm standing in a branch of the Louvre."

"This vase," Lance said, picking up a blue and white porcelain beauty, "is Ming Dynasty. Fourteen grand."

"Holy cow!" I cried. "No wonder Mrs. Van Hooten didn't want any pets around."

I shuddered to think what havoc Prozac would have wreaked on that étagère.

"I'm thinking we'll put up a Christmas tree right here," Lance said, pointing to a space between the limestone fireplace and what looked like a Rodin sculpture.

"We can't put up a tree, Lance. What if we spill pine needles on the rug?"

I pointed to the heirloom Persian rug beneath our feet.

"Don't be silly," Lance said. "We'll put a lining under the tree and be super careful. You know how meticulous I am."

He was right about that.

From his headful of perfectly groomed blond curls down to his spotless white Reeboks, Lance was the poster boy for meticulous. I mean, this was a guy who ironed his undies.

"I brought all my favorite Christmas ornaments," he was saying, "and I found a fabulous article in *Martha Stewart Living* about ornaments we can make by hand. Pine cone Santas. Acorn garlands. Pipe cleaner elves. Won't that be fun?"

Oh, groan. There's nothing more exhausting than Lance in the throes of one of his creative jags.

"C'mon, let me show you to your room," he said, grabbing my suitcase and leading me up a flight of stairs straight out of *Downton Abbey*. I followed him up the steps, desperately trying to figure a way to get out of any future arts and crafts projects.

Upstairs, he ushered me down a hallway past a massive master suite to my room.

"Voila!" he said, showing me inside. "I gave you the room with a view of the garden."

I looked out the window at "the garden," a patch

of green the size of a soccer field. Off in the distance, I could make out a pool and tennis courts.

"Isn't it stunning?" Lance asked, gesturing around the room.

Indeed it was: sumptuous down bedding, quilted silk headboard, thick-as-a-cloud carpeting, all done up in pale peach and dotted with antique furniture.

"That chair over there," Lance said, pointing to a delicately carved beauty, "is an authentic Queen Anne. And so is the matching dressing table."

I looked at the slender legs of the chair and thought how much Prozac would have loved using them as scratching posts.

Yes, it was all for the best that I'd brought Pro to the Fur Seasons.

And yet, I still couldn't help but feel a tad guilty about leaving her there.

True, she'd seemed perfectly content when I'd last seen her chowing down on her charbroiled salmon.

But what would happen tonight at bedtime? I suddenly pictured her all alone on her Fur Seasons bed, her big green eyes wide with fear. How would she ever drift off to sleep without my neck to nuzzle into?

How would I drift off to sleep, for that matter?

"Get your stuff unpacked," Lance said, "while I go downstairs to whip up a batch of hot mulled cider. Won't that be nice? Warming up with a glass of mulled cider on a nippy December day?"

"Lance, this is L.A. The Santa Anas are blowing in from the desert. It's eighty-one degrees."

"Oh, well. I'll just pump up the A/C and soon we'll have Jack Frost nipping at our noses!"

And off he dashed to run up Connie Van Hooten's electricity bill.

After stashing my things in my walk-in closet (bigger than my bedroom at home), I headed back downstairs, where Lance was waiting for me in the living room with the promised mulled cider.

"I just know this is going to be the most fantabulous Christmas ever!" Lance said, as we settled across from each other on two down-filled sofas flanking the fireplace.

"By the time our stay here is over, I'll forget that Justin ever existed. Yes, indeed," he said, sipping at his cider, "this is the perfect place to mend a broken heart."

"Lance, if I remember correctly, you and this Justin guy were dating for a grand total of three weeks."

"Yes, Jaine, but a lot of strong emotional ties can develop in three weeks, something you'd know if you'd had even a scrap of a love life of your own."

"Hey," I protested. "I've had my share of romance."

"A paltry dollop or two, but you've never experienced the depth of true love as I have," he sighed, plastering a soulful expression on his face, Romeo in Reeboks.

And he was off and running, yammering about his love affair gone awry.

As I often do when Lance goes rambling down romance lane, I quickly tuned out, my thoughts drifting back to Prozac, alone and lonely in her room at the Fur Seasons.

"Hey, what's with you?" Lance asked after a while, busting into my reverie. "You forgot the world revolves around me, me, me—and haven't been listening to a word I've said."

Okay, so he didn't say the part about the world revolving around him, but I bet my bottom Pop-Tart he was thinking it.

"I'm worried about Prozac," I confessed. "I'm afraid she's going to be miserable without me."

"Nonsense! I'm sure Pro has made a million kitty friends by now. If I know that cat, she's probably leading them in a conga line."

Lance continued to assure me that Prozac would be absolutely fine and ordered me to stop worrying. And somewhere in the middle of my second mulled cider, I did.

Lance was right. Prozac would survive perfectly well without me.

She was probably having the time of her life letting Lance's dog, Mamie, sniff her tush as she watched Animal Planet on her sixty-inch TV.

I was finally beginning to relax when the sonorous chimes of Mrs. Van H's doorbell filled the air.

"I'll get it," Lance said, springing up to answer the door.

"Jaine!" he called out after a few seconds. "It's for you."

I walked out into the grand foyer and saw the attendant from the Fur Seasons, the one who'd brought Prozac her charbroiled salmon, standing in the doorway holding Prozac's carrier.

Inside the cage, Pro was wailing like a banshee.

"I'm sorry, Ms. Austen," the attendant said, "but we cannot keep your pet any longer."

"Why on earth not?" Lance asked, as I scooped Pro out of the carrier and put an end to her wails.

"I'm afraid she attacked Kathy, our concierge."

"Oh, no!" I gasped.

"In fact, Kathy's in the emergency room right now, having surgery on her pinkie finger."

Lolling in my arms, not the least bit ashamed of what she'd done, Prozac gave a complacent thump of her tail.

I warned her not to call me Pwozie-Wozie.

Chapter 2

"**P**rozac, how could you?" I cried, after the Fur Seasons gal had gone.

The little devil looked up from where she was nestled in my arms.

It was easy. I just chomped down on her pinkie and took a bite.

"Well, we certainly can't keep Prozac here," I said, thinking of the Ming vase and the Persian carpet and the Queen Anne furniture. "She's bound to break, scratch, or tinkle on something."

In my arms, Prozac began to squirm.

Lemme go! I wanna see all the stuff I can break!

"Let's put her in the kitchen for now," Lance said. "She can't do much harm there."

I wasn't so sure about that, once I got a look at Mrs. Van H's stainless steel and marble-countered kitchen, eyeing the fine stemware in glass-fronted cabinets.

"We'd better give her something to eat," I said. "That should distract her for a while."

And indeed, in spite of the charbroiled salmon she'd recently scarfed down, Prozac dived into the dish of caviar Lance had unearthed from the Van Hooten pantry with Olympian gusto.

Leaving her inhaling fish eggs, we headed back out to the living room to figure out what to do next.

"I know!" Lance said. "We'll just keep her in the kitchen all the time."

"Forget it, Lance. Prozac's the Houdini of cats. She'll figure out a way to escape before we've even shut the door."

"Okay, then," Lance said. "We'll box up everything valuable in the house and stow it away."

"Are you kidding? Everything in this house is a museum piece. By the time we box it all up, it'll be time to go home. Look, there's no way out of it. I'm simply going to have to take Pro and go back to my apartment."

"But you can't!" Lance moaned. "Not now, with my heart smashed to tiny pieces. I simply can't bear the thought of spending Christmas alone."

He slumped down in the sofa, all traces of his holiday high leeched out of him.

"Maybe I can call the Fur Seasons and beg them to take Prozac back."

I realized there was exactly zero chance of this happening, but I reached for my cell anyway.

And just as I did, it rang.

I didn't recognize the name on my caller ID, but I answered it anyway, hoping it wasn't one of the army of robocallers who seem to be tailing me these days like a swarm of particularly pesky gnats.

"Hi!" A woman's voice came chirping over my speaker.

Oh, hell. I just knew it was going to be someone trying to sell me solar paneling.

"Is this Jaine Austen?" the chirpy woman asked.

"Yes," I replied warily, waiting for her sales spiel to begin.

"Do you have a cat name Prozac?"

Thanks heavens! No sales spiel. I was off the hook for solar paneling.

"Yes, I have a cat named Prozac."

"I got your name and number from her collar," the chirpy woman said. "The adorable little thing just wandered into our house from our terrace."

"See?" I whispered to Lance. "I told you she's a world-class escape artist." And then, to the chirpy woman, I said, "I'll come right over and pick her up."

When she gave me her address, I realized she was on the same street as Connie Van Hooten. I told her where I was staying, and she told me she was right next door.

"We're the big beige house, just south of Mrs. Van Hooten's."

After hanging up, I charged into the kitchen with Lance and sure enough, one of the windows was slightly ajar. Obviously, Prozac's means of escape.

"I'll go get her," I said, scurrying out of the house, down the front path and over to the house next door.

Like Mrs. Van Hooten's, it was a magnificent piece of architecture. But I could see from the patchy lawn, overgrown bushes, and the water stains on the exterior paint that the house had seen better days.

Heading up the front steps, I spotted a large plastic Rudolph reindeer, lying on a patch of fake snow, fake blood oozing from its head.

Wow. Nothing says "Bah! Humbug!" like a dead Rudolph on your front lawn.

Across the path on the other side of the lawn a menacing mechanical snowman glared at me with beady black eyes.

I rang the doorbell, trying not to stare at my creepy companions.

Seconds later, the door was opened by a leggy blond beauty in baby blue sweats, her lush mane of hair cascading like a waterfall, a Victoria's Secret model come to life.

In her arms, she held Prozac, who was gazing up at her worshipfully, nuzzling her neck, purring in delight.

"You must be Jaine!" the blonde exclaimed. "Are you staying with Connie for the holidays?"

"No, my friend Lance and I are house-sitting for Mrs. Van Hooten while she's yachting in the Mediterranean."

"Well, it's super to meet you. I'm Missy Parker. Excuse the gruesome Christmas decorations," she said, gesturing to Rudolph and the snowman. "My husband thinks they're funny. C'mon in and meet him."

She ushered me into a living room that had

many of the same spectacular features of Mrs. Van H's manse—triple molded ceilings, ornate fireplace, wide-planked hardwood floors.

But here the walls were dingy, riddled with settling cracks, dusty drapes hanging from unwashed windows. The only spot of color in the room was a portrait of a little boy in a sailor suit hung over the fireplace.

"Scotty, say hello to Jaine Austen."

I got my first glimpse of Scotty Parker as he sat in a cracked recliner—a middle-aged guy way older than his twentysomething wife—his eyes riveted on a bulky dinosaur of a TV, watching the Dow Jones ticker crawl across the bottom of the screen on CNBC.

When he finally tore himself away from the Industrial Average to look up at me, I was surprised to see—in spite of his burgeoning pot belly and thinning red hair—the freckled face of an impish teenager.

Think Huckleberry Finn after years of too much booze and not enough exercise.

"Jaine and her friend are house-sitting for Mrs. Van Hooten next door," Missy explained. "Connie's such a doll," she added, grinning at me.

"The woman's a royal bitch," Scotty snapped. "Had her face lifted so many times, her kneecaps are where her chin used to be."

"Oh, Scotty!" Missy said, rolling her eyes. "Don't be that way. He doesn't really mean it," she assured me.

"Yeah, I do," he grumbled.

"I'm surprised Connie's letting you keep a cat in

her house," Missy said, eager to change the subject. "She's so fussy about her collectibles."

"That's just it," I said. "Prozac was supposed to be staying at a pet hotel, but things didn't work out."

I shot Prozac a look of rebuke, but she was too busy rubbing up against Missy's cascading curls to notice.

"That's too bad," Missy said.

"I'm afraid I'm going to have to take Prozac and go back to my apartment. I can't possibly risk having her break something."

"And leave your friend to house-sit all alone?" Missy exclaimed. "What a pity."

Her silken brow wrinkled in dismay.

"I know! Why don't you have Prozac stay here! I've always wanted a kitty. And we don't have any valuables for her to break."

This spoken, I couldn't help but notice, with a tinge of regret.

And she sure wasn't lying about the paucity of valuables, I thought, eyeing the room full of mismatched furniture, decades old, each piece looking like it had been rescued from a second-rate thrift shop.

"I keep my valuables locked up," Scotty said. "Can't trust the help these days."

That last bit shouted at a tiny slip of a Hispanic maid walking by in the foyer, carrying a load of laundry.

Hearing Scotty's zinger, the maid stopped in her tracks just long enough to shoot him a death ray glare.

"So, how about it, Scotty?" Missy was saying,

scratching Prozac behind her ears. "Can Prozac stay with us?"

Scotty looked up, assessing me and Prozac, and from the disgruntled look on his freckled face, I was guessing he found us both wanting. Which is why I was so surprised when he shrugged and said, "Sure. Why not?"

"That's wonderful!" I said. "Thank you so much!"

"And why don't you bring your friend and stop by for dinner tonight?" he added.

Wow. I'd totally misjudged the guy. I had him down as a grouchypants extraordinaire, and here he was turning out to be a real sweetie.

"We'd love to," I said.

"Good," he said. "It's pot luck. You two bring the entrée. Dinner for six."

Whoa. An entrée for *six*? As they say on the Champs-Élysées, *quel chutzpah*!

But he was, after all, taking care of Prozac, and I figured dinner for six was the least I could do to repay him.

"Bye, honey," I said to Prozac as I turned to go. "I'll see you later."

Wrenching herself away from where she'd been nuzzling Missy's neck, Prozac gazed at me blankly.

And you are . . . ?

What can I say? Loyalty's not one of her strong points.

Missy walked me to the door, assuring me I could come visit Pro whenever I wanted.

And then, just as I was about to leave, Scotty shouted out, "Don't forget that entrée! Steaks would be great! Preferably filet mignon."

Filet mignon for six? He had to be kidding! No way was this guy a sweetie. On the contrary, I thought, as I made my way past dead Rudolph and the malevolent snowman.

Ebenezer Scrooge was alive and well and living in Bel Air.

YOU'VE GOT MAIL!

To: Jausten
From: Shoptillyoudrop
Subject: Busy as Bees!

Hi, darling!

Daddy and I have been as busy as bees getting ready for our Holiday Caribbean Cruise. As I probably already told you, a whole bunch of us Tampa Vista-ites are going. Just think how lovely it will be not to have fuss in the kitchen on Christmas Day, listening to Daddy and Uncle Ed arguing over how to carve the turkey! Instead, I'll be basking in the sun with one of those cute rum umbrella drinks! Not that Daddy and I will have much time for basking. There's so much to see and do. All those beautiful islands with magical names. Barbados. Antigua. Martinique! I can't wait to see them all. Especially Martinique. I wonder if that's where they invented the martini.

Did I tell you that darling Isabel Norton will be turning ninety-five on December 30th and that we're having a private party in one of the cruise lounges in her honor? I'm proud to say I was chosen to buy Isabel's gift and I picked out a gorgeous bracelet from the Home Shopping Club. Only $136.48 plus shipping and handling! Which was really a bargain, since it's a genuine diamonette, which is practically the same as diamond at a fraction of the cost!

Not only that, we're going to have our annual Secret Santa exchange on board the ship, too. I drew Ed Nivens from the grab bag, and got him the most adorable Christmas tie (just $24.95, and free shipping!) with tiny Santas all over it.

I only wish you were coming with us to share in the fun.

XOXO,
Mom

PS. I almost forgot! As an extra added attraction, our own Lydia Pinkus, president of the Tampa Vistas Homeowners Association, has been chosen to give a series of onboard lectures on "Christmas Celebrations Around the World." It should be fascinating. Lydia's such a captivating speaker!

**To: Jausten
From: DaddyO
Subject: Insufferable Gasbag**

Dearest Lambchop—

Your mom is in seventh heaven, getting ready for our Caribbean cruise. I haven't seen her this excited since our trip to Dollywood.

Did she tell you about the Secret Santa exchange? You'll never guess whose name I drew! That arrogant battle axe, Lydia Pinkus!! I sent away for the perfect gift: A pair of "Yakity Yak" gag false teeth. You know, the kind that clatter like castanets. It will be my not-so-subtle way of reminding her what an insufferable gasbag she is!

By the way, do not under any circumstances tell Mom about the false teeth. I told her I bought Lydia a potholder.

I can't believe it, but the Battle Axe has actually been hired by the cruise ship to give a series of lectures on Christmas Celebrations around the world. Guaranteed to be royal snorefests. I intend to miss every one of them.

Love 'n snuggles from,
Daddy O

To: Jausten
From: Shoptillyoudrop
Subject: Almost Forgot, Part II

Jaine, sweetheart—I almost forgot the most exciting news of all!

There's going to be a gala costume party on board the ship on New Year's Eve! Daddy and I are going as Scott and Zelda Fitzgerald. I've ordered the

most adorable flapper dress and cloche hat for
me, and a pair of cute knickerbocker pants, the
kind that puff out at the knees, for Daddy!

Won't that be fun?
XOXO,
Mom

To: Jausten
From: DaddyO
Subject: Me Tarzan!

Dearest Lambchop—

Did Mom tell you about the Costume Gala on New
Year's Eve? She actually expects me to show up
as F. Scott Fitzgerald in puffy pants! No way am I
appearing in public in those silly pants. We
Austens have our dignity! Instead I sent away for a
really cool Tarzan costume. Well, it's not much of a
costume. Just a pair of underpants with a loincloth
attached.

No puffy pants for Hank Austen. No, sirree. Me,
Tarzan!!!

Love 'n snuggles from,
Daddy O

Chapter 3

"**H**ow fantastic!" Lance cried when I told him that the Parkers had agreed to take Prozac for the duration of our stay. "What wonderful people!"

"Not exactly. Missy's okay. But Scotty's a piece of work. The guy invited us to dinner tonight and then ordered me to bring the entrée. Filet mignon for six."

"Whoa." Lance blinked in surprise. "Even I wouldn't have the nerve to pull a stunt like that."

"Oh, well. I'll just make a run to Costco and try to save a few bucks."

"Please!" Lance held up his palm, wincing in pain. "Don't talk of Costco. Ever again."

"Why on earth not?"

"That's where Justin and I first met. We bumped carts in the cosmetics aisle. God, he had great skin."

Oh, crud. I cringed at the thought of having to

listen to Lance babble on about Justin for the next two weeks. I swear, the man can turn a handful of dates into a gay version of *Anna Karenina*.

Eager to escape Lance's saga of lost love, I grabbed my car keys and headed off for Costco.

The place was mobbed with holiday shoppers, and after nabbing my filets, I got on a checkout line that seemed several counties away from the cash register.

While waiting on line, I scrolled through the emails on my cell phone and read the latest news from my parents, about to set sail for the Caribbean.

Poor Mom. I hoped she enjoyed those exotic ports of call, because she sure as heck was going to have her hands full trying to get Daddy into a pair of "puffy" pants.

Daddy is nothing if not stubborn, and Mom is a saint for putting up with his antics all these years. Don't get me wrong. I adore Daddy; he's a sweetie of the highest order, but he's a certified disaster magnet—leaving chaos in his wake wherever he goes.

I shuddered to think of Lydia Pinkus opening her Secret Santa gift and finding those castanet false teeth. As president of the homeowners association, Lydia rules Tampa Vistas like a tsarina in support hose, and Daddy has always bristled under her iron-fisted regime.

While Daddy's the main culprit when it comes to family disasters, Mom is not without her quirks, either. She's the one who made Daddy move three thousand miles across country from a perfectly lovely house in Hermosa Beach to live in Tampa

Vistas, Florida, so she could be closer to the Home Shopping Club, under the mistaken notion that her packages would arrive faster that way.

Oh, well. It seemed like a lovely cruise, and I hoped that, aside from castanet clackers and puffy pants, my parents would have the time of their lives.

By now I'd finally made it up to the checkout counter, and minutes later, walked out of Costco fifty-seven dollars poorer.

That night, Lance and I made our way to The House of Scrooge, armed with six of Costco's finest filet mignons—along with Pro's litter box and a shopping bag full of cat food I'd retrieved from my apartment.

I hadn't bothered to cook the steaks. No way was I about to dirty Mrs. Van H's gazillion-dollar oven. I figured the least Scotty could do was have his maid broil the darn things.

It was dark by then, and most of the houses on the street were lit up with holiday decorations. The showstopper on the block was the house across from Scotty and Missy; whoever lived there had gone all out with the kind of pyrotechnic display you see in Disneyland, Rockefeller Center, or an Elton John concert.

It seemed as if every square inch of the lawn was filled with something moving, singing, or glowing. Santa and his reindeer were perched atop the roof, while down on the lawn mechanized elves frolicked near an elaborate Santa's workshop. Frosty the Snowman was belting out his namesake tune alongside a ginormous teddy bear wishing the world *Peace on Earth*. Flashing neon candy canes bordered the lawn as a laser light projector showered the front of the house with a dazzling display of red and green sparkles. All topped off by a snow machine spewing chunks of fake snow in the air.

Lance shook his head in wonder.

"What a glitzfest! And we don't have a thing on our lawn except for an ATD alarm sign."

"It's not our lawn, Lance. It's Mrs. Van Hooten's."

"Not even a wreath!" Lance said, ignoring me. "The very least we can do is buy a Christmas tree."

News of the extravaganza across the street had gotten around. The block was clogged with cars, slowing down to watch the show. Some people had parked their cars and were crowding the sidewalk in front of the display. Others stood to admire it on the sidewalk outside Scotty's house.

Little kids looked on slack-jawed as the phony snow fell to the ground. For most it was probably the only snow they'd ever seen.

Making our way through the crowds, we headed up the path to Missy and Scotty's place.

Once again I saw Rudolph lying dead on the lawn, the menacing snowman now turned on and growling, "You lookin' at me? You lookin' at me?"

"Geez," Lance said, taking it all in. "Who's their decorator—the Marquis de Sade?"

"Scotty's idea. I told you he was a piece of work."

We rang the bell and Missy came to the door, clad in black leggings, a red silk blouse, and matching red stilettos. Clutched in her hand was a rather large tumbler of white wine.

"Hey, guys!" she said, waving us inside. "So good to see you!"

"We brought Prozac's litter box and some cat food," I said.

"Wonderful. Put them down here in the foyer and our maid will get them later.

"You must be Lance," Missy said, turning to Lance and shooting him a blinding smile.

"And you must be Missy," Lance cooed. "Jaine told me how lovely you were, and I can see she wasn't exaggerating."

He was in Neiman's Salesman Mode, the one meant to charm rich biddies into paying a thousand bucks for a pair of Jimmy Choos.

Missy was suitably enchanted.

"C'mon in," she said, taking Lance by the elbow and ushering us into the living room, where Scotty was still glued to his recliner watching CNBC.

"Look who's here," Missy called out brightly. "Jaine and Lance!"

Scotty graced us with a reluctant grunt.

"And this is our friend Dave," Missy said, gesturing to a handsome guy in his thirties seated on a threadbare sofa facing the fireplace.

He'd been staring halfheartedly at the TV when we walked in. Now he jumped up eagerly to greet us, grateful no doubt for the chance to chat with someone other than Scotty.

"Dave Kellogg," he said. "No relation to the cereal," he added with a grin. "Wish I were. Then I could afford to pay off my humongous student loan."

With his lean frame, easy grin, and startlingly

blue eyes, Dave had the wholesome good looks of an extremely hot former Boy Scout.

"Dave's our tenant," Missy explained. "He's studying law at UCLA."

Their tenant? No wonder the house looked so crappy. Scotty and Missy must've been having financial problems if they were reduced to renting out rooms.

"You bring the steaks?" Scotty barked from the recliner.

"Indeed I did," I said, holding up a bag with the steaks. "I hope you don't mind, but I didn't cook them. We thought your maid could do it. That way they wouldn't get cold."

Scotty grunted his disapproval, but Missy smiled brightly.

"What a good idea. Lupe!" she called out. "Come in here for a minute, will you?"

Seconds later, the tiny slip of a maid I'd seen earlier that day came scuttling into the room, wiping her hands on her apron.

"Lupe, honey, meet Jaine and Lance. They're house-sitting for Mrs. Van Hooten next door."

Lupe nodded at us with a shy smile.

"They've brought filet mignon for dinner," Missy said, handing Lupe the bag.

"Dios mio," Lupe muttered as she gazed down into the bag. "Real steaks for a change. It's a Christmas miracle!"

"What's that?" Scotty barked from the recliner.

"Nothing," Lupe said, giving him the stink eye.

Clearly there was no love lost between these two.

"Cook 'em blood rare, Lupe," Scotty commanded. "Just the way I like 'em."

"What if Jaine and Lance don't like their steaks rare?" Missy asked.

"Too darn bad," Scotty grunted. "They're guests in our house. They'll eat what we serve them."

What a charmer, huh?

Grumbling what I'm guessing were a colorful assortment of Spanish curses under her breath, Lupe headed back to the kitchen with our steaks.

"Have a seat," Missy said to me and Lance, pointing to the rumpsprung sofa and two equally shoddy armchairs.

Lance plopped down onto the sofa next to Dave, no doubt hoping to forge a love connection.

But that wasn't about to happen—not the way Dave was gazing at Missy, following her every move with undisguised longing.

I settled down on one of the armchairs, unleashing a small cloud of dust. I hoped it wouldn't take Lupe long to rustle up those steaks. I was starving.

"I just love what you've done with the place," Lance said, eyeing the threadbare furniture. "Shabby chic is all the rage these days!"

"What's so shabby about it?" Scotty growled from the recliner. "Place looks fine to me."

"No, no!" Lance said, putting on his tap shoes. "I just meant it all looks so comfortable and homey."

Scotty shot him a dubious glare and returned to his stock ticker.

"Let me get you guys some wine," Missy said, heading for a big box of wine propped up on a sideboard.

"Not too much!" Scotty shouted as she began to pour wine from the box's spigot.

Missy rolled her eyes and proceeded to pour us each a generous glass of wine.

I had a feeling we were going to need it.

After delivering it to us, she wasted no time topping off her own glass.

"Omigosh!" she cried. "I forgot all about the hors d'oeuvres."

My salivary glands sprang into action. I was hoping for something fun like a cheese ball or franks in a blanket.

But all we got was a bowl of petrified pretzels.

I was trying in vain to bite into one when Missy cried out, "Look who's here! It's Scarlett!"

And there was Prozac prancing into the room.

"Scarlett?" I asked.

"Yes," Missy said, scooping Prozac up in her arms. "Like Scarlett O'Hara in *Gone with the Wind*. We thought 'Prozac' was so depressing, didn't we, Scarlett?"

Prozac looked up at her worshipfully.

You betcha, honey chile!

It seemed as if Dave wasn't the only one smitten with Missy.

"Come say hello to Jaine," Missy said, depositing Pro in my lap.

"Hello, darling," I cooed, sweeping her up to my chest.

A faint glimmer of recognition flickered in her eyes.

Oh, yeah. I remember you. We used to live together,

didn't we? You're the one with the Chunky Monkey stains on your pillow.

She allowed me to hold her and scratch her behind the ears, but the minute Missy took a seat on the sofa, Prozac wriggled free from my arms and hotfooted it across to Missy's lap.

Good Lord. My cat was dumping me for another woman!

I sat there sipping my bargain basement wine, imported no doubt from a vineyard in the Bronx, wishing I'd never brought Prozac to this wreck of a mausoleum.

And I wasn't the only one in a funk.

Over in his recliner, Scotty was grumbling, "Goddamn kids, making such a racket."

Indeed, we could hear the crowds outside the house oohing and aahing over the Christmas lights across the street.

"I ought to sue the Sinclairs for invasion of privacy," he whined. "Their stupid lights are so bright, I can hardly see the TV screen."

"Let me close the drapes, honey," Missy offered.

"And let the Sinclairs win?" Scotty bellowed. "No way!"

No doubt eager to change the subject, Lance pointed to the portrait hanging over the fireplace, the one I'd noticed earlier that day—of a little boy in a sailor suit.

"Is that you?" he asked Scotty.

Now that I took a good look at it, I could see that the little boy in the picture did indeed look like a younger version of the bloated man in the recliner.

"Yep, that's me in my glory days."

"Scotty was a child actor," Missy said. "He played Tiny Tim in a remake of *A Christmas Carol*. They hardly show it here in the States, but it's huge in Japan."

"It would've been big here in the States, too," Scotty said, "if I hadn't been stuck with a bunch of loser costars. The guy who played Cratchit couldn't act his way out of a paper bag."

Scotty shook his head in disgust at the memory of his former costar.

"I was a child actor, all right. Then I got acne and it was all over. But no matter. I showed those Hollywood bastards. I sued my parents for my savings and invested in the stock market.

"Made a bundle," he added with a smug smile.

So he wasn't poor, after all. Just a monumental cheapskate.

Scotty's smile quickly faded as he heard a kid outside shouting, "Look, Daddy. It's snowing."

"I can't take it anymore," he snapped, hauling himself out of his recliner. "I'm going outside and put an end to this nonsense."

"Oh, honey!" Missy jumped up, alarmed. "Please don't make a scene."

And it was at that moment that Lupe came in and averted disaster.

"Steaks are ready," she announced.

Not about to miss out on a freshly broiled filet mignon, Scotty forgot the crowds outside and made a beeline for the dining room, grabbing the seat at the head of the table. The rest of us followed, Missy sitting opposite him, with Prozac/Scarlett in her lap. Lance and I sat on one side of the table, across from Dave on the other.

"How interesting!" Lance said, eyeing the mismatched dishes on the table. "I just love the eclectic look!"

And when I glanced down at my fork, I blinked in disbelief to see the words VITO'S RISTORANTE ITAL-IANO etched at the bottom of the fork.

Good heavens. We were eating with stolen silverware!

Paper napkins (courtesy of Lenny's Deli) spread out in our laps, we all looked up eagerly as Lupe started serving our dinner.

No appetizers. Just the steaks, accompanied by disconcertingly gray green beans and a basket of rolls almost as hard as the pretzels.

It's fair to say that the only thing edible at that table were the Costco steaks, which Lupe had cooked to perfection, ignoring Scotty's orders and broiling them medium rare.

"Hey," Scotty pouted, cutting into his steak. "This isn't blood rare."

"Oops. My mistake," Lupe said with a defiant shrug. And with that, she turned on her heels and marched back into the kitchen.

I was sitting next to Missy, which was both a blessing and a curse. On the one hand, I was as far away from Scotty as possible. On the other hand, I had to sit there and watch her hand-feed Prozac pieces of filet mignon.

"Isn't that just yummity yum yum, Scarlett sweetums?" she cooed to my fickle feline.

Prozac's eyes shone with food lust.

As God is my witness, I'll never eat canned cat food again!

I was so sick at the sight of those two cuddling and cooing, I could hardly finish Lance's leftover steak.

Lance, oblivious to my pain, was telling Missy about his job at Neiman's and yammering on about how he'd love to have her stop by the store.

"I only wish I could shop at Neiman's," Missy said, looking pointedly at Scotty.

"And pay those crazy prices?" Scotty snorted. "No way! Payless shoes are good enough."

Missy sighed and took a healthy slug of her wine. If I wasn't mistaken, this was the third glass I'd seen her pack away.

Then she turned to me, ever the polite, if somewhat sloshed, hostess.

"And what do you do, Jaine?"

"I'm a writer," I replied. "Mostly ad copy for local businesses."

"In a Rush to Flush? Call Toiletmasters! Jaine wrote that!" Lance bragged on my behalf.

Scotty looked at me, a flicker of interest in his eyes.

Then Lance started asking Dave about his courses at UCLA.

Dave was in the middle of some rather snore-inducing chatter about torts, when a fresh batch of oohs and aahs erupted from the crowd outside.

"That's it!" Scotty said, having demolished every morsel of food on his plate. "I've had it! I'm getting my bullhorn."

He slammed down his purloined silverware and stalked off. Minutes later, we heard the front door bang open, and seconds after that, we heard Scotty's voice booming over a bullhorn:

"Everybody get the hell out of here or I'm calling the police! And by the way, kids. This just in. Santa's had a stroke and is in intensive care. So you won't be getting any presents this year."

"He does this every year," Missy groaned. "It's one of our treasured Christmas traditions."

With that, she drained what was left of her wine.

"Dave, honey," she said. "Get me some more wine, and then go outside and see if you can drag Scotty back in."

Dave dutifully poured Missy some more wine from the box on the sideboard, and then headed outside.

"I'll go, too!" Lance said, scurrying out after Dave, unwilling to miss a moment of potential drama.

"God, I hate my life," Missy said the minute we were alone.

In her lap, Prozac meowed.

I know what'll make you feel better. Feeding me some more steak.

"Here you go, Scarlett, honey," Missy said, tossing Prozac a piece of filet mignon.

I couldn't believe she had any left after sharing so much with my greedy cat.

"I would've never married Scotty if I'd known what a miserable cheapskate he'd turn out to be," Missy said with a sigh. "Scotty wasn't lying when he said he made a bundle in the market. He's got money up his ying-yang, and he refuses to part with any of it.

"Of course, he wasn't that way in the beginning," she said, pausing for a slug of wine. "In the beginning, everything was wonderful. I was a cocktail waitress at the Peninsula Hotel when Scotty started showing up and sitting at my table."

For those of you unfamiliar with the Peninsula, it's one of Beverly Hills's most expensive hotels, the kind of joint where you need a cosigner to order room service.

"He was the last of the big-time spenders back then. Gave me fifty dollar tips, and told me how gorgeous I was. In those days, he took me to all the finest restaurants.

"When he first showed me this house, I was shocked, of course, at how crummy it looked. But he said he'd been devastated by his divorce from his first wife and hadn't had the emotional energy to fix things up. He promised I could redecorate once we were married.

"Hah! What a joke. The minute we set off for our honeymoon, which, by the way, was at a Thrifty Inn in Modesto, I realized what a cheapskate he was. I discovered the real Scotty, the cold, angry tyrant with a calculator where his heart should be. So I've been stuck ever since in the House That Time Forgot with a man whose fingers have to be pried from a dime."

"Have you ever thought of leaving him?"

"So many times. But what would I do? Go back to living in a crappy apartment in West Hollywood and being a cocktail waitress? Somehow, as bad as this is, that seemed worse. But now I'm not so sure."

"He does seem like a handful," I commiserated.

"The worst thing was how he'd tricked me. He had me completely fooled."

"I know the feeling," I said, remembering my own marriage, an unmitigated disaster that lasted four years—about three years and fifty-one weeks too long, IMHO.

When I first met my ex-husband, whom I not-so-lovingly refer to as The Blob, he'd seemed like the sweet, sensitive artist of my dreams. He'd told me he was studying Fine Art at the Otis Institute, a prestigious art school in L.A. But the truth was he was taking only one class a week. The rest of the time he devoted himself to studying the fine art of marijuana, which he smoked on a regular basis. Within weeks of our marriage, he'd morphed into a guy who clipped his toenails in the sink and watched ESPN during sex. With himself.

My stroll down marital memory lane was interrupted just then when Scotty returned with his bullhorn.

"Everybody's gone," Dave said.

"Scotty really put the fear of God into those kids telling them Santa was in ICU," Lance added. "Most of them were bawling their eyes out."

Scotty beamed with pride.

"Let's adjourn to the living room for dessert," he said.

Dessert turned out to be a bowl of ancient mints (no doubt pilfered from Vito's or Lenny's). I sucked on one, utterly miserable, watching Prozac nestled in Missy's arms.

It was definitely time for Lance and me to say our good-byes.

I stood up to go, but before I got a chance to open my mouth, all hell broke loose.

Chapter 4

Someone was pounding on Scotty's front door with such force I thought the hinges might give way. Maybe it was a posse of angry neighbors, come to tar and feather the neighborhood Scrooge.

But, no. When Lupe scuttled over and opened the front door, I heard her exclaim, "Ms. Elise!"

"Scotty's ex-wife," Missy whispered to me.

Footsteps thumped in the foyer, and then a haggard blonde in her forties came storming into the living room.

I blinked in amazement.

The woman standing before us was a washed-out, beat-up version of Missy. Her cascading blond hair had long lost its shine. Her baby blues had bags the size of carry-ons. And her undoubtedly once-rocking bod had a bit of a belly.

Nevertheless, the resemblance to Missy was unmistakable.

She could have been her mother.

In a classic Hollywood move, it looked like Scotty had traded in his ex-wife for a younger model.

Now she stomped over to Scotty in his recliner.

"Where the hell's my alimony check, you cheap bastard?" she cried, her face splotchy with rage.

"For crying out loud, Elise," Scotty said with a put-upon sigh. "It's in the mail. I sent it out yesterday. You should be getting it any day now."

"That's what you always say," Elise hissed. "And somehow the check never seems to show up. Every month I have to keep coming here, begging for what's rightfully mine. You really get off on that, don't you, Scotty?" she said, her face now a dangerous shade of puce. "Making me come and beg for my money."

From the smug expression on Scotty's freckled face, I bet he did.

Then Elise turned to Missy, shooting her a warning finger.

"Watch out, honey. Just wait. He's going to screw you over, just like he did to me."

"Okay, that's enough," Scotty said, heaving himself out of his recliner. "Time to go."

Grabbing her roughly by the elbow, he escorted his ex-wife out of the room.

Next to me, Missy sighed.

"Poor Elise," she said, her speech now slurred from all the wine she'd been glugging down. "Scotty used her savings to pump up his investment portfolio, but somehow managed to ace her out of community property in the divorce. She's barely making ends meet, while Scotty is hoarding all his money. And she's right, of course. One of these days, he'll drop me for a new blonde and leave me without a penny."

"Don't worry, Missy!" Dave jumped up to take her hand. "You'll be okay. I'll make sure he can't hurt you."

Any doubts I may have had about Dave's crush on Missy were instantly dispelled. Clearly the guy was head over heels in love.

From Missy's lap, Prozac swatted his hand away.

Watch it, buster. She's in the middle of a very important belly rub.

We all fell silent just then as Scotty returned to the room, smiling blandly as if the whole scene with Elise hadn't happened.

"So who wants another mint? I don't usually give out seconds, but what the heck? It's almost Christmas."

"Actually," I said, eager to get away from this horrible man and his bowl of ancient mints, "it's getting late. Lance and I should be going."

"Right," Lance jumped in. "Must go home and keep an eye on Mrs. Van Hooten's house. After all, that's what we're getting paid for."

I leaned in to pet Prozac good-bye.

"Nighty night, sweetheart."

She gazed up at me through slitted green eyes.

Would you mind not standing so close? You're blocking my view of Missy.

"Thanks so much for taking care of her," I said to Missy, inwardly seething at my fickle feline.

"Our pleasure," Missy replied.

"Yes, indeed," Scotty said. "I checked out the going rates at the pet kennels, and I'm only going to charge you seventy-five bucks a night boarding fee."

"You're charging me?" I asked, reeling in disbelief.

What colossal gall!

"Not necessarily," Scotty said, a sly glint in his eyes, "Seeing as you're a writer, I'll waive the boarding fee if you help me polish my screenplay."

"Your screenplay?"

He nodded proudly. "*The Return of Tiny Tim: Vengeance Is Mine!* It's really in great shape. Just needs a tweak here and there. So how about it? You work with me on my script, and the cat stays for free."

No way was I about to work with this creep on his stupid script. So what if I hadn't had a writing assignment in three weeks? So what if the bills on my dining room table were multiplying like mushrooms in a rainstorm? So what if I was maxing out my credit cards buying Christmas gifts? I could not possibly bring myself to spend one more minute with this dreadful man.

"So how about it, Jaine? Is it a deal?"

"When do we start?"

You knew that was coming, didn't you? What else could I possibly have done? Just like with Elise, Scotty had me by the purse strings.

"Ten o'clock tomorrow morning. And bring your own lunch. No more free meals."

Free meals? I paid fifty-seven dollars for those damn filets!

"Fine," I snapped.

Oh, what a jolly Christmas this was going to be.

"Thank God that's over," Lance said as we walked in Connie Van Hooten's front door, me toting a copy of *The Return of Tiny Tim* that Scotty had given me to read overnight.

"Most miserable meal of my life," Lance was grousing. "Except for Dave, of course. What a cutie."

"You realize he's straight, right?"

"Not in my fantasies.

"After a night like this," Lance said, plopping down cross-legged on Mrs. Van H's Persian rug in the living room, "we absolutely must do some deep breathing exercises and expel the negative vibes from our body."

"Can't we just have a decent glass of wine? That stuff Missy served smelled like 409."

"No, Jaine. We have to deep breathe. Now sit!"

Reluctantly I sat down across from him on the rug.

"We will simply slow down our breathing, lowering our blood pressure, bringing peace and calm to our lives. Come on. It's easy. All you have to do is breathe. Think you can manage that?"

"I'll try," I said, lobbing him back a bit of his own sarcasm.

And so we sat there, breathing in and breathing out. Each breath slightly longer than the last.

And guess what? An hour later, I felt completely calm and centered.

Not from the silly deep breathing, of course.

But from the pint of fudge ripple ice cream I'd scarfed down from Connie Van Hooten's freezer.

Chapter 5

That night I discovered a miracle cure for insomnia: *The Return of Tiny Tim: Vengeance Is Mine!*

I hunkered down in bed, fully intent on reading Scotty's script, but after three pages of his mind-numbing dialogue, I was dead to the world.

I woke up the next morning, the script on my pillow, drool stains on its cover. I was lying there in a mild state of panic, wondering how the heck I was going to fake having read the darn thing, when my cell phone rang.

It was Missy with a last-minute reprieve.

Scotty, she told me, would be tied up with his broker all morning, and wouldn't be able to meet with me until after lunch.

Hallelujah!

That would give me plenty of time to read the script and make notes.

I sprang out of bed, and several minutes later—

face scrubbed and teeth brushed—made my way down to the kitchen to rustle up some breakfast.

Lance was at the kitchen island when I got there, buff as always in shorts and a tank top, whipping up some ghastly green concoction in a blender.

"Good morning, Lazybones!" he chirped. "I've been up for ages. I've already done my morning workout, showered, shaved, and moussed my hair to golden perfection." With that, he shook his headful of tight blond curls, which did indeed look like something straight out of a Michelangelo statue.

"And I made coffee, too!"

Don't you just hate perky morning people?

"Whoa!" he said, as I shuffled over to pour myself some coffee from a fancy stainless steel carafe. "What happened to your hair? Did a bomb go off in your bed last night?"

"This is the way it always looks in the morning," I replied with more than a hint of frost in my voice.

"You poor thing. No wonder you've been so unlucky in love. Here, sweetheart," he said, handing me a glass of the green glop he'd been whipping up. "I made you a rejuvenating energy smoothie. Drink one of these every morning, and your frizzies will be gone in no time."

"What's in this stuff?" I asked, staring down into the green goo.

"Yogurt, wheat germ, kale, and lemongrass."

Oh, glug.

"Thanks, but I never drink salad for breakfast."

"Take just one sip. I guarantee you'll love it."

And like a fool, I took a sip.

Not that I've ever tasted pureed pond scum, but

if I had, I'll bet it would taste a lot like Lance's smoothie.

"Just a little constructive criticism," I said, setting the glass down on the island. "This stinks."

"Suit yourself," Lance shrugged. "But don't blame me if you keep waking up looking like the Bride of Frankenstein."

Eager to get the taste of yogurt, wheat germ, kale, and lemongrass out of my mouth, I headed for Mrs. Van H's massive bunker of a fridge and started rummaging around for something decent to eat. I hit pay dirt in the freezer when I found some frozen croissants. I quickly proceeded to nuke one and slather it with butter and raspberry jam imported all the way from Fortnum & Mason in London.

Then I dug into it with gusto as Lance polished off his ghastly green concoction.

"Busy day today," he said. "Working the late shift at Neiman's. But first, I'm heading off to get our Christmas tree!"

His eyes sparkled with shopaholic fervor.

"Don't go crazy," I pleaded. "The smaller the tree, the less chance of any accidents. We don't want to damage a millimeter of this fabulous house."

"Not to worry, hon. I'll get something perfect! I am nothing if not a master of interior décor.

"I'll save this for you," he said, putting my glass of green glop in the fridge, "in case you want a pick-me-up later in the day."

Yeah, right. I'd rot in hell before I drank that stuff. (Which I'm sure is what they serve down there.)

As Lance skipped off, filled with yogurt-kale-lemongrass energy, I settled down to read Scotty's script. Actually, I settled down for another raspberry jam and butter croissant, but after that, I read the script.

I'll spare you the excruciating details and skip to the gist of the godawful plot: Namely, that the great-great-great-grandson of Tiny Tim sets out to kill the remaining members of the Scrooge clan in order to avenge the indignities suffered by his forebears at the hands of Ebenezer Scrooge. In Scotty's script, the original Ebenezer's transformation from misanthrope to philanthropist was short-lived, and he was soon back to haranguing the poor Cratchits, canceling Tiny Tim's corrective foot surgery, leaving him limping for the rest of his short life.

The script was a bloated two hundred pages of wooden dialogue, unbelievable plot twists, and enough typos to sink the *Oxford English Dictionary*.

I'd mercifully reached the final *Fade Out*, and was soothing my frazzled nerves with the weensiest handful of M&Ms when I heard the front door bang open.

"I'm back!" Lance called out.

Seconds later he came tripping into the living room with a tree stand. Following him was a handsome hunk of a guy in a blue mail carrier's uniform, toting one of the biggest Christmas trees I'd seen outside of a shopping mall.

"Right this way, Graham," Lance said, setting the tree stand between the fireplace and the Rodin sculpture. "Over here."

The handsome mail carrier toted the tree across the room, almost knocking over one of the priceless gewgaws on Mrs. Van H's étagère.

Damn that Lance! Why on earth had he bought such a ginormous tree, when I'd specifically told him not to? But if my annoyance was showing, Lance was oblivious to it, too busy gazing at the hunky tree hauler.

"Jaine, say hello to Graham, our mailman. He saw me trying to get the tree up the front steps and was kind enough to offer to help."

The hunk, who'd now set the tree down into the stand, looked over and beamed me a brilliant smile. He was a studmuffin, all right, with that megawatt smile, rippling muscles, and spectacular tan—a clear candidate for *People* magazine's "Sexiest Man Alive."

Clad as he was in Bermuda shorts (to brave the wilds of L.A.'s Santa Anas), I was able to get a good look at his amazingly well-toned and tanned calves.

He and Lance spent the next few minutes screwing the tree into the stand while I stood around praying the monster pine wouldn't topple over.

"It's so nice of you to help out like this," I said to Graham when he and Lance had secured the tree in place.

"My pleasure," he grinned.

"How can we ever thank you?" Lance said. "I know! How about dinner? At the restaurant of your choice!"

"That's not necessary," Graham said.

"But I insist!" Lance cried, a tad too vehemently.

"Well, okay. How about Chez Jay in Santa Monica? Maybe one night next week?"

"Wonderful!" Lance gushed. "How's Wednesday? Eight o'clock?"

"It's a date," Graham said as he started for the door. "See you both then."

"Oh, Jaine won't be able to make it," Lance piped up. "She's busy that night. It'll be just you and me."

Could he possibly be more obvious? Any minute now, he'd be booking a hotel room.

Lance walked Graham to the door and came floating back to the living room in a goofy daze.

"My God, did you see that smile? That body? Those amazing calves? I think I'm in love."

"What happened to Justin? Just yesterday he was indelibly etched in your heart, if I recall."

"Oh, him," Lance replied with an airy wave. "The more I think about Justin, the more I realize how unsophisticated he was. The man thought Dolce and Gabbana were hit men on *The Sopranos*. A bit of a lamebrain. Especially compared to Graham, who, I can tell, is a man of great depth."

By which, of course, he meant a hottie extraordinaire.

"And to think! He asked me out for dinner!"

I didn't bother to remind him that he was the one who'd done the asking.

"So how about it?" Lance asked, wrenching his thoughts away from Graham and gesturing to the tree. "Isn't it fab?"

"My God, Lance, it's ginormous—a pine tree on steroids."

"A grand house like this deserves a grand Christmas tree. I can't wait to decorate it! I'm going out to the car and get my ornaments. And I stopped off and bought all the supplies we'll need to make our acorn garlands and pine cone Santas!"

Inwardly I groaned, wondering which would be worse: working on Scotty's godawful script or playing arts and crafts with Lance.

After gulping down a PBJ for lunch (with Fortnum & Mason's scrumptious jam), I left Lance in the kitchen boring holes into an unlucky bunch of acorns.

Then off I trotted to start work on *The Return of Tiny Tim: Vengeance Is Mine!*—where I would soon learn that Scotty's script was the clear winner in the Most Dreaded Chore category.

Chapter 6

"This is where the magic happens!"

Scotty ushered me into his office, a dusty room frozen in time somewhere in the 1980s.

A bulky old-fashioned computer monitor sat atop a scuffed desk; rusty metal file cabinets lined the walls; and puffs of stuffing sprouted out from the rips in Scotty's swivel chair. On the corner of his desk were an ancient TV and VCR recorder, the faint hum of a tape running inside the VCR.

And hanging in a prominent place on the wall behind his desk was a framed poster of Scotty's long-forgotten remake of *A Christmas Carol*.

"Sit!" Scotty commanded.

I parked my fanny on a hard metal chair across from his desk.

"Would you care for some coffee?" Scotty asked, plopping down into his chair. "I'll keep a tab of what you drink and bill you later."

Yikes. Any minute now, he'd be charging me to sit on his chair.

"No, thanks. I'm fine."

"So," he said, clasping his hands in front of him, eyes bright and eager as a puppy's. "Did you read the script? What was your favorite part?"

"When it was over."

Okay, I didn't really say that. Instead I fumphered: "I can honestly say I've never read anything quite like it."

And for that, I was beyond grateful.

"How about the scene where Tim mows down everyone at the bachelorette party with an Uzi? Or when he sets fire to Bradford Scrooge's Lamborghini? Or the pit bull scene in the bowling alley?"

His freckled face beamed with pride.

"All so very vivid," I managed to say.

"Frankly, I think the script is perfect as it is," Scotty said, "but it's two hundred pages and most scripts come in at around one hundred twenty. So I need to make some cuts. Did you see any parts we could lose?" he asked, lovingly running his finger over the title page.

"All the stuff between *FADE IN* and *FADE OUT*," were the words I did not have the courage to utter.

"Maybe the decapitation scene," I said. "That might be a bit gruesome for most moviegoers."

"Hell, no!" Scotty roared. "People love beheadings!"

I suggested a few more of the many repulsive scenes scattered throughout the book, but Scotty was horrified at the idea of losing any one of them.

"Let's just go through the script page by page," he said, "and take trims as we go."

And so began my stint in script hell.

Every cut I suggested was met with a howl of protest. I could barely get him to correct his typos. Twenty minutes later, we were still on page one. At this rate, we'd be through by Valentine's Day.

We hobbled along this way, Scotty reacting to my every cut as if I'd just suggested amputating one of his limbs.

I was sitting there, wondering if I should take a cash advance on my MasterCard to pay for Prozac's boarding fee, when the tape in Scotty's VCR clicked to a stop.

"Excuse me," Scotty said. "Gotta change my security tape."

With that he got up and took out the tape, and reached for another from a pile near the VCR.

"I've got security cameras all over the front lawn," he explained. "To catch any neighbors foolish enough to let their dogs poop on my property. Nobody puts anything over on Scotty Parker," he added, a poster boy for paranoia.

After he was through changing the tape, we picked up where we left off, slogging through every syllable of his godawful script.

I'd just about decided to go for that cash advance when the doorbell started ringing in loud, insistent bursts.

"Lupe!" Scotty shouted out. "Someone's at the door."

The fact that his office was right off the foyer just steps from the front door did not prompt Mr. Wonderful to move his lazy tush.

By now our visitor had given up on the bell and was pounding on the door.

"Damn that Lupe!" Scotty cursed. "Laziest maid alive. Get that, will you?" he asked me.

I jumped up, happy for any excuse to get away from *The Return of Tiny Tim.*

Out in the foyer, I saw Lupe rushing out from the kitchen.

"I'll get it," she said, scurrying to the front door and opening it.

Standing there was a refrigerator of a man with a military buzz cut and muscles the size of volleyballs, clad in a T-shirt and sweat pants.

"Mr. Marlon," Lupe said. "How can I help you?"

"I've come to see the sonofabitch you work for."

"Tell him I'm not home!" Scotty bellowed from his office.

"If you're not out here in three seconds, Parker," The Refrigerator said, "I'm gonna come in and beat the living daylights out of you."

"You and who else?" Scotty asked, emerging from his office, eyes narrowed into angry slits, brandishing a pair of scissors.

"I'm not afraid to use these if I have to," he said, waving the scissors.

Scotty had to have been at least five inches shorter and fifty pounds lighter than his angry neighbor, but amazingly, he showed not an iota of fear.

"What the hell do you want?" he asked.

"You ruined my kid's Christmas, you warped sicko," The Refrigerator replied. "Telling him Santa was in the hospital with a stroke and that there wouldn't be any gifts this year. He's been crying all morning."

If he expected Scotty to be touched by this tale, he was in for a big disappointment.

"Boo hoo," Scotty said. "It's time your kid grew up and learned how the world really works."

The Refrigerator's massive fists were clenching and unclenching, like two Rottweilers eager to attack.

"Tell the little wimp to stop being such a crybaby," Scotty added with a sneer.

And that, I fear, was one step over the line.

"Crybaby?" The Refrigerator echoed, his jaw rigid. "Nobody calls my kid a crybaby."

With that, he knocked the scissors from Scotty's hand and sent them skittering across the floor.

For the first time, I saw fear flicker in Scotty's eyes.

The Refrigerator pulled back his arm and was aiming his fist at Scotty's gut.

But Scotty was in luck. Because just then his tenant, Dave, who'd been walking up the path to the house, came rushing in to pull The Refrigerator off Scotty.

"Help me, Lupe!" Dave cried.

Somewhat reluctantly, Lupe came to Scotty's rescue and grabbed hold of The Refrigerator. She was surprisingly strong for such a tiny slip of a thing. Together, she and Dave managed to drag him off Scotty.

"Get out of here," Scotty cried, all bravado now that The Refrigerator was outnumbered three to one, "or I'm calling the cops."

"Okay, I'm going," The Refrigerator said, storming out the front door. "But this isn't over!" he shouted as he headed down the front path. "I'll be back to take care of you once and for all!"

Across the street, two neighbors were standing at their front doors, wide-eyed as they caught all the action.

"Scotty, are you okay?"

We turned to see Missy on the upstairs landing.

"Yeah, I'm fine," he said.

Not from where I was standing. He looked pretty darn shaken.

"Bring me a scotch, Lupe," he said. "Not the watered down stuff I serve to guests. The real thing.

"And you can go home," he said to me. "I need to call my attorney to take out a restraining order against that guy."

I sent out a silent prayer of thanks to Marlon, The Refrigerator. For the time being at least, I did not have to look at one more word of Scotty's script from hell.

I grabbed my purse from Scotty's office, but I did not go home as directed.

Instead I headed upstairs to pay a little visit to Missy and Ms. "Scarlett."

I almost gasped when I saw Prozac.

There she was sprawled out on the Parkers' bed,

lolling on a faux mink throw, surrounded by a sea of cat toys.

But it wasn't the cat toys or the faux mink that had me bug-eyed.

It was the knitted hat on her head. Yes, perched on her head was a bright red crocheted cap, the kind babies wear, tied under her chin, with holes for her ears. And right in the center of the cap, popping up from her head, was a plastic sprig of mistletoe!

You've got to understand. This is a cat who's gone ballistic every time I've tried to put a Santa hat on her head to pose for our Christmas photo. Her mantra ever since I've known her has been, *No Hats Ever in a Zillion Years.*

And now, after only two days with Missy, she was sporting a sprig of mistletoe on her noggin.

"Isn't that hat the cutest thing ever?" Missy gushed. "Doesn't Scarlett look adorable?"

"Yeah, adorable," I muttered, glancing around the bedroom, last furnished sometime in the Carter administration, its dingy walls adorned with bad flea market art.

"I went shopping this morning and bought Prozac all these toys," Missy said, bursting with maternal pride. "And the mink throw, and that adorable hat. I spent my whole allowance on the little darling."

Prozac looked up, preening, from the throw.

I'm worth it.

"She just loves Rhett Butler," Missy said, picking up a plush catnip-filled skunk.

I shot her an exceedingly anemic smile, which

no doubt clued her in to the fact that I had not
stopped by to admire her pet store purchases.

"Look who's come to visit you, Scarlett!" she
cooed, gesturing to me.

Prozac yawned.

Oh, yeah. It's you again. June? Jean? Janet?

I wanted to throttle her.

Instead, I couldn't help myself. As much as she
didn't deserve it, I sat down beside her on the bed
and began petting her. Immediately I detected the
scent of tuna in the air.

"Has she been eating human tuna?" I asked.

"She just finished her afternoon snack," Missy
nodded. "She certainly loves her snacks, doesn't
she?"

"If it's not nailed to the floor, she'll eat it."

"Not really. She didn't seem to like the cat food
you brought. In fact, she turned up her nose every
time I tried to feed it to her."

*Of course she did, when she knew there was a plate of
human tuna waiting in the wings!*

"You really should try to get her to eat the cat
food," I said, dreading having to wean Prozac off
her extravagant diet once we got back home.

"I'll try," Missy promised, "but it's so hard to say
no to darling Scarlett."

"Oh, look," she said, as Prozac took a lazy swipe
at a couple of toy mice. "Now she's playing with
the Tarleton Twins."

Missy gazed at her precious Scarlett for a worshipful beat, then plopped down cross-legged on the
bed to join us.

"That was pretty scary what happened downstairs just now," she said, her brow furrowed in concern. "I hope he's going to be okay."

"Scotty was a bit shaken up, but I think once he has his scotch and calls his lawyer, he'll be fine."

"Scotty?" Missy wrinkled her tiny nose in distaste. "Who cares about him? I was talking about Dave. The poor thing weighs a hundred sixty pounds soaking wet. Marlon could've pulverized him."

Worry shone in her eyes.

I'd already seen Dave look at Missy limp with longing. Apparently, he was not alone on the Love Boat.

"Don't worry about Scotty," Missy was saying. "He'll be just fine. The guy's got the hide of a rhinoceros. Although, confidentially, and I know this is going to sound awful, I wouldn't have minded if Marlon had roughed him up a bit. Nothing serious. Just enough to send him to the hospital for a couple of days and get him out from under my feet. I honestly don't know how much longer I can stand living with him. Always complaining and bossing me around. I feel like I'm one step above Lupe."

"If you're this unhappy, Missy, you really should think about leaving him."

"I've got to do something, that's for sure," she said, a determined spark in her eyes.

A spark I would remember only too clearly in the days to come.

YOU'VE GOT MAIL!

To: Jausten
From: Shoptillyoudrop
Subject: A Sight to Behold!

Ahoy, sweetheart!

I'm happy to report our ship, the *Caribbean Queen*, is absolutely spectacular—gleaming woodwork and ocean views everywhere you look. Our cabin is gorgeous, with our own private balcony. I just wish Daddy would stop referring to himself as "The Captain," and calling me his "matey."

The swimming pool is magnificent, and there are so many restaurants and lounges. There's even a miniature golf course! Most spectacular of all is the Christmas tree in the main atrium, which soars up practically two stories. What a sight to behold. I'm positively in awe!

XOXO,
Mom

To: Jausten
From: DaddyO
Subject: A Sight to Behold!

Well, Lambchop—I've got to admit this ship is really quite a beauty. The pool, the lounges, the casino—

all fantastic. And the most magnificent sight of all, as I'm sure Mom has already told you—the twenty-four hour buffet!

Just think! Anything you want to eat, any time, day or night. What a spread! Salads, hand-carved meats, all kinds of potatoes and pasta, and desserts to die for. The chef here is famous for his chocolate éclairs, which he only makes on certain days.

Of course, you've got to be careful at these buffets. Your old Daddy happens to be a Buffet Master. You've gotta skip the salads and froufrou stuff and go straight for the big ticket items like roast beef and lobster. That's where most people make their mistake. They load up on salad, don't save room for roast beef, and the cruise line makes a profit. Well, they're not going to cash in on Buffet Master Hank Austen. I happen to have a black belt in strategic buffet planning.

In fact, Mom and I are heading off right now to grab some lunch. I heard the chef's chocolate éclairs are on the menu today.

Love 'n munchies from,
Daddy O
Aka The Buffet Master

To: Jausten
From: Shoptillyoudrop
Subject: Back from Lunch

Back from lunch, sweetheart. Very delicious
indeed. But I refuse to be one of those people who
gain weight on cruises. I'm determined to stick to a
healthy diet. I had a sensible low-cal tuna salad,
with just the weensiest cookie for dessert. (Okay,
two cookies.)

Daddy, on the other hand, piled his plate with
enough food to feed a small South American army.
I kept telling him he could go back for seconds,
but he insisted on cramming as much food as possible onto one plate, blathering some nonsense
about being a "buffet master."

He was most miffed however, when they ran out of
éclairs for dessert.

XOXO,
Mom

To: Jausten
From: DaddyO
Subject: Annoying Little Brat

The most annoying thing happened at lunch today,
Lambchop. My triple-decker turkey and roast beef
sandwich and potato salad were delicious, but
when I got to the dessert section, there was only

one chocolate éclair left. I was just about to grab it, when a bratty redheaded kid came racing out of nowhere and nabbed it out from under me.

"Hey!" I shouted. "I was about to take that."

"Better luck next time, gramps!" he sneered.

And to make matters worse, he took one bite of the éclair and, staring me straight in the eye, tossed the rest of it in the trash. He didn't even want the darn thing. Just took it to spite me. What an annoying little brat.

Oh, well. I've got to look on the bright side. The clattering false teeth I ordered for Lydia Pinkus's Secret Santa gift are tucked away safe in my suitcase, and now, while your mom is off listening to one of The Gasbag's lectures on Christmas Celebrations Around the World, I'm going to wrap it. You'll be very proud of me, Lambchop. I went down to the ship's gift shop and asked for one of their jewelry gift boxes. I'm going to take the false teeth out of its original Yakity Yak wrapping and put it in the fancy gift box, so Lydia will think she's getting something really nice.

Ah, yes. What's a missing éclair compared to the joy of watching Lydia's face when she opens her Secret Santa gift and sees those Yakity Yak false teeth clattering away?

Love 'n snuggles from,
DaddyO

Chapter 7

I got a break from script hell the next morning when Missy called to tell me that Scotty would be out all day Christmas shopping.

Freedom, blessed freedom!

No more Tiny Tim and his heinous acts of vengeance on the English language.

I used my time wisely to catch up on missed episodes of *House Hunters* and do one last bit of Christmas shopping.

Determined to avoid the mobs at the mall, I'd already done the rest of my shopping online. Holiday shopping is quite stress-free, I find, when done in the comfort of one's own home, with a credit card and a glass of chardonnay at one's side.

And at that very moment my carefully curated gifts (peanut butter fudge for everyone!) were winging their way to their soon-to-be grateful recipients.

Due to Lance's misguided conviction that fudge

is not one of the seven basic food groups, I'd ordered him a Hugo Boss tie.

Every year, Lance picks out a tie he wants me to buy him, and I pick out a book I want him to buy me. Every year, Lance ignores my wishes and gets me a cashmere sweater instead.

Which is one of the reasons I love the guy.

Normally, I give Prozac a pair of brand new pantyhose to destroy, but this year, having seen all the toys Missy had lavished on her, I really had to up my ante.

So—after reading about my parents' buffet adventures on the SS *Caribbean Queen*—I spent a good hour at Mrs. Van H's kitchen island, surfing the web on my laptop, before finally plunking down one hundred dollars for something called a Mowse, an egg-shaped toy with a feathery tail that was guaranteed to scamper around, mimicking the movement of an actual mouse. Surely, this piece of computerized wizardry would put any gift of Missy's to shame.

I'd finished processing the order, paying twenty-seven dollars extra for express delivery, my Master-Card groaning in protest, when Lance came rushing in the kitchen with a bag of groceries.

"I just ordered the most fabulous fifteen-pound goose for our Christmas dinner!" he announced.

"A fifteen-pound goose, for two people? Are you crazy?"

"What's the big deal? We'll have leftovers!"

"What about Mrs. Van Hooten's oven? What if you get it dirty?"

"If there are any spills, I promise I'll clean them up. You've got to stop being such a worrywart."

With that, he started unloading groceries from his bag, a most unappetizing lot of rice cakes, wheat germ, and soy milk.

"And I've got some very exciting news!" he beamed, shoving a hunk of tofu in the fridge. "While I was on line at the supermarket, I met the most adorable guy."

"What happened to Graham, the mailman? I thought you were in love with him."

"Not for me, silly. For *you*! He's absolutely gorgeous, and most amazing of all, he actually wants to meet you."

"And exactly why is it so amazing that an adorable man would want to meet me?" I huffed.

"You know what I mean, honey. You're a darling woman, attractive as any woman could possibly be in a CUCKOO FOR COCOA PUFFS T-shirt, but you're not exactly walking the runway at Milan."

"Thanks loads. I'll be sure to print that out and save it for my epitaph."

"Anyhow, I've got you all set up. His name is Randy and you're meeting him for coffee next Wednesday night. That's the same night I'm going out with Graham. Isn't that exciting?"

"Forget it, Lance. You know how I feel about blind dates. They're nature's way of telling you that nuns don't have it so bad."

"Okay," he shrugged. "Be that way. Stay home, grow old and lonely with only your cat to comfort you. Oh, wait. I forgot. Your cat seems to have dumped you for another woman."

Ouch. He had me there.

I must admit that Prozac's burgeoning love affair with Missy had wounded me to the quick.

How could she be so fickle?

I thought back to all the belly rubs I'd given her, the love scratches, the hairballs I'd picked out of my freshly washed laundry, the anchovies I'd ordered on my pizzas especially for her. After all that devotion, all that pampering, all that love (and shrimp with lobster sauce) we'd shared, here she was deserting me for a flashy blonde with a catnip skunk and a faux mink throw.

Well, two could play at that game.

Lance was right. It was time I got out there and made a little love connection of my own.

"Okay, I'll do it!" I cried.

"Good for you! I just know Randy's going to adore you. Especially after your makeover."

"What makeover?"

"You don't think I'm going to let you go on a date looking like that?" he said, with a dismissive wave at my sweats. "When I get through with you, you'll look fantab, not the least bit like yourself!"

Grrrr.

All I can say is it's a good thing he had that cashmere sweater waiting for me under the Christmas tree.

"No more procrastinating, Jaine!"

Dressed for work in Armani splendor, Lance plopped a shopping bag on the sofa beside me where I was watching Kevin and Luanne, a couple on *House Hunters*, decide between a charming Victorian and a hip city condo.

Looking inside the shopping bag, I saw it was filled with pine cones, cotton balls, swatches of felt, and a tube of something called Wacky Glue, guaranteed to stand up under fifty pounds of pressure.

"It's time for you to tackle those pine cone Santas!"

Oh, foo. I'd forgotten all about Lance's Christmas crafts projects.

"I'd do it myself," he said, "but I've still got the pipe cleaner elves to make."

Lance had gone all out on the Christmas decorations, and I must say the tree was looking pretty darn terrific, with crystal snowflakes, glittering white and silver balls, sprigs of holly—all finished off with his acorn garlands, which added quite a festive touch.

He'd put in so much effort, the least I could do was glue some cotton balls onto a couple of pine cones.

And so, as Lance trotted off to work, I bid Luanne and Kevin good-bye and headed off to the kitchen to make pine cone Santas.

After covering the kitchen island with newspaper, I set out all the supplies: twelve pine cones, cotton balls, felt, and a bunch of what's known in crafting circles as "goo-goo eyes," white plastic buttons with small black pupils encased inside them. When shaken, the pupils move around to give a goggle-eyed effect.

And finally, there was the Wacky Glue, the vital ingredient that would hold it all together.

Lance had printed the directions from a crafts website, and much to my relief, they looked reasonably easy to follow. All I had to do was glue two goo-goo eyes to each pine cone, cut out a pink felt nose and attach it under the eyes, and a red felt mouth under the nose. The final touch would be cotton balls shaped into a mustache and beard.

Simple, right?

Wrong. Oh, so very wrong.

Have you ever tried to glue a goo-goo eye to the tip of a pine cone? Well, don't. It's darn near impossible. Those pine cones had really tiny tips, and the goo-goo eyes kept sliding off. I had to slosh on the Wacky Glue like crazy before those pesky eyes finally stuck to the cones.

Afraid to jostle any of the eyes, I decided to let the glue set for a while before I returned to complete the job—time spent in the entertaining company of a *Real Housewives of Beverly Hills* marathon. I meant to spend only an hour watching those doyennes of drama, but I got caught up in some riveting wine-tossing scenes, and wound up watching their antics for several episodes. Three hours later I looked up in the middle of a hair-pulling match, and realized I'd forgotten all about my pinecone Santas.

I hustled back to the kitchen where, one by one, I went down the line of would-be Santas, happy to see the goo-goo eyes were firmly attached to the pinecones.

Even without the rest of the face, the Santas were beginning to look really cute.

This crafting thing wasn't so bad, after all. Maybe I could take it up as a hobby. For all I knew, I had a wellspring of creativity just waiting to be tapped.

With a song in my heart, and an Oreo in my mouth (a gal's got to keep up her energy), I began industriously cutting twelve felt noses for my Santas.

When I was through, I reached for one of the Santas to glue on his nose.

And that's when disaster struck.

When I tried to pull the pine cone, it wouldn't budge. I yanked and yanked. But that damn cone stayed stubbornly welded to the marble. Frantically I went down the line, only to discover that each and every Santa was welded to the island. On careful inspection, I saw that all the Wacky Glue I'd sloshed on the pine cones to keep the goo-goo eyes in place had trickled down the cones and through the newspapers onto Mrs. Van H's priceless marble island!

Oh, hell. Why had I used so much damn glue? Why hadn't I used something stronger than newspaper to protect the marble? And why had I wasted three hours on those damn Beverly Hills housewives?

I tugged frantically at the cones, trying to jar them loose, but they just snapped off in my hands, and I soon wound up with an island full of pine cone stubs.

I couldn't risk scraping them off with a knife and marring the surface of the marble, mined no doubt from some ancient quarry in Rome.

By now I was in a mild state of panic. I had single-handedly ruined Connie Van Hooten's kitchen island!

I was totally flipping out, wondering how many lifetimes I would have to work to reimburse Mrs. Van H for the cost of her island, when I thought of a possible way out of this mess:

Lupe! After all, she was a maid. Surely she'd know how to get pine cone Santas off kitchen islands.

Like a flash I was knocking at the Parkers' back door.

"Ms. Jaine. What's wrong?" Lupe asked, when she came to the door and saw the look of panic on my face.

"Santas are Wacky Glued to the island!" was all I was able to gasp out.

"Sorry." She shook her head. "No comprende."

I forced myself to take a deep breath and tell her exactly what had happened.

Once she'd heard the whole story, she nodded her head in comprehension.

"No problemo," she assured me with a big smile. "Lupe can fix."

With that, she scurried to one of Scotty's creaky cupboards and pulled out a can of WD40.

"This is wonderful," she said, holding it aloft. "Works miracles."

Minutes later, we were back in Mrs. Van H's kitchen, and, as promised, the WD40 did indeed work miracles.

Lupe sprayed the stuff under the base of each pine cone, gradually freeing them from captivity.

Of course, by now the kitchen smelled like the inside of an auto repair shop, but I didn't care.

We scrubbed the island free of WD40, and opened the windows and door to air out the room.

After tossing the pine cone detritus into the trash can outside, I headed back to the kitchen to shower Lupe with profuse thanks—not to mention a pint of Ben & Jerry's Chocolate Chip Cookie Dough, which we shared, sitting side by side at the kitchen island.

Lupe dug in with gusto. Not as much gusto as me, of course—nobody beats me in the ice cream gusto department—but she was pretty darn enthusiastic.

"Mr. Scotty won't buy ice cream unless it's on sale," she said, spearing a spoonful. "His favorite flavor is 'Expired.'

"Such a miserable man. When he hired me, he promised he'd pay me five hundred dollars a week. But when I got my first paycheck it was only $100. He said he took out the rest for room and board. He works me day and night and gives me only one day off every other Thursday."

"That's awful! Have you tried looking for another job?"

"Impossible," she sighed.

"Why? Surely there are plenty of jobs for housekeepers in Bel Air."

She shook her head sadly.

"I can't believe how foolish I was. In the beginning, when I thought Mr. Scotty was my friend, I told him all about my sister, Norma, and my nephew, Raul. I'm so proud of Raul, he's starting college this year. Raul was born here in the United States, so he's a citizen. But Norma, she is illegal like me.

"Mr. Scotty hired a detective and found out all about Norma and Raul. Where they live. Who their landlord is. Where Raul goes to school. Now, when I threaten to quit, he tells me he's going to turn me and Norma over to La Migra. I don't care for myself. I can always run off and hide somewhere. But Norma can't run. She has to be here for Raul.

"So I'm trapped with Mr. Scotty. I keep hoping that when Raul graduates from college, he will get a good job and make enough money to find a lawyer who will keep Norma safe. In the meanwhile, I'm stuck with the Evil One."

"You poor thing!" I said, my heart going out to her.

By now we'd scraped the last of the ice cream from our bowls.

"Thank you so much for all your help," I said, as she got up to leave.

"Why don't you come back with me?" Lupe said. "Missy is away jogging. You can visit with your cat."

Leaping at the opportunity to spend some alone time with Pro, I accompanied Lupe back to Scotty's house, where I gave her a hug and thanked her again for being my rescuing angel.

Then I made my way upstairs to Missy's bedroom, where I found Prozac lolling on her faux mink throw, playing with her catnip skunk, Rhett Butler, batting him about with girlish glee.

Oh, Rhett. I do declare. You are one hunky skunk!

Great. Not only was she cheating on me with Missy, now she had a thing going with the skunk.

"Hi, sweetheart!" I called out, plastering a hopeful smile on my face.

She looked up to shoot me a blank stare.

Oh. It's only you.

"I just dropped by to say hi."

I plopped down on the bed next to her and began scratching her behind her ears, something that normally sends her into spasms of ecstasy. But today, she ignored my loving strokes and continued pouncing on Rhett.

When I reached over to take her in my arms she wriggled free.

Yuck! You smell like WD40.

I sat there for a few more minutes, hoping Prozac would tire of Rhett and turn her attention to me. But no such luck. I might as well have been part of the faded wallpaper.

With a pained sigh, I hauled myself up from the bed.

"Bye, darling," I called out as I headed for the door, hoping for at least a farewell meow.

But Prozac was too busy pouncing on Rhett to notice I was leaving.

I was halfway down the stairs, feeling utterly rejected, when the front door banged open and Scotty came charging into the house, loaded down with a bunch of plastic bags from the 99 Cent Store.

"Hey, Jaine," he said, catching sight of me. "I finished all my Christmas shopping. I got all this," he said, holding up the plastic bags, "for less than twenty bucks!"

He beamed with pride.

"I just hope nobody expects me to wrap their presents. No way was I spending an extra ninety-nine cents for three rolls of wrapping paper.

"Come see what else I bought," he said, beckoning me into the kitchen, where Lupe was busy stretching a small mound of hamburger meat into dinner for four.

Scotty whipped out a large bakery box and set it down on a well worn kitchen table. Then he lifted the lid with pride, revealing a scrumptious looking Yule log, thick with chocolate frosting.

"It's a chocolate Yule log!" he beamed. "And I got it half price!"

I had no doubt that he did. Because written on the log in red and green icing was the inscription MERRY CHRISTMAS, AUNT HARRIET!

"Put it in the freezer," he commanded Lupe. "We'll defrost it on Christmas Day."

"Speaking of Christmas, Mr. Scotty," Lupe said, nervously fingering the edges of her apron, "I'm hoping I can have the day off to be with my family."

"Are you kidding?" Scotty replied, as if she'd just asked for a Tesla. "I just gave you Christmas off last year."

And with that, he lumbered off.

"Sometimes," Lupe hissed, her eyes blazing fury, "I feel like killing that man."

At the time, of course, I didn't dream she actually may have meant it.

Chapter 8

I left Lupe stewing under Scotty's dictatorial reign and made my way back to Casa Van H. Passing the trash cans where I'd stashed the mangled pinecones, I felt a stab of guilt. Poor Lance would be so disappointed to know they were now destined for a landfill.

I had intended to while away the rest of the afternoon with the Beverly Hills Housewives, but instead I got in my Corolla and spent the next forty-five minutes battling Christmas traffic to drive out to Lance's favorite vegetarian restaurant in Santa Monica—the kind of eco-chic joint where women in one-hundred-dollar yoga pants sip chai lattes between workouts.

I'd decided to get Lance his favorite kale and tofu salad for dinner that night.

Yes, I know that kale and tofu on the same plate is enough to make a normal person upchuck. But for some strange reason, Lance actually liked the stuff, and I figured getting him the salad was the least I could do after ruining his pine cone Santas.

The parking lot was full of Mercedes SUVs when I got there, so I wound up parking five blocks away. When I finally got to the restaurant, I had to wait in line to place my order. (Can you believe people wait in line to buy kale and tofu?) What seemed like eons later, I made it to the head of the line and ordered Lance's godawful salad. I'd been planning to make a pit stop at Ralphs supermarket for some of their yummy fried chicken for my own dinner, but drained of all energy, I decided to order something at the vegetarian joint instead.

Working on the tried and true principle that you can never go wrong with cheese, I chose the least objectionable item on their menu: an avocado and mozzarella sandwich.

At long last, my eco-friendly order was ready and I headed back outside. I was about a block away from the restaurant when I suddenly noticed a pop-up Christmas store, chock-full of Christmas ornaments. I'd been so frazzled from my rush hour trek to the restaurant, I guess I hadn't noticed it earlier.

Now I wandered inside and saw the most adorable felt Santas hanging from a tree. With white cottony beards and bright red Santa caps. Best of all, the clerk assured me, they were handmade! And on sale! I bought up a whole bunch, thrilled that I would be able to hand Lance some handmade ornaments, after all.

Maybe slogging through all that hellish traffic had been a blessing in disguise.

I was quite pleased with myself when Lance came home from work that night.

I had his ghastly salad laid out in Mrs. Van H's breakfast nook, along with a glass of his favorite (glug!) coconut water.

"Kale and tofu salad! Yum!" he cried when he saw the revolting pile of greens on Mrs. Van H's fine china.

"I drove all the way to Santa Monica to get it."

"Aren't you an angel!" he said, sitting down and digging into it with relish

How he got that stuff past his gullet, I'll never know.

"And look at you," he beamed, "eating something reasonably healthy for a change."

I had to admit the avocado and cheese sandwich wasn't so bad, except for the icky sprouts they'd shoved in.

"So," Lance asked, spearing a hunk of tofu, "how'd it go today with the pinecone Santas?"

"Not exactly as planned," I admitted.

I proceeded to tell him about my nightmarish adventure with the goo-goo eyes and the Wacky Glue on Mrs. Van H's kitchen island.

I thought for sure he'd be disappointed, but strangely enough, he took it all in stride.

"Dear, sweet, incompetent Jaine," he said, tsking in pity. "Worry not. Uncle Lance will take care of everything. By the time I'm through decorating, this house will look like a real-life issue of *Martha Stewart Living.*"

"Actually, Lance," I said, smarting more than a tad at his "incompetent" crack, "I found some really cute Santas we can use instead."

I raced into the kitchen and got the felt Santas I'd bought that afternoon.

"Aren't they great?" I said, laying them out on the table. "And they're handmade. Just not by me."

Lance looked down and wrinkled his nose.

"We can't possibly use these," he said, holding up one of the Santas like it was a dead mouse. "Way too tacky."

"Hold on," I said, beginning to really regret driving all the way over to Santa Monica for Lance's stupid salad. "Let me get this straight. Felt Santas are tacky, but pine cones with goo-goo eyes and cotton beards are the height of good taste?"

"The pine cone Santas were kitsch," Lance said, as if explaining the letters of the alphabet to a four-year-old. "There's a fine line between kitschy and tacky. Someday I hope I'll be able to teach it to you."

By now, I was ready to dump his stupid kale salad on his head.

But he just chattered on, oblivious.

"You're not the only one who did some shopping today," he said, reaching into his pocket and pulling out a small jewelry box.

"For you," he said, handing it to me. "For your date with Randy."

I opened it to find a pair of beautiful silver teardrop earrings.

See? This is why I can't ever stay mad at the guy.

"Oh, Jaine!" he cried, hope in his eyes, kale in

his teeth. "Things are really looking up for us! I've got a date with Graham, and with any luck, you'll hook up with Randy. Wouldn't it be wonderful if we both wound up with dates on New Year's Eve? For once we won't be stuck home watching *30 Rock* and eating diet popcorn!"

"I keep telling you, Lance. It doesn't have to be diet popcorn. This year, we could get popcorn with salt and cheddar cheese."

"This year," he said gleefully, "we could get lucky!

"To us!" he said, raising his glass of coconut water in a toast. "May we both wind up with the man of our dreams."

I raised my glass of chardonnay, but just as we were about to clink glasses, we heard shouting coming from Scotty's house.

"You miserable sonofabitch!" a woman was yelling.

Never one to miss a minute of drama, Lance was up and out of his seat like a rocket. I'm ashamed to admit I was hot on his heels right behind him.

We peeked out the front door at Scotty's house. Standing in the porch light under his portico was a tall, aristocratic sixtysomething woman in Katharine Hepburn slacks and a flowing wool cape. Her thick crop of silver hair was swept back from the sides of her head in soaring wings.

I couldn't make out her features at this distance, but her voice was ringing loud and clear.

"It was you, you bastard! You cut the electrical cords on our Christmas display."

And indeed, I looked across the street and saw that the extravagant display we'd noticed the other night was unlit, unmoving, dead to the world.

Scotty stood there, his chin and gut both jutting out belligerently.

"I don't know what you're talking about."

"It had to be you," said the silver-haired aristo. "You've been making such a fuss about our Christmas display, scaring everybody off with your ridiculous bullhorn."

"Your decorations are a blight on the neighborhood," Scotty shot back. "Invading our privacy with your blinding lights. And clogging the street with traffic. Whoever cut those cords did everybody on the block a favor."

"I know it was you."

"Oh, yeah?" I could hear the sneer in Scotty's voice. "Prove it."

With that, he stepped back inside and slammed the door in her face.

The furious aristo stormed across the street to her darkened front lawn. As she hurried up her front path, I couldn't help but notice the irony of her unlit "Peace on Earth" teddy bear.

Peace on earth?

Not in Bel Air. Not that night.

Not that Christmas.

YOU'VE GOT MAIL!

To: Jausten
From: Shoptillyoudrop
Subject: Exciting Day!

What an exciting day in Antigua! So much to see.
Daddy and I took a fabulous catamaran ride, sailing past historic Nelson's Dockyard (named after
Admiral Horatio Nelson, or Willie Nelson, I forget
who), the magnificent Pillars of Hercules cliff for-
mations, quaint fishing villages and exotic banana
trees. Plus a delicious lunch on board the catamaran. Now we're back on the ship and off to hear
Lydia Pinkus's lecture on Holiday Traditions
Around the World. (Today she's doing Latvia.)

XOXO,
Mom

To: Jausten
From: DaddyO
Subject: Off to the Pool!

Hi, Lambchop. Back from Antigua. Took a boat
ride, saw an old dock, a couple of banana trees,
and some guys out fishing. Pretty good lunch on
the catamaran, but not up to the standards of the
Buffet Master.

Your mom actually expected me to go with her to
listen to Lydia bore us senseless with her lecture
on Holiday Traditions in Latvia.

But your old DaddyO put his foot down and said
No Way. Right now I'm headed over to the pool to
soak up some rays.

Later, gator!
Smooches from,
DaddyO

To: Jausten
From: DaddyO
Subject: The Brat Is Back!

Most aggravating incident at the pool. I was having
a perfectly pleasant time, lying in my deck chair,
feeling the warm ocean breezes waft over my body,
when I decided to take a dip. I swam a few laps—
doing a very impressive crawl stroke, if I do say so
myself—then got out and walked back to my chaise
to towel off. But when I opened my towel, I found a
hairy black spider lurking in the folds. I don't mind
telling you, my heart did a couple of flip-flops.

Taking a closer look, however, I saw that it was a
rubber spider, one of those gag items, probably
from the same joint that sold me Lydia's Yakity Yak
castanet false teeth. Just as I was just plucking it out
from the towel, I heard an obnoxious giggle. I turned
to see the same redheaded kid who'd stolen my
éclair grinning at me from the other side of the pool.

Clearly, he was the one who'd shoved the spider in
my towel. He was laughing so hard, it was all I

could do not to run over and slap him silly. But, seeing as he was with his mother, I had to refrain from any capital punishment.

Instead I sat back down in my chaise and plotted revenge.

It didn't take long for me to come up with a plan. I bided my time until the kid and his mom went into the pool—The Brat diving underwater, his mom doing laps. Once I was sure they were both distracted, I zipped over to their deck chairs and hid the spider in his mom's towel.

Then I sat back and waited. Sure enough, when they got out of the pool, the kid's mom reached for her towel to dry off, found the spider, and got the shock of her life. Then, just like me, she realized it was a fake. Instantly, she knew where it had come from. She turned to The Brat and started chewing him out, wagging her finger, and taking away the sundae he'd ordered from the poolside café.

As The Brat sat on his chaise and sulked, I gave him a jaunty wave.

Vengeance is mine!
Nobody crosses your DaddyO and gets away with it.

Love 'n snuggles from,
DaddyO
aka The Avenger

To: Jausten
From: Shoptillyoudrop
Subject: Such an Edifying Chat!

Darling, did you know that Latvia is the home of
the first Christmas tree ever? According to Lydia,
whose lecture was simply spellbinding, the first
documented use of an evergreen tree at Christmas
was in the town square of Riga, the capital of
Latvia, in the year 1510. I can't believe Daddy
chose to miss out on such an edifying chat!

By the way, I found him at the buffet, eating
something he called his Victory Éclair. Heaven
knows what that was all about.

I stopped by for a sensible apple. (True, I picked
up a cookie instead, but it was really a very small
cookie.)

XOXO,
Mom

Chapter 9

After inhaling my breakfast croissant and reading about Daddy's latest skirmish with The Brat, I was back at the salt mines with Scotty the next morning, slaving over *The Return of Tiny Tim: Vengeance Is Mine!*

And I do mean slaving.

The aging Huck Finn sat across from me, feet propped on his desk, the freckles on his scalp peeking through his thinning hair, still refusing to let go of a single syllable of his script.

Glugging down cans of something called Econo-Cola and nibbling at individually wrapped Saltines (filched, no doubt, from Lenny's Deli), he clung to his godawful dialogue like a barnacle on a sinking ship.

We'd come upon a five-page passage where Tim was tying the noose he was going to use to hang one of his victims, rambling on about avenging the honor of the Cratchits.

"Scotty," I said, plastering on a placating smile, "surely we don't need to waste five pages making a noose."

Scotty looked up from his Saltine, irritated.

"We're not wasting pages," he snapped. "We're building tension."

Trust me, the only tension we were building was the headache throbbing in my temples.

By now I was ready to reach over and ram a Saltine up his nose.

But as much fun as that would have been, I didn't get a chance to do it, because just then there was a commotion at the front door. And the next thing I knew the aristocratic neighbor I'd seen yelling at Scotty last night came sweeping into the room.

Today her Katharine Hepburn slacks were topped off with a cashmere sweater that cost more than a Kia. Underneath her helmet of perfectly sculpted silver hair were icy gray eyes and cheekbones so sharp they could slice tomatoes.

In her hand, she was waving a piece of paper.

"Hello, Olivia," Scotty said. "Wish I could it say it was nice to see you, but I'd be lying through my teeth. Have you met my indentured servant, Jaine?"

(No, he didn't really call me his indentured servant, but we all know that's what I was.)

"Jaine, this is Olivia Sinclair, who's been a pain in my butt ever since she and her husband moved in across the street."

I shot her a weak smile, which she totally ignored.

She was there for one reason and one reason only: to have it out with Scotty.

"My electrician just finished rewiring my Christmas lights. Here's the bill for the damages." She slammed the paper down on Scotty's desk. "I expect you to pay every bit of it, plus five hundred dollars for pain and suffering."

Scotty glanced at the bill and snickered.

"I won't be paying you, Olivia. Not one penny."

With that, he took the bill, wadded it up into a ball, and tossed it across the room at his wastepaper basket.

"Slam dunk!" he cried as it landed in the rusty wire receptacle.

"On the contrary," he said, turning to Mrs. Sinclair with a sly smile, "you're the one who's going to be paying me. Big time."

Mrs. Sinclair's granite features turned even stonier with rage.

"That's it. I'm calling the police."

"Not so fast, Olivia. Before you make that call, I have a present for you."

Opening his top desk drawer, he took out a manila envelope.

"A little something for your memory book," he said, handing it to her.

She grabbed the envelope and pulled out what looked like an eight-by-ten photo. And suddenly all the anger drained from her face, fear radiating from her eyes. As if in a trance, she walked out of the room, the envelope clutched to her chest.

I'd tried to get a peek at the picture, but to no avail. All I knew was that whatever Scotty put in that envelope had scared the stuffing out of the stony aristo.

Something told me I'd just witnessed an ace black-mailer at work.

Lance was waiting for me when I got home that night, pouncing on me like an eager puppy.

"Oh, Jaine!" he cried. "Aren't you excited?"

"About what?"

"Don't tell me you've forgotten. Tonight's Double Date Night. Your date with Randy and my date with Graham."

As a matter of fact, after eight hours of working with Simon Legree—I mean, Scotty—I had forgotten all about the date Lance had set up for me with the guy he'd met on line at the supermarket.

"You're meeting him at seven for coffee at the Starbucks on Pico Boulevard in Westwood."

"Coffee? But I'm starving. I haven't had a thing to eat since lunch."

(Except for a Saltine I'd filched while Scotty was in the loo.)

"You don't have time for food now!" Lance replied. "You need every available minute to make yourself presentable."

"I'm not leaving this house," I said, arms planted firmly across my chest, "without something to eat."

"Oh, all right," he conceded. "I'll go get you a snack."

Off he raced to the kitchen, while I plopped down on the living room sofa, exhausted from my day at the salt mines.

Minutes later, Lance returned with a teensy container of no-fat, no-fruit, no-fun yogurt.

But I ate it with good grace and a smile on my face, mainly because while he'd disappeared to the kitchen to get it for me, I'd chowed down on an emergency Almond Joy I had stashed in my purse.

After scraping the last of the yogurt from the container, I hauled myself up from the sofa and headed upstairs to get ready for my date. Much to my regret, Lance hurried after me, hot on my heels.

I was hoping he'd be too busy primping for his date with Graham to pay any attention to me, but I was sadly mistaken.

He'd nailed down his outfit for the evening (California Preppy, whatever the heck that was) and—given that he wasn't meeting Graham until eight ("Such an elegant time to dine!")—he was, most unfortunately, devoting all his primping energies to me, making good on his earlier threat to give me a complete makeover.

He'd actually driven back to my apartment and ransacked my closet to choose an outfit for me to wear: my most uncomfortable skinny jeans (with a gut-pinching set-in waist), black silk blouse, faux suede blazer, and my one and only pair of Manolo Blahniks.

He had the whole outfit laid out on my bed in the guest bedroom, along with the new teardrop earrings he'd bought me.

"Now hustle into the shower," he commanded, very Henry Higgins, "and wash your hair. We need to straighten out every last curl on that mop of yours."

"Do I have to? I think my curls look fine."

Indeed, with zero humidity in the Santa Ana

winds, my curls were silky-shiny, at their Botticelli best.

"It's straight hair for you, young lady. We're going for the sleek, sophisticated look. Remember," he said, wagging a most irritating finger. "You've got only one chance to make a fab first impression."

So I plodded into the shower and washed my hair, after which I spent a good half hour ironing out every last curl with my dryer, so it rested on my shoulders in a curl-free bob.

When I was through, Lance eyed me appraisingly.

"On second thought," he said, "you're right. I think I like the curls better."

Argggh. Is he the most aggravating man ever, or what?

And so, under great protest, I went back into the shower, rewashed my hair, and had it scrunched dry to curly perfection by Lance, with the help of some expensive glop from Neiman Marcus he uses for his own hair.

I have to admit, the end result was worth it. My hair looked pretty darn terrific.

Having conquered my curls, Lance hovered over me as I applied my makeup.

"You don't use lip liner?" He looked on, aghast, as I slapped on some lipstick straight from the tube. "And don't tell me you're using drugstore lipstick! My God, hookers in Calcutta buy better makeup than you."

At last he left me alone to get dressed. (And to suck on an ancient Life Saver I'd rescued from the bottom of my purse.)

When I was finished, Lance hurried back to my side and spun me around for inspection.

"Perfect!" he pronounced, fussing with a stray curl. "You actually look presentable! Now, whatever you do, don't be yourself! Try for someone sexy and alluring."

"Gee, thanks for the vote of confidence."

"No problem, hon," he said, oblivious, as usual, to my sarcasm.

Then, after checking his watch, he added, "Guess it's time for me to make myself fabulous. Which should be easy. I've got so much to work with!"

Frankly, I was surprised there was enough room in the Van Hooten mansion for me, Lance, and his outsize ego.

Wishing him good luck with Graham, I grabbed my car keys and headed downstairs, off to my blind date with Lance's Supermarket Special.

Chapter 10

Driving over to Starbucks, I was overcome with doubts. Lance, after all, was a master of hype. For all I knew my "gorgeous" blind date would be Quasimodo's homelier brother. With a rampaging personality disorder.

Why on earth had I ever let him talk me into this?

I arrived at the appointed Starbucks, parked my car in a nearby municipal lot, and after struggling with a meter to accept my credit card, came dashing into the café a good five minutes late.

Looking around, I saw the usual assortment of writers banging away on their screenplays, readers engrossed in their books, and a group of geeks lost in a board game.

Then one of the readers looked up and waved at me.

My God. Lance did not lie. How could I have ever doubted him?

The dollburger waving at me was a world-class stunner. I was so taken back by his movie star good looks, I almost stumbled onto the lap of one of the gamer geeks.

The next thing I knew Lance's supermarket special was standing up and beckoning me to his table.

Although Lance had mentioned his name was Randy (or Andy; I really wasn't paying attention), for the purposes of my little story, and to get an idea of just how scrumptious he was, let's just call him Ryan Gosling II.

I gulped as I took in his tawny, blond-streaked hair, emerald green eyes, and the sexiest smile west of the Marlboro Man.

"You must be Jaine!" Ryan II said, treating me to his high-testosterone smile.

"Um . . . uh . . . er . . ."

Okay, what I meant to say was "yes," but I was a tad overwhelmed. You would have been, too. Honest.

Finally, I regained my powers of speech.

"Yes, I'm Jaine."

"What a pleasure to meet you!" Ryan II said, pulling out a chair for me.

A dollburger—with lovely manners! I was in blind date heaven!

"What can I get you?" he asked.

My brain cells, busy focusing on the blond streaks in his hair, couldn't be bothered with ordering.

"I'll have what you're having," I managed to say.

So entranced was I with his spectacular good looks that I did not even think about ordering my usual chocolate chip muffin.

As he walked over to the counter, I glanced

down at the book he'd been reading and gasped in delight.

Omigosh. It was *Joy in the Morning*. By P. G. Wodehouse.

P. G. Wodehouse just happens to be one of my favorite authors. And not many guys I've met even know who he is.

To think that Ryan Gosling II was a fan! Clearly we were literary soulmates.

And I soon discovered we had even more in common when Ryan II returned to our table with two Mocha Frappuccinos—and a double chocolate chunk brownie.

A P. G. Wodehouse reader—and chocoholic, too!

At that moment, I was certain that Cupid was hovering over us, getting ready to ping us with his arrow of love.

"Hope you like chocolate," he said, setting the brownie down on the table between us.

"Kinda sorta," I replied in the understatement of the year.

Under normal circumstances, I would have already plowed halfway through that brownie. But that day, all I did was sit there with a goofy smile on my face, afraid of biting into the thing and winding up with a glob of chocolate on my teeth.

"I can't tell you how excited I am to meet you," Ryan II said, flashing me his heart-stopping smile. "It's not every day I get to meet a famous TV writer."

A famous TV writer? What on earth did he mean? True, last year I got roped into working on a Grade Z reality show, and years ago, I'd done some time on an equally forgettable sitcom, but that hardly made me famous. Where had he gotten that idea?

And then it hit me: Lance! Lord knows what lies Lance, the master of hype, had spewed to land me this date.

"Actually," Ryan II said, reaching down into an attaché case by his chair, "I was hoping you might be able to get me a job on one of your shows."

And with that he whipped out a publicity head shot and résumé.

"I'm an actor," he said, treating me to another glimpse of his dazzling smile. Which suddenly seemed a lot less dazzling that it had just a minute ago.

Now it all made sense. The guy wasn't looking for a date. He was looking for a job. I should've known this whole thing was too good to be true.

"So you want me to hire you," I said.

Now his smile turned sheepish. "Well, actually, yes. But we could go out on some dates, too, if you like."

Above me, I felt Cupid putting his arrow away and flying off to Club Med.

"I'm sorry to disappoint you," I said, grabbing the brownie before he could get his scheming paws on it, "but I'm not really a TV writer. I write ads for small businesses here in L.A."

Ryan's smile froze.

"But it said in your profile that you were a famous TV writer, an accomplished bungee jumper, with a PhD in Celtic Literature from Vassar College!"

"Profile? What profile?"

"On Smatch.com, the dating website. That's where I saw your profile. It also said you were a chocoholic into P. G. Wodehouse."

"Is that why you brought this book?" I asked, gesturing to *Joy in the Morning*.

"Yeah," he nodded. "I haven't actually read any of it."

By now, I was in a state of shock. I simply couldn't believe that Lance had the monumental gall to sign me up on a dating website without my permission.

"Well, it's all a pack of lies. Except for Wodehouse and chocolate. A friend of mine apparently put up my profile without my knowledge. I haven't been near a TV studio in years. I spend most of my time writing toilet bowl ads for Toiletmasters Plumbers.

So, no, I'm not really a famous TV writer."

"That's okay," Ryan II said with a sigh, slipping his head shot back into his attaché case. "I'm not really single."

At which point, his cellphone rang, and he grabbed it.

"Oh. Okay, honey. I'll be right there.

"That was my wife," he said, clicking off his phone. "Gotta run. Her water just broke."

Grabbing his attaché case, he scooted for the door.

"Do you me a favor, willya?" he called out on his way out the door. "Return the book to the Venice Library. I think it's overdue a couple of weeks."

And so he left me, alone with my chocolate chunk brownie and an overdue library book.

No doubt about it. Cupid had definitely left the building.

I was so disgusted, I could barely nibble at my double chunk chocolate brownie.

Oh, who am I kidding? I scarfed down every last crumb, and scraped all the stray frosting off the napkin, too.

I wish I were one of those frail creatures who "can't eat a thing" when they're upset, but somehow my tummy always makes room for double chunk chocolate.

Slurping the last of my Frappuccino, I hauled myself up and made my way back to my Corolla.

Not only had I driven down from Bel Air to Westwood to meet the unscrupulous Ryan Gosling II, I now had to battle traffic out to Venice to return his stupid library book, which I dropped into the return box outside the library.

I only hoped they slapped him with a hefty fine.

All the way back to Bel Air, I thought of Lance and the many ways I'd like to throttle him for putting my profile on Smatch. Back at Casa Van Hooten, I climbed into bed, just waiting till Lance got home so I could read him the riot act.

Normally I'd have Pro's warm body to comfort me in my hour of need, but now all I had was the second double chocolate chunk brownie I'd bought at Starbucks.

I ate it in bed, careful not to spill a crumb on Mrs. Van H's zillion-thread-count sheets.

Channel surfing on the guest bedroom TV, I came across an episode of *My Cat from Hell*. But it was way too painful to watch, evoking, as it did, so many tender memories of Prozac. Instead, I opted for a Christmas special with the *Property Brothers* (who, I bet my bottom Pop-Tart, never showed up on a blind date with head shots and résumés!).

During the commercial breaks, I took particular pleasure in drawing pot bellies on the models in Lance's Jockey for Men underwear catalog.

At last I heard the front door open.

"Yoo hoo, Jaine, honey. I'm home!"

Seconds later, he was bursting into my room, clearly having glugged down a mighty swig of Love Potion #9.

"Oh, Jaine! I had the best dinner date ever! Graham and I sat in a romantic corner booth, thigh to thigh, candlelight flickering in Graham's eyes. We ordered chateaubriand and the most heavenly bottle of pinot noir and talked and talked all night!

"I told him about my job at Neiman's. I may have exaggerated just a tad. If he should ever ask, I'm the general manager.

"He told me all about himself, his boyhood in Kansas, his job as a postal carrier and about his dead boyfriend Peter, who passed away a few years ago, and who he kept calling his 'honey bunny.' Which so warmed my heart. Shows you that underneath those fabulous pecs beats a heart of gold.

"To be perfectly honest, I wasn't paying all that much attention to everything he said. I was just so distracted by his eyes! I don't know if you noticed, but they're a spectacular shade of Tiffany blue. Which is where I hope we'll be buying our engagement rings. Yes, I know what you're thinking, that I'm going way too fast. But he's the one. I can feel it in my bones."

I was quite certain that Lance's nauseating enthusiasm was spewing not from his bones, but from a more centrally located part of his bod.

Finally he realized I was just sitting there, stony-faced.

"Silly me. I've been babbling on about Graham and forgot all about you. How did your date go?"

"Not quite as well as yours," I said, barely restraining myself from bopping him over the head with his Jockey catalog.

"How was Randy?"

"For starters, he was married."

"Oh, no!"

"He showed up at Starbucks with his head shots hoping I would give him an acting job. Apparently my Smatch.com profile claims that I am a famous TV writer."

Still lost in Graham-land, Lance failed to detect the fury in my voice.

"How could you go behind my back and sign me up for a dating service?" I shrieked, finally getting his attention.

"I wanted to surprise you."

"I was surprised all right. You told me you met Randy on line at the supermarket."

"Technically, I did. I saw his profile on the Smatch app while I was waiting on line at the supermarket."

"And those lies you made up about me! Bungee jumping and going to Vassar!"

"I know! Weren't they great? No need to thank me, hon. That's what friends are for. You're going to love Smatch! So Randy was a bust. Big deal. Now you have a vast database of men just waiting to be discovered."

"Forget it, Lance. No way am I staying on Smatch. I'm going to delete my profile right now!"

Lance's eyes widened in dismay.

"But you can't! I paid a hundred and twenty bucks for six months' membership."

And just like that, I started melting.

I don't know if you're keeping a tally, but so far, Lance had bought me a cashmere sweater, dangly earrings, and now a $120 membership in an on-line dating service.

He'd spent a small fortune on me.

"I only want what's best for you, sweetie," he said, smiling at me hopefully.

And the thing of it is, he really did. He may be the most aggravating man on earth, but he really cares about me.

"Just give it a chance, will you?" he begged. "Somewhere out there, there's got to be someone just right for you."

"Okay," I conceded. "I'll give it a chance. But first thing in the morning, I'm rewriting my profile."

"You'll probably want to take out the part about you being a body double for Scarlett Johansson."

"What??!"

"Just taking a little poetic license."

"Oh, all right. And speaking of poetic license, I took the liberty of making some creative changes to your Jockey catalog."

And I must admit it was quite soothing lying back against Mrs. Van H's eiderdown pillows listening to Lance's yowls of dismay as he discovered the pot bellies I'd drawn on his Jockey studs.

Yes, most soothing, indeed.

Chapter 11

You can't imagine the utter pap Lance had made up about me on Smatch.com. In addition to the Vassar/bungee jumping/Scarlett Johansson body double thing, I was also apparently a Cordon Bleu cook and part-time lingerie model.

I quickly set about correcting these whoppers and reading the many messages I had received from lingerie fetishists and Scarlett Johansson stalkers. Not to mention the boatload of bilge from scammers professing to be brain surgeons/attorneys/nuclear physicists writing such Pulitzer Prize–winning billets-doux as:

You are pretty ladie. I will like to know you very much.

After cleaning up my Smatch profile, I spent the next several days back in the trenches with Scotty, desperately trying to trim the fat from his bloated epic.

Work was even more intolerable than usual due to the fact that the Santa Anas had not let up and the temperature was climbing well into the eighties. Scotty, ever the cheapskate, refused to turn on his A/C. Even with all the windows and French doors open, the House of Scrooge was a veritable sauna.

Thank heavens I managed to have some fun at night with Lance.

We popped in at a couple of Christmas parties, the most festive being the annual Toiletmasters Christmas bash (where my boss and genial host, Phil Angelides, served eggnog from a claw-footed bathtub), took in the Christmas boat show at the marina, and saw the spectacular display of Christmas lights in Beverly Hills. (None of which, according to Lance, were as brilliant as the twinkle in Graham's Tiffany blue eyes.)

No matter where we were, Lance simply could not get Graham off his mind.

After their first date, Lance assumed he'd be spending scads of time with his new flame. But Graham told Lance he'd be tied up until after Christmas—which sent Lance spiraling into an eddy of doubt, bombarding Graham with emoji-laden texts, parsing every reply with the gravity of a monk studying an epistle from Saint Paul.

"What if he doesn't really like me?" he'd moan as I worked my way through my annual supply of Christmas fudge. "What if he's just trying to let me down gently? What if he's lost interest? What if I never get to see him again?"

"What if I take this piece of fudge and shove it

in your mouth so you'll give me two minutes of blessed silence?"

Of course I didn't say that. I was far too kind a person, and far too busy eating my Christmas fudge.

On Christmas Eve, Lance and I went to his hipster Unitarian church in Santa Monica, a great old Spanish sanctuary with a bell tower, red tile roof, and wood-beamed ceilings. A striking raven-haired minister, who looked like she might have graced the cover of *Vogue* a decade or two ago, presided over a series of inspirational poems and readings while a world-class choir, no doubt full of Hollywood backup singers, belted out a medley of soaring hymns.

Sitting there, breathing in the bracing scent of the pine garlands adorning the pews, I was filled with a sense of peace. Next to me, Lance was staring off into space, either contemplating the wonder of the season or parsing the hidden meaning in Graham's latest text.

Back home at the Van Hooten manse, we stopped in the living room to admire Lance's Christmas tree with its eclectic mix of traditional ornaments, handmade baubles, and strands of fresh acorns.

After enough oohs and aahs from me to stroke Lance's ego, we adjourned to the den, cups of mulled cider in our hands, to watch our favorite holiday movie, *Christmas in Connecticut*.

Normally I adore this flick with Barbara Stanwyck as a kitchen klutz pretending to be a Martha Stewart clone. But this year, my heart wasn't in it. In spite of the mulled cider and deluxe TV with surround sound, I felt an empty spot in my lap. A spot where Prozac should have been, demanding her Christmas Eve belly rub.

Try as I might to shove her out of my mind, I missed the little rascal.

Lance, too, was distracted, obsessively checking his phone for messages from Graham.

So, longing to see Prozac, I left Lance—eyeballs glued to his phone—and headed next door to check in on Christmas Eve at The House of Scrooge.

Lupe greeted me at the Parkers' front door, a wan smile on her face.

"How's it going, Lupe?"

"Not so *bueno*," she sighed. "I'm stuck here with Mr. Wonderful when I should be home with my family for Christmas."

I remembered how Scotty refused to give Lupe time off for the holiday. What a bum.

"Everybody's in the living room watching Scotty's movie, the one he made when he was a little boy. *Dios mio.*" Lupe shook her head in disgust. "He was every bit as—how you say, stinky?—then as he is now."

She led me to the living room where Scotty, Missy, and their tenant, Dave Kellogg of non-cereal fame, were gathered around watching Scotty's long forgotten remake of *A Christmas Carol.*

Scotty was stretched out on his recliner, clutching a tumbler of discount booze, while Missy sat perched on the sofa, Dave in an adjacent armchair.

In the corner of the room was a massive artificial tree with built-in lights.

Whaddya know? For once it looked like Scotty had actually forked over some dough for the holidays.

But then I noticed a price tag dangling from the tree.

"He buys a fancy artificial tree every year," Lupe whispered, following my gaze. "Then he returns it on January second."

Yikes. The man defied belief.

"Ms. Jaine is here," Lupe announced, shooting Scotty a filthy look before flouncing off to the back of the house.

"Jaine!" Missy cried, turning around to greet me. "How nice of you to stop by. C'mon in. We're watching Scotty's movie."

As I walked around to the front of the sofa, I saw something that made me gawk in astonishment.

There, curled up in Missy's lap, was Prozac—with a pair of fuzzy reindeer antlers strapped to her head!

First, the mistletoe cap. Now this—from the cat who puts up a battle royale when I even try to change her flea collar! I could not believe she was sitting there, with Bullwinkle's headgear strapped to her noggin, docile as a Stepford cat.

"Come sit here, Jaine." Missy patted a spot on the sofa next to her. "Scarlett, honey, look who's here!"

Prozac tore her eyes away from Missy and glanced up at me lazily.

Oh, yeah. It's whatshername.

"You hold her," Missy said, setting Prozac in my lap. "You must miss your little darling."

Indeed I did. Unfortunately, the feeling was not mutual.

Although Prozac remained on my lap, granting me the privilege of scratching her back in the sweet spot right behind her tail, never once did she take her eyes off Missy, gazing at her with the same kind of reverence I gaze at my Christmas fudge.

And Prozac wasn't the only one under Missy's spell.

Dave was having a hard time keeping his eyes on the TV, stealing covert glances at Missy every few seconds.

The only one paying attention to the clunker on the TV screen was Scotty, busy trashing all the other actors, reserving most of his scorn for the guy playing Bob Cratchit, an actor named Everett Chambers.

"Have you ever seen such a wooden performance?" Scotty bellowed at the screen as Cratchit begged for a day off from Scrooge. "I've seen better acting from a ventriloquist's dummy. What a doofus!"

Prozac eyed him appraisingly.

Takes one to know one.

Scotty caught her looking at him.

"Why, even that cat could turn in a better performance."

Was he kidding? Prozac could give Meryl Streep a run for her money.

We all sat there, uncomfortable, as Scotty continued to rant at the screen, glugging down shots of booze between zingers.

"He does this all the time," Missy whispered in my ear. "Blames the failure of the movie on everyone else in the cast, instead of his own terrible performance."

And indeed, as I looked at the young freckle-faced Scotty on the screen, I practically needed a diabetes shot to get through his syrupy portrayal of Tiny Tim.

"Care for some popcorn?" Dave asked, holding out a bowl, in one of the rare moments he wasn't gazing, rapt, at Missy.

"Be careful," he warned as I reached out to grab some. "It's discount popcorn. Most of the kernels haven't popped."

So there I was, gnawing away at unpopped popcorn, gazing down at my cheating feline, Scotty bellowing in the background—wishing I could just take Prozac, rip off her stupid antlers, and drive back home to my apartment.

But my escape plans were interrupted just then by an angry banging on the front door.

By now I was used to angry banging at Scotty's front door. This did not seem to be a house where people popped by for friendly chitchats.

Missy, alarmed, jumped up to get it.

Seconds later, she returned with Scotty's ex-wife, Elise, who looked even angrier than when I'd first seen her barging into Scotty's living room the other night.

"You miserable piece of slime!" she screeched at Scotty. "I still haven't gotten my alimony check."

"Really?" Scotty said, with a patently phony look of surprise on his face. "It must've gotten lost in the mail."

"My God," Elise groaned, "you're almost as bad a liar as you were an actor. You never wrote me a check."

And off she marched toward the foyer.

"Where the hell are you going?" Scotty cried out.

"To your office, where I will find your check-book and write myself my alimony check."

Alarmed at the thought of parting with his money, Scotty started to haul himself out of his re-cliner.

"You take one more step, Scotty, and I swear I'll beat the living daylights out of you." With that, Elise rushed to the fireplace and picked up a rusty poker, waving it in the air, itching to bop her for-mer husband on the bean.

Clearly cowed, Scotty sat back down in his re-cliner and made no attempt to stop her as she headed out of the living room.

Dazed by the drama that had just played out be-fore us, we returned to watching the movie. Scotty continued trashing the actors, but with not nearly as much gusto as before, periodically glancing at the foyer, awaiting Elise's return.

Elise was gone for what seemed like an eternity, but then, any time in Scotty's company seemed like an eternity. Finally she came back, waving a check, which she thrust, along with a pen, in Scotty's hand.

"Now sign the damn thing."

Reluctantly, Scotty placed the check on a TV tray by the side of his recliner and signed it.

Elise snapped it up without missing a beat.

"I don't know how long I can keep putting up with this, Scotty. I've had it with you and your heartless determination to keep me living in poverty."

She started to stalk off but stopped to glance at the TV.

"What an egotistical little ham," she said, eyeing young Scotty. "The worst Tiny Tim ever. And the years have done you no favors. It's time somebody shut down your act once and for all."

With that, she turned on her heel and stormed off into the night.

In my humble op, the best performance of the night.

YOU'VE GOT MAIL!

To: Jausten
From: Shoptillyoudrop
Subject: The Nerve of That Man!

You're not going to believe what Daddy bought Lydia for her Secret Santa gift! A pair of clacking false teeth! Have you ever heard of anything so awful? And he actually had the nerve to put them in a fancy box from the ship's gift shop before wrapping them in the gift wrap paper I'd brought from home for last-minute emergency gifts. It was just a stroke of luck on my part that I found the original packing for the false teeth stuffed away in his suitcase.

Well, I rushed right down to the gift shop and bought Lydia a lovely scarf. Daddy almost bust a gasket when he found out it cost sixty dollars, but that's what he gets for buying those false teeth in the first place.

The nerve of that man! He claims he was making a statement about Lydia being an "insufferable gasbag."

We're headed off to the Secret Santa exchange. Thank heavens I found out about Daddy's devious plan in time to stop it. I shudder to think how embarrassed I would have been if poor Lydia had seen those clacking teeth.

Merry Christmas, sweetheart! I only wish you were spending it with us!

XOXO,
Mom
PS. Hope you got the adorable Capri set Daddy and I sent from the Home Shopping Club. I just love the cat on the T-shirt who says "Meowy Christmas!" The minute I saw it, I thought of you and your precious Zoloft.

To: Jausten
From: DaddyO
Subject: Operation False Teeth Foiled!

Bad news, Lambchop! Mom found out about my plan to give Lydia Pinkus those Yakity Yak false teeth for Christmas. Not only that, she went down to the gift shop and spent sixty bucks on a replacement gift! The thought of spending sixty dollars on The Gasbag is almost as nauseating as the thought of listening to one of her snorefest lectures.

To: Jausten
From: DaddyO
Subject: Silver Lining

Back from the Secret Santa exchange. Lydia, needless to say, loved her sixty-dollar scarf. I was all set to write the whole thing off as another Christmas fiasco. That is, until I opened my own Secret Santa gift. There, nestled in a wad of tissue paper, was a bright purple fright wig! The perfect accessory for my Tarzan loincloth!

I can't wait to wow everybody at the costume party.

In the meanwhile, Lambchop, I'm sending you a load of extra hugs and kisses for Christmas. No present I ever get will be as special as my little Lambchop.

Love 'n snuggles from,
DaddyO

Chapter 12

I slept in till nine on Christmas morning.

Which was not surprising. After all, I no longer had Prozac, my personal alarm clock, to pounce on my chest and claw me awake for her breakfast.

As much as I tried, I simply could not erase the memory of her in those ridiculous fuzzy antlers last night, gazing longingly at Missy.

I had to face facts. My cat was cheating on me with another woman. And my heart was breaking. Why, I didn't even feel this bad when I found out that my ex, The Blob, had been sexting with his tai chi instructor.

After brushing my teeth and splashing some cold water on my face, I checked my emails and was happy to learn that Mom had foiled Daddy's dastardly plan to embarrass Lydia Pinkus with a pair of castanet false teeth.

Relieved that all was well on the high seas, if not here in Bel Air, I headed downstairs to the kitchen where I found my roomie whipping up one of his ghastly green smoothies.

You'd think he'd give himself the day off on Christmas, but no, he was determined to slug down that pureed grass no matter what.

"Merry Christmas!" I said, forcing a bright smile.

"You too, hon!" Lance grinned, a tiny green mustache on his upper lip. "Smoothie?" he asked, holding out the blender.

"Not if I want my Christmas to stay merry."

"Suit yourself, but you're missing out on a treat. I added nutmeg and extra wheat germ!"

Oh, glug.

Giving the blender a wide berth, I nuked myself some coffee and one of the cinnamon raisin bagels I'd laid in for the duration of our stay.

Then I told Lance about last night's festivities at The House of Scrooge, about their "borrowed" Christmas tree, their half-popped popcorn, Prozac's obsession with Missy, and how Scotty's ex-wife showed up and almost bonked him over the head with a fireplace poker.

"I've had more fun at a bikini wax," I sighed.

"You poor thing," Lance said, gulping down the last of his smoothie. "I know what'll cheer you up. Let's go open our Christmas presents! And remember. Act surprised!"

And so we adjourned to the living room to open our gifts.

I oohed and aahed (with utmost sincerity) over my cashmere sweater, a luscious baby blue beauty with a jewel neck and three-quarter sleeves. And after gushing "What a surprise!" Lance proceeded to admire the tie he had so painstakingly picked out for himself.

"If all goes right," he said, eyes shining, "I'll wear it on New Year's Eve with Graham. He just texted me a little while ago to wish me a Merry Christmas! Which means he's thinking about me! Hopefully naughty thoughts if that winking emoji at the end of his text meant anything."

Buoyed by images of future snugglefests with his hunky mailman, Lance sprang up from the sofa.

"Better hustle off to the kitchen and get started on my Christmas goose. I'm making a special tofu cranberry stuffing to go with."

Double glug.

"Need any help?" I asked, praying he'd say no.

My prayers were answered.

"I don't think so, hon. After that pine cone Santa disaster, I think it's best to keep you as far away from the kitchen as possible, and leave everything to the master chef."

Puh-leese. This from a man whose idea of gourmet cooking is serving his Lean Cuisine on fine china.

But I was grateful to be relieved of cooking duty, and as the pots and pans started clanging away in the kitchen, I headed upstairs to get dressed. In spite of last night's painful encounter with Prozac, I was eager to pop by next door and deliver her Christmas gift.

The one-hundred-dollar Mowse I'd ordered had arrived and now, after getting dressed, I put in the batteries and tested it out. I watched in awe as the egg-shaped toy with the feathery tail darted around my bedroom like a living critter.

Surely, my Mowse would outshine anything Missy had bought.

I trotted next door with the Mowse tucked away in a festive shopping bag, hoping for a much-needed show of affection from my fickle feline.

Just as I was about to ring the bell, the door swung open to reveal Lupe in jeans and a T-shirt, her purse slung over her shoulder, her arms full of presents.

"Ms. Jaine!" she whispered, quickly slipping outside to join me. "I was just about to sneak away to spend a few hours with my family. That's my nephew," she added, waving at a slim, dark-haired young guy standing at the curb beside a blue Nissan.

He waved back, a sweet smile on his face.

"Promise you won't tell Mr. Scotty?"

"Of course not!" I assured her. "Your secret's safe with me."

"You know what that *bastardo* got me for Christmas?" Lupe said, eyes blazing. "A used apron!"

"No!"

"Yes! With a big gravy stain on it. He said, 'It's already broken in.' "

"How awful!" I commiserated.

"You come to work with him today?" Lupe asked, holding the door open.

"God, no! I came to see my cat."

"Scarlett's upstairs in Missy's bedroom."

I cringed at the sound of Prozac's new name.

"And Missy?" I asked.

"She's out on her run."

Thank heavens. Now I'd get to spend some precious time alone with Pro.

"I'd better be going," Lupe said. "My nephew's waiting. Merry Christmas, Ms. Jaine."

"You too, Lupe. And have a wonderful time with your family."

I watched as she hurried down the path to her nephew's car and rode off, safe, for the time being, from Scotty's wrath.

Then I tiptoed inside, determined to steer clear of Mr. Wonderful.

As I crossed the foyer to the staircase, I happened to glance into the kitchen and saw something that made me stop dead in my tracks.

Something that always makes me stop dead in my tracks:

Chocolate.

Sitting on the kitchen counter on a cardboard bakery platter was the chocolate Yule log that Scotty had bought at a discount, the one with the words MERRY CHRISTMAS, AUNT HARRIET! blazoned across its chocolate frosting.

Heaven only knew how stale it was underneath, but my, that frosting looked scrumptious.

And before I knew it, I'd scampered into the kitchen for the weensiest taste.

If I do say so myself, I have mastered the fine art of spackling over holes I've made after frosting taste tests. But when I went to dig my finger into the luscious chocolate goo, it was hard as a rock.

Lupe must've just taken it out of the freezer to defrost.

Oh, well. I couldn't afford to be thinking about chocolate anyhow, not when I had Prozac's affections to win back.

Upstairs, I found my pampered princess on Missy's bed, playing with the catnip-filled skunk Missy had given her, the one she'd called Rhett Butler.

Prozac was pouncing on the toy with the wild abandon of a pole dancer in heat.

"Merry Christmas, sweetheart!" I said, plopping down next to her on the bed. "Look what Mommy bought you."

I whipped out the Mowse from my shopping bag.

"It's a Mowse!" I said putting it on the floor.

I was thrilled to see Prozac drop Rhett from where she had him clenched in her jaw and stare at the Mowse, who was now scampering about the room, feathery tail wagging in its wake.

"See? It's just like a real mouse, Pro! Go get it."

She watched it for a few more seconds, then turned to gaze at me with the same kind of look Samson must have given Delilah when she asked him how he liked his haircut.

If that thing's a mouse, I'm Albert Schweitzer.

And back she went to molesting poor Rhett Butler.

I was sitting there, cursing the day I ever allowed Prozac to stay here at the House of Scrooge, when I thought I heard a soft thud downstairs, followed by footsteps. Oh, hell. What if Scotty was coming upstairs? What if he found me here and expected me to work on his miserable script on Christmas

Day? Or what if he was looking for Lupe? What the heck was I supposed to tell him?

I sat there, frozen, for what seemed like a small eternity, but thank heavens, I didn't hear his footsteps on the stairs. Maybe he just went to the fridge for one of his Econo-Colas.

Finally spent from her antics with Rhett Butler, Prozac stretched out in a satisfied stupor and allowed me to scratch her back.

"Does that feel good, sweetie?" I murmured as I scratched. "Does it?"

She looked up and gazed at me sternly.

Less yakking and more scratching, please.

After enough scratching to cause carpal tunnel syndrome, I managed to get her nestled in my arms, and was holding her there, just like in the old days, when the door burst open and in trotted Missy, breathless and sweaty, ponytail tousled, in shorts and a tank top.

"Just got back from my run," she said.

At the sight of Missy, Prozac wriggled free from my arms and raced over to her, rubbing against her ankles with the same wild abandon she'd lavished on Rhett Butler.

"Did my precious Scarlett miss me?" Missy asked, scooping her up in her arms.

A worshipful gaze from Pro.

More than a can of freshly opened human tuna!

At which point, Prozac began licking her with enough passion to qualify for a same-sex marriage license.

"Wait till you see the cute gift I bought you for Christmas!" Missy chirped.

With that, she reached into her vanity drawer and pulled out a cheap rubber squeaky mouse.

Prozac took one look and went bananas, pouncing on the toy, still oblivious to my Mowse performing near acrobatic feats not two feet away.

"What's that?" Missy asked, noticing the Mowse.

"Just a little gift I picked up for her. But I'm afraid she's not very interested in it."

"That's funny," Missy said. "Scarlett seems to be crazy about everything I buy her."

By now I was ready to upchuck. Even Lance's breakfast smoothie wasn't this nauseating.

"Time for me to go," I said, getting up from the bed.

"I almost forgot," Missy said, as I headed for the door, "Scotty mentioned something at breakfast about wanting to talk to you about the script. Would you mind popping in his office on your way out?"

Of course I'd mind.

I couldn't think of anything worse, except staying one more minute watching Prozac's lovefest with Missy.

I headed downstairs, girding my loins, prepared to tell Scotty I was not about to do a stitch of work. Not today. Not on Christmas.

As it turned out, I would not have to work with Scotty that day. Or any other day, for that matter. Because when I stepped in his office the first thing I saw was Scotty Parker slumped over his desk, blood trickling from his scalp—bashed in the head with Aunt Harriet's frozen Yule log.

Chapter 13

Soon after I called 911, the place was swarming with cops dusting for fingerprints, checking the body, and doing whatever else cops do when a guy has been bonked to death with a chocolate Yule log.

One of the officers, a brawny African-American dude who looked like he could moonlight for Lance's Jockey underwear catalog, took down my statement about finding the body.

I assumed I could then skip off to freedom but was informed that I'd have to stick around until the detective on the case showed up. I don't know what the detective was doing that morning—investigating another murder, or opening Christmas presents—but I wound up waiting two hours before he finally strolled in.

Hours I spent huddled in the living room with Missy, Dave, and Prozac, the latter nestled—where else?—on Missy's lap.

I'd called out to Missy right after I'd phoned the police. She'd come running down the stairs and gasped at the sight of Scotty, blood pooling on his desk. I did not have to warn her not to touch the body; she made no attempt to go near it, just stared at it, eyes wide, and then turned away.

Now as I sat across from her, she looked like a novice actress auditioning for the role of The Grieving Widow, wringing her hands and blinking back nonexistent tears. Every once in a while she managed to work up an actual drop of moisture but I sensed it was taking a lot of effort.

I remembered how she'd badmouthed Scotty, how trapped she'd felt in the marriage and how desperately she'd been trying to figure a way out.

Maybe the way out she'd taken was murder.

Meanwhile, Dave was glued to her side, patting her hand, assuring her that everything was going to be okay.

I couldn't help but notice how his hand lingered on hers with each pat. It had been clear from the first night I met him that the Parkers' tenant was crazy about Missy. Now I wondered: Was it possible he bumped off Scotty to get rid of his competition?

And Dave was not the only one on the Missy Sympathy Bandwagon.

Most galling was Prozac, nuzzling Missy under her neck, comforting her in her time of stress. How aggravating was that? Whenever I stressed out, all she ever offered me was her belly to rub. But today she was a bundle of affection.

Who did she think she was, anyway—a dog?

At last the detective on the case showed up: Lt. Max Muntner, a lumbering round-shouldered fellow with a bit of a pot belly and heavy-lidded eyes that looked like they'd seen it all—and then some.

After offering condolences to Missy, he asked permission to use the den as headquarters, and summoned her first for questioning. Working up a few tears for the occasion, she rose from the sofa, still clutching her "darling Scarlett," and headed off across the hall.

With Missy gone, Dave realized I was actually there in the room and began chatting with me. He told me how shocked he was over Scotty's death, how he'd been in his room all morning, studying his law books. He said he'd wanted to fly home to spend Christmas with his family, but finances were tight.

Frankly, I got the feeling he was just where he wanted to be—in close proximity to his luscious landlady.

His eyes lit up the minute she came back from her session with the detective.

"How'd it go?" Dave asked.

"Okay, I guess," she shrugged. "Apparently Scotty was killed sometime between a little after ten when he ended a phone call with his broker and eleven when Jaine found the body."

Oh, brother. Can you believe Scotty had the gall to bother his broker on Christmas Day?

"I told the detective I was out running the whole time," Missy was saying, "but he didn't seem convinced."

Frankly, neither was I.

I flashed back on Missy returning to her bedroom, sweaty in her shorts and tank top. She well might have been out running. But who knows if she hadn't burned off a few extra calories knocking off her hubby?

I didn't have time to ponder Missy's guilt or innocence, however, because just then I was summoned to chat with Lt. Muntner.

"Come in," he said, waving me into the Parkers' den, a musty affair with threadbare furniture from the Left-Out-on-the-Curb-on-Garbage-Day Collection.

The detective sat on a recliner, a recorder and a notepad on an end table by his side.

I plopped down on a nearby sofa, trying to steer clear of the many stains adorning its cushions.

In his lap Lt. Muntner had a copy of *The Return of Tiny Tim: Vengeance Is Mine!* He rifled through the pages, shaking his head in disbelief.

"What a stink bomb," he pronounced.

"I'm afraid so."

"Mrs. Parker tells me you were helping Mr. Parker write it."

"No, I was helping Scotty edit it. I was trying to get him to cut out the really awful parts."

"I'd say that's just about everything."

I was beginning to like this guy.

"So," he said, pulling his notepad from the end table and getting down to business. "You're the one who discovered the body."

"That's right. I was upstairs visiting my cat when

Missy came home from her run and told me Scotty wanted to see me. So I stopped by his office and that's when I found his body."

"Did you see or hear anything unusual while you were upstairs?"

"As a matter of fact," I said, "I thought I heard a thud, and then some footsteps. I figured it was Scotty going to the kitchen to get himself a snack."

"And the thud. What did you think that was?"

"I had no idea. But now I realize it was probably Scotty's head hitting his desk."

I was shuddering at the memory of Scotty crumpled over his desk when the Jockey model cop showed up.

"Excuse me, sir," he said to Lt. Muntner. "I thought you should know that the victim's security surveillance tape is missing. Also, we checked the murder weapon for fingerprints. Looked like the killer was wearing gloves. But somewhere along the line he or she got sloppy, because we managed to find a print on the Yule log. We just sent it off to the lab for identification."

I sat up with a jolt. Because I suddenly realized that the fingerprint in question was none other than mine.

If only I hadn't tiptoed into the kitchen to get a taste of that frosting!

In no time, they'd match up the print with the one on my driver's license, and bingo, I'd be sharing a cell with a gal named Bruce.

Oh, hell.

I had to play it cool and monitor my speech. I'd

seen enough cop shows to know that anything I said could be held against me in a court of law.

And so, with all the sangfroid of a Yorkie on uppers, I shrieked:

"Omigod! It was me! All I wanted was a taste of the frosting. The Yule log was out on the kitchen counter when I got here and the frosting looked so yummy, nice and creamy just the way I like it, and I couldn't resist. After all, it was chocolate and I mean, who says no to chocolate? But when I tried to scoop some up with my finger I realized it was frozen so I went upstairs to Prozac with my Mowse and I swear I never touched it after that."

I tend to babble when I'm nervous.

"Let me get this straight," Lt. Muntner said, a bit dazed. "You saw the Yule log on the kitchen counter and tried to eat some frosting but it was frozen solid, and you were so upset, you had to go upstairs and calm down with a Prozac."

"No, Prozac is my cat."

"And your mouse? Is that another one of your pets?"

"No, Mowse is a toy I bought Prozac for Christmas. The cutest little thing. It scampers around just like a real mouse, but Prozac hardly looked at it; all she cares about is Missy and Rhett Butler!"

Omigod. Why was I babbling like this? Would somebody please shut me up???

"I see," said Lt. Muntner, no doubt making plans to book me in the nearest psycho ward. "Maybe it's time for you to take a Prozac for real. You're probably going to need it."

Oh, dear. I didn't like the sound of that.

"Ms. Austen, you were found at the scene of the crime. And if, as you claim, yours is the fingerprint on the murder weapon, you're definitely a suspect in this case."

"But why? Why would I want to kill Scotty?"

"That's for us to find out, isn't it?" the good detective said with a genial smile.

Okay, now I didn't like him so much.

"In the meanwhile," he cautioned, "don't leave town."

Thoroughly shaken, I staggered out of the den and back to Casa Van Hooten, where Lance greeted me in a cranberry-stained apron.

"Just in time!" he grinned. "My goose is cooked!"

And so, it appeared, was mine.

Chapter 14

Lance led me to the kitchen, beaming with pride. "Doesn't it smell yummy?"

"Actually," I said, taking a sniff, "it smells like smoke."

Sure enough, the minute we walked in the kitchen we saw wisps of smoke seeping out from the oven.

"Lance, I think your goose is on fire!"

Grabbing an oven mitt, Lance raced to the oven and yanked open the door, where flames were leaping up from the roasting pan.

And before I could stop him, he'd filled a glass of water and tossed it on the fire, which made the flames shoot up even higher.

Apparently, the very worst thing you can do in a grease fire is to try to put it out with water.

And a grease fire was precisely what was going on in Connie Van Hooten's oven. As I was later to learn, Lance, the master chef, had cooked his goose without reading a single recipe, figuring, as he put it, "it would be just like roasting a turkey."

But as all you gourmet cooks out there undoubtedly know, roasting a goose is *not* like roasting a turkey. It seems these geese love their cholesterol, would never dream of joining Weight Watchers, and thus are chock full of fat—fat that must be periodically removed from the roasting pan with a baster, a step Lance neglected to do as he busied himself watching yet another rerun of *Christmas in Connecticut.*

So, after several hours in the oven, the goose was swimming in a bed of fat that got hot enough to ignite.

Frantic, I now raced to the kitchen pantry and pulled out a fire extinguisher I'd noticed a few days ago when I was rummaging around for Double Stuf Oreos.

Of course, finding a fire extinguisher is a lot different from knowing how to use one. After a few desperate attempts, we pulled out a pivotal pin, which released the trigger.

Lance then took aim, blasting the oven like Wyatt Earp at the OK Corral.

The good news was the fire was out.

The bad news was the oven was now a mountain of foam.

We spent the next several hours exfoliating Connie Van Hooten's oven of all goose fat and fire extinguisher foam.

Which gave me plenty of time to tell Lance about Scotty's murder.

"Are you kidding me?" he said when I told him

I'd discovered the body. "If you find one more corpse, they're going to name you honorary coroner."

(It's true. I've found more than my fair share of bodies in my day, spine-tingling adventures you can read all about in the titles at the front of this book.)

"If you ask me," Lance said, scraping foam into a hefty bag, "the killer's got to be Missy. From my short time at dinner with them, it was clear she hated Scotty."

"Actually, the police think I might have done it."

"You?" He looked up, shocked, from a particularly nauseating clump of charred goose fat. "Why on earth?"

"Because I left my fingerprint on the murder weapon."

Somewhat shamefaced, I explained how I'd tried to nab some frosting off the frozen Yule log.

"Honestly, Jaine," Lance tsked. "How do you manage to get yourself into these crazy scrapes?"

"Look who's talking," I said, waving at the mess around us.

"Yes, but I'm not the one with an orange jumpsuit in my future."

"You don't really think it'll come to that, do you?"

"No, hon. Of course not. I'll get you the best lawyer money can buy. My attorney, Raoul. You remember him, don't you? The guy who got me five hundred bucks when I tripped over a chopstick at PF Chang's?"

I remembered Raoul Duvernois, Esq., all right, a sleazebag graduate of the Wile E. Coyote School of Law. I sincerely doubted this clown would be able to get me out of a parking ticket, let alone a murder rap.

No, if anyone was going to get me off the hook, it would be yours truly. I made up my mind then and there to do a little snooping and clear my name.

But I murmured some feeble words of thanks to Lance, knowing that his heart was in the right place.

We took turns scraping and scrubbing, knocking back a lovely bottle of pinot noir during our breaks, and at last, Connie Van Hooten's oven was sparkling clean.

It was then, and only then, that we noticed a "self-cleaning" button on the control panel.

Cursing ourselves for not discovering this handy little doodad hours earlier, we tossed our blackened goose in the trash, and sat down to eat the only thing that survived the fire: Lance's godawful cranberry tofu stuffing.

No doubt about it: Worst. Christmas. Dinner. Ever.

It took an entire pint of Chunky Monkey to get the taste out of my mouth.

Oh, who am I kidding?

Two pints.

Chapter 15

Normally, I am a bath girl. I like nothing better than to lie up to my neck in strawberry-scented bubbles, soaking my blues away.

But that was before I'd laid eyes on Mrs. Van H's guest bedroom shower, a marble extravaganza, complete with four wall jets and a ginormous rainfall showerhead.

The next morning, I stood under its heavenly spray, my body massaged from all angles, and thought about my suspects in Scotty's murder. There was Missy, of course, who was desperate to get out of her marriage. And Dave, who was desperate to get into Missy's panties. There was also Marlon, the bruiser of a neighbor whose little boy Scotty had traumatized. He sure looked like he wanted to kill Scotty the day he'd stopped by to ream him out for ruining his kid's Christmas.

And for a brief instant I considered Lupe. After all, she loathed Scotty for keeping her apart from her family. But I had to rule out the diminutive maid. The Yule log was on the kitchen table, untouched, when Lupe snuck out of the house to visit her loved ones.

After every inch of my body had been sprayed to oblivion, I got dressed and headed down to the kitchen where Lance, dressed for work, was packing the remains of last night's tofu and cranberry stuffing in an unlucky plastic container.

"Morning, hon! How about a smoothie?" he asked, pointing to the blender, half full of green grassy gook.

The guy was never going to give up, was he?

"Maybe some other lifetime."

After a disapproving "tsk," he handed me the stuffing.

"Here's the rest of my cranberry tofu stuffing. I thought you could bring it over to Missy Parker as a condolence offering."

Condolence offering? Was he kidding? Condolences were what you needed *after* you ate the stuff.

Funny how eager he was to get rid of it, after he'd raved about it at dinner last night, calling it "the yummiest stuffing ever."

But now it occurred to me: He probably hated the glop just as much as I did!

"Sure you don't want to keep some?" I asked. "Just to snack on? After all, you really love it so."

"That's okay," he said, putting on his martyred saint face. "You know me. Always willing to sacrifice."

Oh, puh-leese. This from the guy who gives up broccoli for Lent.

"Gotta run, sweetie." He plunked a grass-scented peck on my cheek. "After-Christmas sale starts today. Bound to be a zoo."

As Lance trotted off to work, I settled down with my morning CRB and checked my emails, where I found a Smatch.com message from *NiceGuy* in Santa Monica.

I've spared you the harrowing details until now, but even after I'd de-Lancified my Smatch profile, I'd been barraged with missives from the world's least eligible bachelors, the bottom of the barrel, guys one step up from the penitentiary. Such as the Tantric Papa Seeking Acrobatic Mama. The five-foot-three bald gnome in search of a Charlize Theron lookalike. And the research librarian still living with his mom and into handcuffs and hot fudge sundaes.

But *NiceGuy* didn't seem bad. Not bad at all.

According to his profile, he was a stockbroker living in the marina, into movies, Brazilian jazz, and daily gym workouts.

And those workouts had really paid off.

His profile pictures showed a guy with a ripped muscular bod, slicked-back hair, and the kind of chiseled Clint Eastwood laugh lines I find so appealing.

Having at last heard from someone who bore a passing resemblance to a human being, I wasted no time and wrote him back.

After a brief exchange of messages, we arranged to meet the next day for lunch at the pool area of his condo. He was off from work for the holidays and laid up with a sprained ankle (no doubt from all those gym workouts), so he'd asked me to meet him where he lived. In a public space, of course, for safety's sake.

Feeling buoyed by my upcoming date (I might have been facing a murder rap, but at least I'd have a boyfriend to visit me in prison), I headed into town to pick up something edible to bring to Missy. I couldn't possibly show up to pay a condolence call with only Lance's ghastly stuffing.

A half hour later, armed with the stuffing and a lovely take-out roast chicken, I was knocking at Missy's front door.

Lupe answered it, positively beaming.

"Ms. Jaine! Come in! Did you hear the terrible news?" she asked, still smiling. "Mr. Scotty is dead! But of course you heard. You were the one who found the body!"

So happy was she that I was beginning to wonder if Lupe had something to do with Scotty's death after all. But it couldn't be. When she left the house, that Yule log was in pristine condition on the kitchen table.

"I guess I should feel bad," Lupe said, probably realizing that now was not the time for a smiley face, "but Mr. Scotty was a terrible man."

Couldn't argue with her there.

"I brought some food for you guys in your time of . . . um . . . mourning," I said, holding out my sympathy chow.

"Muchas gracias!"

Staring somewhat dubiously at the stuffing, Lupe led me to the living room where Dave was on the sofa engrossed in some paperwork.

t aside from any biological forebears, there
only one human in that room with the right to
lled Pro's mommy, and that was yours truly.

ou don't mind, do you, Jaine, if Scarlett
s to visit every once in a while? I don't know
I'm going to do without her."

How about going to the pound and getting a
of your own?" were the words I did not utter.
stead I mumbled something along the lines
We'll see."

Meanwhile, Prozac, in Missy's arms, clearly en-
ced with the idea of her own bedroom, was
owing up a storm.

*d like a canopy bed, please, with an extra soft down
forter. And a nice fluffy pillow to claw to shreds.*

I can't wait to fix up this mausoleum," Missy was
ng, decorating fever shining in her eyes. "The
hen. The bathrooms. They all need makeovers.
I my God, if these walls could talk, they'd
eam, 'Paint me!' So much to do. I can't wait to
started!"

ll this redecorating, I figured, would take a lot
oolah.

So Scotty left you a nice inheritance," I said.
et another motive for murder.)

ctually, Scotty refused to make a will. Insisted
as way too young to even think about dying.
s his wife, I get everything!"

e couldn't help busting into a jubilant grin.

nd forgive me for sounding so crass, but I
d every penny."

e certainly did," Dave chimed in. "When I

"Look who's here, Mr. Dave!" Lupe announced.
"It's Ms. Jaine."

And off she trotted to the kitchen.

Dave looked up, startled, and quickly shoved
the papers he'd been reading into a folder. Whatever it was, he didn't want me seeing it.

"I just stopped by to pay my respects, and I
brought some food, too. A roast chicken and a
side dish."

I figured the less said about the cranberry tofu
nightmare, the better.

"How kind of you," he replied with a weak smile.
"Come, sit down," he added, waving me to a rumpsprung armchair. "Missy's upstairs. She should be
down any minute. Scotty's death has been quite a
blow."

To Scotty, anyway. Right on the noggin.

"I don't suppose you heard anything yesterday
morning, when you were in your room studying?
Any footsteps? Or any other signs of an intruder?"

If I'd heard the noises, surely he had, too.

"Nope," he said, shaking his head. "Didn't hear
a thing. But then, I wouldn't. I wear earplugs when
I study. Helps me concentrate."

"Oh, that's too bad. I thought I heard someone
in the house, but at the time I figured it was Scotty."

Now, of course, I wondered if it might have
been Dave nipping down the hallway to knock off
his rival in romance.

"Luckily it's Christmas break and I don't have
any classes this week," Dave was saying. "This way I
can stay close to Missy in her hour of need."

At which point we could hear the grieving widow,

at the apex of her hour of need, tripping down the stairs, calling out:

"Guess what, darling! I booked us into the Four Seasons Maui next month. I'm sure the whole Scotty thing will have blown over by then. Won't that be fun?"

Looking over at Dave's folder, I could now see the Four Seasons logo peeking out from one of the pages. No wonder he hadn't wanted me to see what he was reading.

"Oh, sweetie," Missy crooned. "I can't wait to get there and—"

But I never got to hear the rest of her Hawaiian plans because she had now entered the room and clammed up at the sight of me, flummoxed, like a blond deer caught in the headlights.

For a minute, I thought she was going to try to reprieve her Grieving Widow act. But even she could see what a waste of time that would be.

"Oh, dear," she said with a sigh. "I suppose you must think I'm awful. Planning a vacation right after Scotty's death. But I told you, Jaine. Our marriage was the pits. I'm sorry he died the way he did," she added, trying to work up a soupçon of grief, "but frankly, I'm glad to be rid of him. Don't take that the wrong way. I didn't kill him. As much as I wanted him out of the picture, I would never have the nerve to commit murder."

Maybe. Maybe not. The jury was still out on that one.

"Of course you didn't kill Scotty," Dave piped up, outraged. "No one in their right mind would think you did."

That accompanied by a warning s̶ rection.

Missy snuggled down next to him and took his hand in hers.

"I suppose I should tell you," she "Dave and I have fallen in love."

So what else was new?

"We'd appreciate it if you wouldn't to the police, though. It sort of gives us tive to murder Scotty."

Ya think?

I was sitting there looking at the love dering if they could have possibly teame Scotty (Missy distracting him while Dave and bopped him over the head with the when Missy's other true love showed scene.

Yes, just then "Scarlett" came prancing us, tail swishing, very lady of the manor.

Hey, y'all! I'm here! So stop what you're pay attention to moi!

I'd long given up hope that she'd eve edge my presence with Missy in the roo deed she didn't, zipping right past me a a beeline for her new squeeze.

"Darling Scarlett!" Missy said, scoop in her arms. "Do you know what Mo to do? She's going to make over the room just for you!"

Mommy?

I choked back a curse.

If anyone was Prozac's mommy, highly promiscuous alley cat.

think of all the indignities she put up with from that miserable excuse for a human being . . ."

Dave was about to embark on a list of Scotty's many faults but was interrupted just then by the doorbell.

Seconds later, Lupe was ushering a short stumpy guy in a shiny sharkskin suit into the living room.

"Mr. Carmichael," Lupe announced. "Mr. Scotty's attorney."

"Of course," Missy said, getting up to shake his hand. "We met when I signed my prenup."

"I'm so sorry for your loss," Mr. Sharkskin said, with all the sincerity of a Jack in the Box clown.

"Sit down, won't you?" Missy said, gesturing to a spindly armchair.

Mr. Sharkskin squeezed himself into it, and took out some paperwork from an attaché case.

"I stopped by to offer my condolences," he said, "and to go over Scotty's will with you."

"But Scotty didn't make a will," Missy protested.

"Oh, he made one. Back in his twenties. When he was still married to Elise and madly in love with her. Perhaps he forgot about it in the ensuing years. Or just didn't want you to know about it. But I've got it right here in my files."

"And?" Missy asked, more than a tad anxious.

"I'm sorry to be the bearer of bad news," Mr. Sharkskin intoned, "but Elise gets everything."

"But that's impossible!" Missy cried, a look of utter disbelief on her face.

And I couldn't help wondering if it was the look of a woman who just realized she'd taken the ultimate risk and killed her husband—all for nothing.

Chapter 16

So Elise had hit the jackpot. She'd inherited everything.

You should have seen the look on Missy's face when Mr. Sharkskin told her how much it was all worth: More than five mil in Scotty's brokerage account, plus the house in Bel Air.

For the first time since Scotty's death, Missy genuinely looked the part of the grieving widow.

I bid her and Dave and Mr. Sharkskin good-bye and beat a hasty retreat back to Casa Van Hooten, armed with a hot new murder suspect.

Namely, Elise Parker.

With more than five mil at stake, Elise made a very viable suspect indeed.

Had she known all along about the will and, at the end of her rope, decided to cash in with a frozen Yule log?

Possible, but not likely. If Elise knew she was

going to inherit everything, why risk losing it all engaging in ongoing battles with Scotty? Why not keep the good will flowing until he popped off?

Then I remembered her visit on Christmas Eve when she'd ransacked Scotty's office looking for his checkbook. It had taken her quite a while before she'd returned to the living room, check in hand. What if, while poking through Scotty's desk, she'd found a copy of the will? And what if, discovering how much she had to gain by Scotty's death, she returned the next day to collect on her inheritance?

Back in Mrs. Van Hooten's kitchen, I logged on to my computer and found Elise's address on whitepages.com.

Time to pay the newly minted heiress a little visit.

Hopping into my Corolla, I made my way to Elise's apartment in Hollywood—a shabby, water-stained affair perched atop a kabob restaurant.

I checked the directory in a grimy doorway next to the kabob joint and buzzed Elise's apartment, hoping she'd be home. I'd decided to drop in on her unannounced, hoping to catch her off guard.

Luckily, she answered my buzz.

"Who is it?" she asked, her voice scratchy over the intercom.

"Jaine Austen."

"Do I know you?"

"Not really, but—"

"Then forget it. Now's not a good time."

That's what she thought. I wasn't about to get turned away so easily. Time for a weensy fib.

"I'm Mr. Carmichael's assistant," I blurted out. "He asked me to stop by with some legal papers for you to sign."

"Why didn't you say so? I'm in 202."

And just like that, she was buzzing me in.

What can I say? Sometimes it pays to be devious.

A creaky elevator etched with an imaginative display of male genitalia delivered me to the second floor, where Elise was waiting for me outside her apartment in a faded silk bathrobe, her hair uncombed, in bedhead mode.

"Come in," she said, waving me inside.

The first thing that hit me when I walked in the room was the overwhelming aroma of onion and garlic.

"Excuse the smell," Elise said. "It's from the kabob joint downstairs. I'm right above the kitchen. And it never goes away. I can douse myself in perfume, and I still smell like baba ganoush."

I followed her past a small dining area into her living room, furnished very Early Motel 6, with a drab oatmeal sofa and particle board furniture.

The focal point of the room was a blow-up photo of a young Elise hanging on the wall, looking absolutely exquisite in a flowing sundress, her silken hair fanning out in the wind.

"That's me," she said, following my gaze. "Back when I was a model."

What a knockout she'd been.

"Gosh, you were beautiful. And you still are," I hastened to add, in case she still thought she was.

"Wait a minute," she said, squinting at me. "Don't I know you from somewhere?"

"We've never been formally introduced," I said, "but I was at Scotty's house when you showed up for your alimony check."

"You were working on Christmas Eve? I don't believe it."

Oh, hell. I was about to be busted.

"So typical of Scotty," she went on, "expecting people to be on call three hundred and sixty-five days a year. You poor thing."

I sighed with relief as she led me over to her oatmeal sofa.

"So," she asked, "where are those papers Mr. Carmichael wanted me to sign?"

Planting myself firmly on the sofa so I'd be harder to evict, I began rummaging through my purse.

"Darn it all," I said with feigned frustration, "I left them at the office. Mr. Carmichael's going to kill me. I've got to go back and get them."

"Okay, hon," Elise said, running her fingers through her none-too-clean hair. "Come back when you've got them."

No way was I actually about to leave.

"Um . . . before I go, could I trouble you for a glass of water?" I asked with my most winning smile. "These Santa Anas make my throat so dry."

"Okay, sure," she said, walking all of five steps to her kitchen. Seconds later she was back with a glass of cloudy tap water.

"Thanks," I said, taking a tiny sip, hoping to avoid any free-floating carcinogens.

"What a shocker about Mr. Parker getting killed, huh?" I threw out as casually as I could.

"Not really," Elise said, sitting down across from me on the sofa, curling her long legs under her. "Pretty much everyone who knew Scotty detested him. So I'm not surprised he was knocked off. I just hope the cops don't suspect me, what with my inheriting all his money."

"I'm sure they won't. Especially if you have someone who can vouch for your whereabouts at the time of the murder."

"Unfortunately, no," Elise sighed. "The police told me Scotty was killed sometime between ten and eleven on Christmas morning. I was home alone all morning that day. Didn't leave my apartment till eleven-thirty to go to noon mass. Which means I have no alibi whatsoever.

"But of course I didn't do it," she hastened to assure me, taking a sip from a coffee mug on an end table. "As much as I hated him, Scotty was my meal ticket."

She gazed down into her coffee mug and sighed.

"Things haven't gone well for me since our divorce. I've stumbled from one job to the next. Somehow I just can't seem to hold on to them. So if anyone wanted to keep Scotty alive, it was me. I had to fight for every dime of my alimony checks, but in the end, I always got them. With Scotty gone, I would have been toast.

"And then," she said, shaking her head in wonder, "I found out that he'd left me everything. My

God, you could've knocked me over with a lamb kabob. I still can't believe it. I figured he'd leave it all to some porno site, or a charity named after himself. Maybe even to Missy. But me? Never."

Up close I could see the roots of her blond hair were coming in gray and her face was crosshatched with a web of fine lines—lines I suspected would soon be erased at the hands of a skilled plastic surgeon.

"It's funny," she was saying, "you'd think I'd be delirious with joy, now that I'm going to be set for life. And don't get me wrong. I'm happy. But I still can't help feeling sad that Scotty's dead."

And it was true. Unlike Missy, there appeared to be real sorrow in Elise's eyes.

"Sure, he put me through hell. But it wasn't always like that. When we first married," she said, her eyes glazing over at the memory, "he was sweet and caring. Showered me with love. I gave him the savings from my modeling career to help him out with his investment portfolio. And that's when it all started going bad. The richer he got, the less he seemed to care about me. I was devastated when he dumped me for Missy. And enraged by the way he treated me. But on some level, I guess I never stopped loving him. Or at least the man he used to be."

By now tears were running down her cheeks, and I was having a hard time believing she was the killer.

"Excuse me," she said, unfurling her legs from the sofa. "I hate the way I look when I cry. I'm just going to splash some water on my face."

She headed off down a hallway to her bathroom.

Touched by her tears, I was just about to cross her off my suspect list when I looked over at her coffee mug.

I expected to see dregs of coffee at the bottom, but instead I saw a half an inch of some pale bubbly stuff.

I took a sniff.

Champagne.

Whoa. It looked like somebody had been doing a little celebrating when I'd buzzed her on her intercom. Perhaps Elise wasn't quite as heartbroken as her poignant performance had led me to believe.

A feeling that was reinforced just then when her phone rang. Still in the bathroom, Elise let her machine get it.

A chirpy woman's voice came on the line.

"Elise, it's Bitsy Clayton at Coldwell Banker. I've found you some fabulous properties in Bel Air to look at this afternoon. Call me!"

Returning to the living room at the tail end of her realtor's message, Elise had the good grace to blush.

"The first thing I did when I learned about my inheritance was to call a realtor," she said. "As I'm sure you can understand, I can't wait to get out of this hellhole. But I'm still really sorry Scotty's dead."

Somehow this time her words didn't seem quite so convincing.

"Well, I guess I'd better be going," I said, hauling myself from the sofa.

"What time will you be back?" Elise asked.

"Back?"

"With the legal papers."

Really, I had to start keeping better track of my lies.

"Oh, right. In about an hour or so."

And with that, I skedaddled out the door.

But not before glancing over at Elise's dinette table and seeing a box of surgical rubber gloves— the same kind of gloves you'd use if you didn't want to leave fingerprints on a lethal Yule log.

Chapter 17

By the time I reached my car, Elise had catapulted to the top of my suspect list.

With more than five million bucks to gain, no alibi, and a box of fingerprint-masking rubber gloves on her dinette table, she was shaping up to be quite a contender.

More and more, I was convinced she could have found a copy of Scotty's will in his office on Christmas Eve and done away with him the next day.

All thoughts of Elise were shelved, however, when I pulled up in front of Casa Van Hooten and saw Marlon, Scotty's hulking refrigerator of a neighbor, out on his front lawn.

I remembered the day he'd rushed at Scotty, furious at his misanthropic neighbor for ruining his little boy's Christmas, how he'd aimed his cantaloupe-sized fist at Scotty's gut and had been restrained only by the combined efforts of Dave and Lupe.

Most of all, I remembered how he'd left the house hollering that he wasn't through with Scotty.

I'll be back to take care of you once and for all! were his exact words, if memory served.

Now I wondered if he'd popped by on Christmas morning to make good on his threat.

Clambering out of my Corolla, I hurried over to Marlon's front lawn, where he was bent over a large Rudolph reindeer ornament strung with fairy lights. Many of the lights, I could now see, were missing, including a larger bulb for Rudolph's nose.

Marlon was busy replacing them from a pile on the lawn, muttering a string of muffled curses.

"Hi, there!" I said, at my very chirpiest, hoping to avoid the storm cloud brewing over his head. "I'm Jaine Austen. I'm house-sitting for Mrs. Van Hooten."

"Yeah, I know who you are," he said glancing up at me. "You were there the day I almost busted Scotty's chops."

He picked up a fairy light and began screwing it in, the tiny bulb dwarfed by his sausage-like fingers.

"Would you believe some vandal stole the lights off my Rudolph the other night? Wouldn't be the least bit surprised if it was that sonofabitch Scotty. Had to go all the way over to the Home Depot in Burbank to get replacement bulbs."

"I suppose you know about Scotty's murder," I said, thrilled with the opening he'd just lobbed me.

"Couldn't have happened to a more deserving

guy," Marlon said, kneeling under the sun, a sweat stain the size of New Jersey blooming on the back of his T-shirt.

"And by the way," he added, "I'd be happy to be a character witness for you if you need me."

"A character witness?"

"Yeah, I heard the police found your fingerprint on the Yule log."

Wow. News sure traveled fast here in the land of the one-percenters.

"I can assure you," I said, with no small degree of indignation, "I'm not the one who killed Scotty."

"I didn't really think you were," Marlon said. "Figured you wouldn't have the nerve. But I'm prepared to help out anyone who bumped off that bastard."

"Have any ideas who might have done it?" I asked.

"My money's on Missy."

"Missy?"

"Anyone could see she hated the guy. Can you imagine what it must have been like to have been married to him?"

He shuddered in disgust.

"But Missy was out running at the time of the murder," I said, repeating Missy's alibi. "She left the house a little after ten and was gone almost an hour."

"Not true," Marlon said. "I happened to be looking out the window and saw her coming back home at about ten minutes past ten. I remember the time because I'd just finished doing a hundred squats and I checked my watch to time myself."

So Missy had been lying. She'd snuck back into the house. Maybe she'd forgotten something. Or maybe she'd popped back in to bludgeon her hubby to death.

"I do a hundred squats every day," Marlon was saying, beaming with pride.

Judging from the thigh muscles bulging from his shorts, I didn't doubt it for a minute.

"How very impressive," I said, eager to stay on his good side.

By now Marlon had finished screwing in Rudolph's missing lights, all but the one for Rudolph's nose. He picked up a big red bulb from where it was lying on the grass and was just about to screw it in when Graham came up the front steps with the mail.

"Hi, there," Graham said, flashing us a friendly smile. "Here's your mail, Marlon. I see Marlon Jr. got another letter from Santa."

"Just drop it in the slot." Marlon pointed to a mail slot alongside his door. "My wife's been writing letters to Marlon Jr. every day," he explained to me, "pretending to be Santa, trying to convince him that Santa is alive and well. We were finally getting him to believe it, and then Rudolph's nose got stolen. Now little Marlon is convinced Rudolph is sick, too, and that any day now he's going to be sharing a room with Santa in St. John's intensive care unit.

"Damn that Scotty for ruining little Marlon's Christmas!

"What's worse," he said, his face flushed with anger, "he had the nerve to call my boy a crybaby!"

I looked up just then and saw a little boy's face

peering out the window, a slight boy with delicate features.

To a man like Marlon, a veritable wrecking machine, the thought of his son being a crybaby must have been intolerable.

Suffused with rage at the memory of Scotty's taunt, Marlon clenched his cantaloupe fists, and I heard the unmistakable sound of glass splintering.

"Hey, Marlon!" Graham cried. "Be careful!"

As if waking from a trance, Marlon opened his fists, revealing the red light bulb smashed in the palm of his hand, blood seeping out from a nasty gash.

This was one angry man.

Angry enough, I felt certain, to have delivered a fatal blow to the skull of the Neighborhood Scrooge.

As Marlon lumbered inside his house to bandage his hand, Graham and I headed down to the sidewalk.

"Wow," I said. "Did you see the blood on Marlon's hand? What a temper."

"I guess that anger management class he took didn't do much good."

"Anger management class?"

"Marlon Jenkins used to be a professional football player and had a reputation for being a very volatile guy. A couple of years ago he got jailed for beating up a rival player. He got out after a few months, but part of the deal was that he had to go to an anger management class."

Holy moly. The guy did jail time for assault and battery. Talk about your history of violence.

By now Marlon was running neck and neck with Elise in my Most Likely to Have Bonked Scotty to Death sweepstakes. Maybe he lied about seeing Missy coming home early from her run to deflect suspicion away from himself. Or maybe he did see her come home—not from his living room window, but from where he was hiding in Scotty's house after having just offed his neighbor with a frozen Yule log.

"You know Scotty Parker was murdered, right?" I asked Graham.

Graham nodded.

"I heard it on the news on my way to work. Frankly, I'm not surprised. Scotty was a pretty terrible guy. Always fighting with the Sinclairs about their Christmas lights. Spying on the neighbors' dogs to make sure they didn't poop on his lawn. Mrs. Van Hooten told me he'd call the police and file a noise complaint every time she had a dinner party! And cheap? He once asked me to lay out postage for a package to Canada, promising to repay me.

"As if that was going to happen!" he added, rolling his eyes.

"The man was amazingly tight with a buck," I agreed.

"No kidding," Graham snorted. "Money had to be surgically removed from his wallet."

By now he'd forgotten all about his mail cart, lost in memories of Scotty's cheapskate ways.

"Technically, mail carriers aren't supposed to receive gifts worth more than twenty bucks. But people in this neighborhood are so rich I often get fifty and hundred dollar tips at Christmas. Not Scotty. You wouldn't believe the gifts I got from him—free toothbrushes recycled from his dentist, stale chocolates—even a pair of used socks! Unwashed!"

"Eeeew! How gross!"

"Scotty was one for the books, all right," Graham said.

"Do you have any idea who might have killed him?"

"Not really. But from what I just saw, I'd say Marlon is a prime suspect."

My sentiments exactly.

YOU'VE GOT MAIL!

To: Jausten
From: Shoptillyoudrop
Subject: Glorious morning!

What a glorious morning we just spent in
Martinique! After boarding our tour bus, we were
whisked off to see a beautiful old church, Sacré-
Coeur de Balata. Then off we tooled to the majes-
tic Mount Pelée volcano. And I was wrong about
Martinique being home of the martini. On the contrary, we made a most refreshing pit stop at a rum
distillery where they treated us to some yummy
samples! Afterward, we visited a fishing town
where artist Paul Gauguin once painted. All this in
four fascinating hours!

The only glitch on the tour was a visit to a gift shop
where Daddy picked up the most hideous tiki
mask he insists on hanging on our living room wall.
As if that will ever happen.

Must take a tiny nap. Then off to Lydia's lecture on
Christmas traditions in Guam. It should be thrilling.

XOXO,
Mom

To: Jausten
From: DaddyO
Subject: A Shoo-In to Win!

Spent the morning in Martinique, Lambchop, visiting some dusty old church, a dustier volcano, and a podunk fishing village where Paul Gauguin once lived. No wonder he moved to the South Pacific. Had a great daiquiri at a rum distillery, though, and picked up a super tiki mask for our living room.

Now Mom's gone to one of Lydia's gasbag lectures. And I'm heading downstairs to join some of the Tampa Vista guys for a scavenger hunt the cruise ship has organized. Each member of the winning team gets a $500 shipboard credit.

With me at the helm of our team, we're a shoo-in to win. I've always had a knack for following a trail. In a former life, I must have been a Himalayan Sherpa.

Ciao for now!

Love 'n hugs from,
DaddyO

To: Jausten
From: DaddyO
Subject: The Brat Strikes Again!

I should have known there'd be trouble when I saw The Brat on one of the other teams at the scavenger hunt.

From the minute the starting whistle blew, Team Tampa Vistas was off to a roaring start. In no time at all, we managed to find and take pictures of a magazine with a Kardashian on the cover, an animal carved out of fruit, someone wearing a seasickness patch, two people with matching T-shirts, and a Santa Claus lookalike. We were way ahead of all the other teams. All we needed was a deck chair "reserved" sign. At last we came across one. But just as I was about to snap a picture of it, The Brat came bolting in out of nowhere, grabbed it off the chair, and dashed away with it. There was nothing we could do but keep searching. We finally found another sign, but by that time Team Brat had already won the grand prize, and the little monster was posing for pictures with his teammates.

If that volcano we saw today was still active, I know just who I'd like to toss right in.

Your extremely frustrated,
DaddyO

To: Jausten
From: Shoptillyoudrop
Subject: Determined to Stay Happy!

Did you know that Guam is the home of the annual Jingle Bells 5K run? And their Christmas sweets are coconut pies and yam doughnuts! Isn't it amazing how Lydia digs up these fascinating facts? Such a knowledgeable woman!

XOXO,
Mom

PS. Daddy's in a very bad mood. I found him at the buffet, eating a chocolate éclair and muttering about throwing a little boy into a volcano. I have no idea what that's about. And I don't want to know. I'm determined to stay happy on this trip. Can't wait for darling Isabel Norton's 95th birthday. And, of course, for the exciting New Year's Eve costume party.

To: Jausten
From: DaddyO
Subject: Insult to Injury!

is there no end to The Brat's evil doings? I just went down to the lobby to check out the official ship photos taken of the passengers on Christmas Day. They're all displayed on racks in the lobby. When I looked at the pictures of Mom and me, I was horrified to see that somebody had blacked out my teeth and crossed my eyes with magic marker in all the pictures.

And I know exactly which little monster did it. I complained to the ship's purser who promised they'd make new copies of the photos, but refused to take action against The Brat, seeing as I have no actual proof that the kid was the one who defaced the photos.

But he did it, all right.
And one of these days, he's going to pay. This fight isn't over yet.

Love 'n snuggles from,
DaddyO
aka The Avenger

Chapter 18

Thank goodness Lance was away at work the next day when I got ready for my date with *NiceGuy*. The last thing I needed was my self-appointed fashion guru micromanaging my outfit.

What with *NiceGuy* being a stockbroker, and probably somewhat of a straight arrow, I'd decided to abandon my usual Fresh-from-the-Ice-Cream-Aisle-at-the-Supermarket look.

Instead, I chose a pair of elastic waist skinny jeans, Eileen Fisher white silk tee, and strappy sandals. Topped off with a pair of tasteful silver hoop earrings. Then I applied my drugstore mascara and lipstick, thrilled not to have to listen to a Greek chorus of disapproval from Lance.

When I checked myself out in the mirror, I liked what I saw: Curls suitably shiny. Hips and tush suitably camouflaged. Drugstore lipstick pleasingly pink. Pronouncing myself dateworthy, I grabbed my car keys and took off for *NiceGuy*'s condo in the marina.

On the ride over, my mind drifted to Daddy's shipboard battle with The Brat. Yes, I realized that as a grown man, Daddy should have risen above such childish antics, but frankly, the kid seemed like an insufferable little snot, and I didn't blame Daddy one bit for being steamed about the stunt the kid had pulled in the scavenger hunt. Not to mention defacing Daddy's photos. In the Battle of The Brat, I was definitely rooting for Team Daddy.

All thoughts of Daddy quickly faded, however, when I pulled up at *NiceGuy*'s condo. Dubbed the Marina Palms, it was more like a city than any condo I'd ever seen—a complex of three behemoth buildings with a guard station out front.

I gave my name to the guard at the gate, who had instructions to let me in. He pointed the way to the pool area, and after parking my car, I trekked down a winding brick path until I reached what can only be described as the Garden of Eden with deck chairs.

The grounds were lush with hibiscus and bougainvillea, swaying palms dotted throughout— all surrounding a glittering turquoise pool. Residents lolled in designer chaises, snack tables at their sides, enjoying the view of the sailboats docked in the marina at their feet.

Because of the warm weather, there were a number of people scattered around the pool. Three young boys frolicked in its turquoise waters with their dad, a burly bald guy, who elicited squeals of delight by picking up each boy one by one, holding him aloft in the air, and then tossing him into the water.

I spotted *NiceGuy* (whose real name was Phil) right away, sitting on a chaise in aviator sunglasses, reading *The Wall Street Journal*, his slicked-back black hair gleaming in the midday sun. Clad in baggy sweat pants and a tight tank top (revealing a divine set of abs), he was a Grade A cutie pie.

Looking around at everybody in their shorts and bathing suits, I suddenly felt a tad over-dressed. But any awkwardness about my outfit vanished when Phil looked up from his paper and flashed me a smile that could melt the ice off a Minnesota snow plow.

"Jaine!" he cried, getting up from his chaise.

When he walked over to greet me, I noticed he was limping.

"Excuse the limp," he said. "As I told you, I sprained my ankle. Bandages come off next week."

He pointed down to a bulge around his ankle under his sweat pants.

"Anyhow, thanks so much for driving out here to meet me."

"Not a problem," I assured him with utmost sincerity.

"Well, I appreciate it," he said, wrapping me in a warm bear hug.

Oh, goodness. I liked the feel of that.

"C'mon." He gestured to a chaise adjacent to his own. "Sit down and we'll order lunch."

He handed me a Marina Palms menu.

"Wow," I said, blinking in disbelief. "Your condo has its own restaurant?"

What a world apart from my life, where room service means a quick call to Domino's.

"The food's really very good," Phil said.

It sure looked it. They had a whole bunch of salads, which I pretty much ignored, zeroing in on the Marina Burger, a half-pound beauty with bacon and mushrooms and thick-cut fries. But then I had second thoughts. I really needed to make a good impression and order something delicate and ladylike. Like the tuna niçoise salad. Or the mango and chutney on a bed of arugula. Something that would give Phil no clue to the pepperoni-pizza-and-chicken-chimichanga gal lurking beneath my elastic waist jeans.

The mango and chutney salad, it would be.

"So what would you like?" Phil asked.

"Marina Burger with fries."

You didn't really think I was going to order something on a bed of arugula, did you?

"Good choice," he grinned. "It's my favorite, too."

Phil took out his cell phone and placed an order for two Marina Burgers, plus a beer for himself and a glass of chardonnay for me. Normally, I don't drink during the day, but normally, I'm not sitting next to my potential future hubby.

While we waited for our food to show up, we started chatting. Much to my relief, Phil was easy as pie to talk to.

That is, when I could tear my eyes away from his fabulous abs.

He told me about going to college at Dartmouth and getting his MBA from Stanford and how he'd spent the past seven years as a VP at his brokerage firm.

And all I had to brag about was my Golden Plunger Award from the Los Angeles Plumbers Association for my Toiletmasters slogan: *In a Rush to Flush? Call Toiletmasters!*

With a lame smile, I told him about it.

"You wrote *In a Rush to Flush?*" he asked. "I've seen it on buses all over town!"

He actually seemed impressed!

I was in such a glow of good will I didn't even mind when one of the tykes in the pool accidentally splashed water on my Eileen Fisher silk tee. I smiled and laughed it off, to show Phil what a good sport I was.

When our burgers arrived, I tried not to swan dive into mine, but I couldn't help myself.

It was divine.

Soon ketchup was oozing from my bun and onto my fingers, grease dotting my chin as I scarfed it all down.

Phil was telling me how much he enjoyed his work, helping people plan their financial futures, making sure they were safe in their retirement years.

What a great guy, huh? The Mother Teresa of brokers.

"I'm also really into charity work," he told me, managing to eat his burger, his fingers miraculously ketchup-free.

"In fact, that's how I sprained my ankle," he was

saying. "Fell off a ladder while working for Habitat for Humanity."

My gosh, he really *was* a saint!

I felt like a bit of a slacker in comparison.

I give clothes to the Goodwill and money to worthy causes when I can afford to (Go, ASPCA!), but that's about the extent of my charity work.

True, one year I volunteered at a soup kitchen at Thanksgiving. But I was told my services were no longer needed after I'd scarfed down a tad too many slices of pumpkin pie.

I fumphered something about my gig at the soup kitchen, careful to leave out the part about the pumpkin pie.

Meanwhile, at the pool, the kids were still splashing away, and a fresh crop of droplets landed on my blouse. Once again, I brushed them away with gay insouciance, secretly longing to lob what was left of my hamburger bun at the inconsiderate tykes.

But Phil was oblivious to the kids in the pool. Instead, he took off his sunglasses, revealing emerald-flecked hazel eyes, and gazed at me with grave intensity.

"So?" he asked. "Have you ever been married?"

"Once," I admitted, repressing all thoughts of The Blob, refusing to allow him to ruin a perfectly lovely lunch. "But it didn't work out.

"And you?" I asked.

"I've had a few relationships, but I haven't found that special someone yet."

Then he reached out and took my ketchup-stained hand in his.

"But I'm hoping that's all about to change."

Yikes! Did that mean what I thought it meant? Was my philanthropic financial guru actually interested in me? It sure looked like it.

Phil retrieved his hand to finish his burger and we continued talking. Well, Phil continued talking, telling me more about his job. But I have to be honest; my mind drifted just a tad when he got to the part about deferred income annuities.

My hand was still tingling from the touch of his fingers, my heart still doing flip-flops over what he'd hinted about me being that special someone in his life.

Soon I was daydreaming about living a fabulous new life here at the Marina Palms, with a restaurant on the premises and the marina at my feet. I could just see myself as the wife of a respected stockbroker/philanthropist, going to soigné dinners in slinky black dresses and my one and only pair of Manolo Blahniks (who soon would have lots of baby brother and sister Manolos).

Gone would be my old haphazard ways. I would be the kind of woman who got her hair styled once a month and her nails done once a week. The kind of woman who wouldn't dream of keeping a half-eaten Almond Joy at the bottom of her purse. (Not without wrapping it up in a Baggie, anyway.) I'd be organized, on top of my game, networking at Phil's many business dinners and building up my client list. Instead of toilet bowl ads, I'd be writing for major corporate clients.

I was lost in a delicious reverie of me accepting a Businesswoman of the Year award when I heard an outburst of squeals coming from the pool. The three little boys were all shrieking with glee as their dad mounted the steps to the diving board.

Now that he was out of the water, I could see that he was a mountain of a guy, with a gut the size of a beer keg.

The diving board groaned in protest as he walked to the edge.

Then he jumped up and down a few times, threatening to break the springs, assumed a diving pose, and plunged into the water.

Unfortunately, his dive went wildly awry and he landed in a massive belly flop, sending a tsunami of a wave crashing over the edge of the pool, dousing both me and Phil.

We leaped from our chairs, Phil jumping with surprising agility for a guy with a sprained ankle. And as he jumped, the leg of his sweat pants yanked up.

I blinked in surprise to see that there were no bandages around his ankle.

No, the bulky object taking up space under his sweat pants was a black ankle monitor. I recognized it right away. I'd seen plenty like it watching *Cops*, one of the many insipid reality shows I'd been planning to give up in my new incarnation as Businesswoman of the Year.

"That's an ankle monitor!" I cried. "You don't have a sprained ankle. You didn't want to leave your condo because you're under house arrest. You're a crook!"

"White collar," he assured me. "Just a wee bit of insider trading. But I'm sure to get my broker's license back after my five hundred hours of community service. In the meanwhile, do you think you could loan me forty bucks to cover the cost of lunch?"

Oh, crud. The man of my dreams was a criminal. Even worse, my fries were all wet.

I was so upset, I could barely finish them.

Chapter 19

I drove back to Casa Van Hooten, thoroughly disgusted with Smatch.com. Didn't they even screen their members?

In desperate need of solace, I decided to pay a visit to Prozac, longing to hold her in my arms and feel the comforting warmth of her fur against my cheek.

After parking my car, I took my chances and rang Missy's doorbell, praying she'd be out on a run or applying for a job as a cocktail waitress somewhere.

Lupe answered the door in a happy glow. Gone was her maid's uniform. Instead, she wore a simple black pencil skirt, buttoned cardigan, and conservative stacked heels. Around her neck, a strand of what had to be faux pearls.

"So nice to see you, Ms. Jaine!" she grinned.

"You too, Lupe. You look terrific."

"Gracias. I'm getting ready for a job interview.

Missy can't afford to keep me on anymore, but she recommended me to a family up the street. I'm going to meet them in a half hour."

"That's wonderful!"

"The pay is good, with two days off each week, and my own private patio! Say a prayer that I get the job."

"Oh, I will."

After all the hell Lupe had gone through working for Scotty, the poor thing deserved a break.

"I'm afraid Missy isn't here right now. She's at the gym."

Yes!!

"Actually, I came to see my cat."

"Scarlett? I think I saw her wander into Mr. Scotty's office," she said, waving to Scotty's former lair. "Now, if you'll excuse me, I've got to fix my hair and put on my makeup."

And as she scooted off down the hall, I made my way to Scotty's office.

A shiver ran down my spine as I stood in the doorway, flashing back to the day of the murder and the sight of Scotty's body slumped over his desk, blood oozing from his freckled scalp.

Never a bastion of neatness, the room looked as if a small tornado had swept through it—drawers open, items strewn across Scotty's desk, his ancient TV and VCR brushed with traces of fingerprint powder, his computer missing—no doubt carted off to some forensic crime lab.

Clearly, the police had gone over the scene of the crime with a fine-tooth comb.

Showing impeccably good taste, they'd opted to

ignore Scotty's magnum opus: *Vengeance Is Mine: The Return of Tiny Tim*, which still sat on his desk, Prozac napping atop its mountain of unreadable pages.

As I approached the desk, I gulped to see dried blood staining its surface.

With no small degree of trepidation, I sat down in Scotty's squeaky swivel chair, hoping his bad karma (and musty body odor) wouldn't rub off on me. I reached out for Prozac, who gazed at me through slitted eyes.

Oh. It's you again.

"Prozac, honey!" I cried, nestling her in my arms. "I just had the worst date ever! For once I thought I finally met a decent guy, a stable, responsible man of unassailable ethics and fab abs, and then, poof—out of nowhere—he turned out to be a criminal! With an ankle bracelet!"

She gave me a solicitous sniff.

Yeah, right. Whatever. Is that burger I smell on your breath?

I sat there basking in Prozac's attention, trying to convince myself it was me she was sniffing and not my Marina Burger breath, when I happened to glance out the window and see Mrs. Sinclair, the neighbor with the elaborate Christmas decorations, pull into her driveway and get out of her car.

As the silver-haired aristo walked up to her front door, arms laden with Bloomingdale's shopping bags, I thought back to the day she stormed into Scotty's office, accusing him of cutting the cords on her Christmas display. I remembered how she'd tossed him her electrician's bill, demanding that he pay it. And how, totally unfazed, Scotty had reached in his desk drawer and pulled out a manila envelope—with the photo that had turned Mrs. Sinclair's face ashen.

Scotty said he had no intention of paying her electrician's bill. On the contrary. He said she'd be the one making payments to him.

Scotty had been blackmailing Mrs. Sinclair, of that I was certain. But what on earth was his hold over her?

I looked around his office, searching for clues. And then it hit me:

The VCR—the one Scotty used to spy on his neighbors, to make sure their dogs weren't pooping on his lawn. What if his security camera had captured more than just dogs pooping? What if Scotty had inadvertently captured some damaging footage of Mrs. Sinclair?

According to the police, the killer had taken the tape in the machine on the day of the murder. But what if there was an earlier tape that Scotty had saved, with incriminating footage of the decorating diva?

Indeed, there were two other tapes near the VCR, and I wasted no time picking up one of them and shoving it in the machine, watching the results on the ancient black-and-white TV. After what seemed like hours of nothing but passing cars and scampering squirrels, at last I hit pay dirt.

A Mercedes convertible pulled up in front of Scotty's house. Mrs. Sinclair was in the passenger seat next to a balding guy behind the wheel. Then the bald guy reached over and wrapped Mrs. Sinclair in his arms. Eventually they pried themselves apart, and Mrs. Sinclair got out of the car, blowing a kiss to the man as he drove off. After which she headed out of the frame, crossing the street to her own house.

Was the man in the Mercedes Mrs. Sinclair's husband, dropping her off en route to another destination?

Or, more likely, was he her lover?

Had Scotty taken a screen shot of their torrid embrace and handed it to Mrs. Sinclair that day when she came storming into his office?

I looked outside and saw two cars parked in the Sinclairs' driveway. Neither of them was a Mercedes.

Of course, it was possible there was a Mercedes stowed in the Sinclairs' garage and the man on Scotty's security tape was indeed Mrs. Sinclair's hubby. But what if there was no Mercedes in that garage, and Mrs. Sinclair had been deep in the throes of an illicit affair?

Desperate to keep the news of her affair from her husband, and unwilling to meet Scotty's black-mail demands, had Mrs. Sinclair crept across the street on Christmas morning to whack the life out of her rapacious blackmailer?

Those were the thoughts flitting through my brain when I heard the front door open and Missy call out, "Yoo-hoo, Scarlett! I'm home!"

Prozac, who had been dozing comfortably in my lap, now sprang to her feet and practically flung herself into Missy's arms as she showed up in the doorway, looking a bit disheveled in yoga pants and tank top.

"How's my precious Scarlett?" Missy cooed, scooping her up.

Pro gazed up at her adoringly.

Oh, so lonely without you! Got any snacks?

"Hi, Jaine," Missy said, turning to me. "Forgive the way I look. I was just at the gym. I'm a mess."

"You look fine," I assured her.

This woman could walk through a car wash and come out looking terrific. If she weren't so sweet, I'd really hate her.

And yet, I couldn't forget what Marlon said about seeing her sneaking back into the house the morning of the murder. Was it possible Missy was not nearly as sweet as she seemed, that a cold-blooded killer lurked underneath those yoga togs?

As she stood there in her tank top, I suddenly became aware of how muscular her arms were. Those biceps of hers looked hard as steel. Certainly strong enough to have delivered a fatal blow to her overbearing husband.

"I'm so happy you stopped by," she was saying. "I bet you miss your darling Scarlett."

"Her name is *Prozac!*" were the words I refrained from shouting.

"Actually, Missy, I need to talk to you."

"Sure, but let's go to the living room. This room gives me the creeps," she said, eyeing the dried blood on Scotty's desk. "It's all too gruesome."

Minutes later, I was sitting across from Missy in a thrift shop armchair, she and Prozac cuddled cozily on the sofa.

"Can I get you something to eat?" Missy offered.

"Now that Scotty's gone we have really nice cookies, not factory seconds."

"No, thanks," I said, for one of the few times in my life turning down empty calories, eager to question my prey.

"Look, I'll get straight to the point. Your neighbor Marlon says he saw you sneaking back to the house on Christmas morning when you were supposedly out running."

If I expected her to be flustered or caught off guard, I was sadly mistaken.

"It's true," she admitted with a sheepish shrug. "I already told you about me and Dave. We're in love. I snuck back in the house and tiptoed straight to his room where we spent the next forty-five minutes or so having ex-say."

The latter whispered so as not to taint "Scarlett's" delicate ears.

"Did you hear anything at all when you were with Dave?" I asked. "Any footsteps? Scotty crying out?"

"Nope, not a thing. All I heard was the pounding throb of my beating heart."

Puh-leese. Spare me the romance novel glop.

"Dave says he's going to take care of me now that Scotty's gone. We're going to get married and everything. He says I don't even have to get a job."

I found it hard to imagine how Dave was going to support Missy as a struggling law student, but frankly, like R. Butler, I didn't give a damn.

Missy was sitting there, caught up in the wonders of her newfound love. Clearly her life was acres better now that Scotty was gone. Even without the money she'd expected to inherit, she was in seventh heaven.

And once again I couldn't help wondering if Missy was the killer—taking time out from her frantic dipsy doodle to end her miserable marriage with a frozen Yule log.

Chapter 20

I left Missy and Pro smooching on the sofa, cursing the day I ever agreed to let Pro stay with the blond beauty.

But I couldn't moon over my unfaithful feline.

I had another cheating couple to investigate. Namely, Mrs. Sinclair and her cuddle buddy in the Mercedes.

I needed to get a gander at Mrs. Sinclair's husband and see if he was the bald guy I'd seen on the security tape.

What with two cars in the Sinclairs' driveway, I figured Mr. Sinclair had to be home. So I headed across the street, past the Disneyland extravaganza on their front lawn, and rang their doorbell.

Mrs. Sinclair came to the door in her Katharine Hepburn slacks, her silver hair perfectly coiffed.

"May I help you?" she asked, looking me over like a pesky Jehovah's Witness she couldn't wait to get rid of.

"Hi, I'm Jaine Austen. I'm staying across the street at Mrs. Van Hooten's house."

"I know who you are," she replied, with nary a trace of a smile. "I saw you that day in Scotty's office when I came to give him my electrician's bill. You're Connie Van Hooten's house sitter."

"Actually, Connie and I are very close friends."

"Really?"

She shot me a look of utter disbelief, as if there was no way on God's green earth a woman like Connie Van Hooten would be pals with the likes of *moi*.

Thank heavens I was still in my Eileen Fisher top, and not my CUCKOO FOR COCOA PUFFS T-shirt.

"Oh, yes," I said, lying with abandon. "Connie and I have been friends ever since we met on the board of St. John's Hospital."

I'd seen a letter addressed to Connie from the board of directors of St. John's, so I tossed out that whopper.

"What is it I can do for you?" Mrs. Sinclair asked, still making no move to invite me in.

And I had to get in if I expected to get a gander at Mr. Sinclair.

Time for another weensie fib.

"Connie told me what a marvelous job you've done decorating your house."

"Did she?" At last, a chink in her armor. A faint smile managed to work its way to her lips. "How nice of her. Of course it's been a few years, but I think it's held up very well."

"Actually, I'm thinking of making some changes

to my own home." (As if. The only thing I'd planned on changing in my apartment was the toilet paper.) "And I was wondering if I could have a tiny peek at what you've done. For inspiration, you know."

She hesitated a beat, but eventually house pride won out.

"Of course," she said, at last stepping back from the doorway and ushering me inside. "Let's start with the living room."

I followed her into a living room awash in floral prints and coordinating stripes, dotted with priceless antique gewgaws. Very Bel Air Meets the Cotswolds.

I made lots of appropriate oohs and aahs.

"This is perfect! Just the look I was going for!"

If I had the hundred grand it would undoubtedly take to put it together.

But the pièce de résistance in the room, the thing I most wanted to see, was Mr. Sinclair.

And there he was, sitting in an armchair, reading something on his iPad. A tall man, with a hawklike nose and—most important—a full mane of thick silver hair.

Definitely not the bald guy in the blackmail picture.

Whoever Mrs. Sinclair had been embracing that day, it hadn't been her hubby.

Clearly the grand dame of Bel Air had been having an affair.

"Evan, this is Jaine Austen. She's a good friend of Connie Van Hooten's. Jaine, my husband, Evan."

"How nice to meet you," Mr. Sinclair said, ever the gentleman, getting out of his chair to shake my hand.

"I'm showing her our remodel. Connie told her what a wonderful job we'd done."

"You have marvelous taste!" I exclaimed, continuing to slather on the compliments with a trowel. "And I love your Christmas decorations. They're absolutely breathtaking!"

"They've been featured in *Sunset* magazine," Mr. Sinclair beamed.

"Come, Jaine," Mrs. Sinclair said. "I'll show you the kitchen. You're going to love the island.

"I'll get some wine and hors d'oeuvres, hon," she called to her husband as we headed off.

"Thank you, darling," he replied, beaming her a loving smile. "You're the best."

If he only knew.

I trotted after Mrs. Sinclair into her gargantuan kitchen, practically a carbon copy of Mrs. Van Hooten's. I'm guessing all one-percenters have massive islands, stainless steel appliances, and sub-zero refrigerators.

Now that I had her alone, I needed to question her about the incriminating footage I'd found on Scotty's VCR.

But I had to be careful and ease my way in.

"What a shame about Scotty, huh?" I said, as she removed a plate of depressingly low-calorie cru-dités from her fridge.

"Not really," she said, selecting a bottle of wine from her built-in wine cooler. "As you probably could tell the day I stopped by his office, I detested the man. A most disagreeable fellow. By the way, what were you doing there that day?"

"Oh, um, Scotty hired me to help him with a

script he was writing. I'm a screenwriter. TV and movies."

One more lie, and I'd be struck by lightning.

"Scotty hired you?" Mrs. Sinclair blinked in surprise. "He was paying you real money? Not the Monopoly kind?"

I couldn't possibly tell her the truth—that I'd bartered my services for Prozac's room and board—and blow my cover as a rich person.

"Actually, he hadn't gotten around to paying me when he was killed," I said, tap dancing around the truth.

"He never would have come through with the money. The man would sooner part with a kidney than a dollar."

"I suppose the police have come to question you," I said, steering the subject back to the murder.

"Yes. They were here. They wanted to know if we saw anyone going into the Parkers' house the morning of the murder."

"Did you?"

"No, Evan and I were at church that morning, then Skyping with the kids in Aspen."

"No other questions from the police?" I asked.

"No. Just routine inquiries."

"I thought they might have asked you about that rather loud quarrel you had with Scotty outside his house about your Christmas decorations."

Her smile grew stiff then. Very stiff.

"We discussed it briefly. But the police didn't take it seriously. Scotty fought with all the neighbors."

Okay, now was the time to move in for the kill.

"What about the blackmail photo? Did the police take that seriously?"

"What blackmail photo?"

She barely batted an eyelash, playing it cool.

"The envelope Scotty gave you that day in his office. He told me it contained a compromising photo of you with another man. Not your husband."

Of course, Scotty had told me no such thing, but she didn't need to know that.

"You mean that picture of me and Lucas?"

She rolled her eyes, exasperated.

"For heaven's sakes. Lucas is my brother. He was up from Orange County visiting. He took me to lunch and I hugged him good-bye. End of story. Only Scotty would turn a loving brother/sister embrace into an extramarital affair."

She blew off the whole thing so convincingly, I was tempted to believe her. But I couldn't forget her reaction the day she saw the picture, how her face turned ashen at the sight of it.

"If that was your brother, why were you so upset when you saw the picture? Why didn't you say something to Scotty?"

And then suddenly, all the granite in her turned to mush. Her face crumpled, her eyes misting with tears.

"If you must know," she said, sinking down onto one of the island stools, "that was the day Lucas first told me he had been diagnosed with cancer. He's been having chemo and radiation and it looks like he's going to pull through, thank heavens. But when I saw that picture, I remembered how terrible I'd felt when I'd first learned the news, how terrified I'd been at the thought of losing him.

"Suddenly my quarrel with Scotty over a stupid electrician's bill seemed meaningless. So I got my priorities straight and walked out the door."

Mrs. Sinclair may have been a bit of a snob, and she may have had ghastly taste in hors d'oeuvres, but for what it's worth, I believed her.

Scotty had been all wrong about that embrace in the Mercedes. It hadn't been an affair. Mrs. Sinclair was still very much in love with her husband. Of that I was convinced, especially when she returned to the living room with the wine and crudités.

She set them down on the coffee table, and kissed her husband lightly on the forehead. In return, he squeezed her hand.

They were in love, all right.

I thanked Mrs. Sinclair for her time, assuring her I'd gotten more than enough decorating ideas to inspire me and my fictional decorator. Then I made my way down their front path, hoping someday I'd be lucky enough to find the kind of love the Sinclairs shared.

Chapter 21

Back at Casa Van Hooten, Lance was waiting for me with dinner on the kitchen island—a low-cal meal of broiled salmon and asparagus. Much to my surprise, it was really quite delish, but barely made a dent in my appetite.

As I always say, a meal without starch is like a day without Oreos.

I hankered for some bread or potatoes, but Lance quickly put the kibosh on any starchfest.

"We need to slim down if we want to be in shape for our dates on New Year's Eve."

"What dates? We don't have any dates."

"Don't be such a Debbie Downer. Just toss your wishes out to the universe, and the universe will make it happen!"

"Lance, you've got to stop believing the messages in your fortune cookies."

"I must admit," he said, a cloud of doubt in his eyes, "I'm getting a tad worried. It's been ages since my dinner date with Graham, and aside from that Merry Christmas text, I haven't heard a word from him."

"Actually," I said, "I ran into him yesterday."

"Really?" Lance sat up with a jolt, ignoring the asparagus he was about to spear. "How did he look? Was the sun glinting off the hair on his calves?"

"I don't know, Lance. I wasn't checking his calf hairs."

"I don't understand," Lance sighed. "We had so much fun at dinner. Why hasn't he asked me out?"

"Why are you sitting around waiting for him to make the next move? Why don't you ask *him* out?"

"No way. Absolutely not. I asked him out first. Now it's his turn to ask me. I made up my mind after Justin and I broke up that the next time I met an interesting man, I was going to play hard to get. I was much too eager with Justin and I'm convinced that's why it all went south. I've got to play it cool with Graham and retain my air of mystery."

"Then maybe you'd best cut down on your seventeen texts a day."

"Point well taken. Just this last one," he said, taking out his phone, "to send him the picture I took of our salmon and asparagus."

After dinner we retired to the living room with cups of no-cal tea, admiring the Christmas tree and breathing in the slightly woodsy aroma of its acorn garlands.

"Yes," Lance mused, stirring his tea, "I've absolutely got to play it cool with Graham. I refuse to be seen as desperate and needy. And speaking of desperate and needy, how are things with you, hon? How did your date go with *NiceGuy*?"

"Don't ask," I sighed. "He turned out to be a white-collar criminal. Under house arrest at his marina condo for insider trading."

"A condo in the marina? Sounds like a keeper to me!"

"Forget it, Lance. No way am I going out with him. In fact, I think I've had it with Smatch. I've made up my mind to take down my profile."

Lance put down his teacup, alarmed.

"That's ridiculous! You can't give up on Smatch because of one crappy date."

"Two crappy dates. Don't forget about the married actor."

"You can't give up because of two crappy dates. Did Madame Curie give up when she was trying to discover the radio? Did Orville Redenbacher give up when he was inventing popcorn? Did Henry the Eighth give up after his first five wives?"

"First of all, Orville Redenbacher did not invent popcorn, and Madame Curie discovered radium, not the radio."

"I hate it when you nitpick. My point is: You're never going to find Mr. Right if you give up the search. You've got to kiss a lot of frogs to find your prince."

If I kissed one more frog, I'd be an honorary amphibian.

But Lance had a point. I thought about the Sinclairs and how happy they were. I wanted what they had. Especially now that I'd been jilted by Prozac.

"Okay, you're right," I conceded. "I'll stay on Smatch."

"Good for you, sweetheart!"

Bolstered by my decision to give love another chance, I sprang from the sofa and headed for the kitchen to celebrate with one of the several pints of Chunky Monkey I'd stocked in Mrs. Van H's freezer.

But much to my horror, when I opened the freezer door, I discovered it was a Chunky Monkey– free zone. Not a pint to be found. No frozen goodies of any kind.

"What the hell happened to my Chunky Monkey?" I demanded, storming back into the living room.

"Oh," Lance said, not even bothering to look up from where he was no doubt shooting Graham another text, "I gave all our desserts to a homeless shelter."

"What??!"

"Like I said before, it's time to shape up for our New Year's Eve dates!"

Resisting the urge to strangle him with an acorn garland, I grabbed my car keys and set off for the nearest supermarket—Ralphs in Westwood, right across the street from the UCLA campus.

Because most of the students were home for winter break, the parking lot was fairly empty, and I hustled inside, where I was soon cradling two pints of Chunky Monkey in my arms.

In no time I was at the checkout counter, paying ten cents extra for a plastic bag I would possibly use later to suffocate Lance.

Back outside, I made my way across the nearly deserted lot to my Corolla and was just about to open the door when I felt what seemed like an iron clamp on my shoulder, spinning me around. I turned to find myself face to face with former football star and jailbird, Marlon Jenkins.

Holy Mackerel! Up close he was like two stories tall!

And from the way his unibrow was bristling, I could tell he was not a happy camper.

"Hi, Marlon," I managed to squeak.

"Don't 'Hi, Marlon' me," he snapped. "The cops came to talk to me today. Apparently somebody blabbed about my fight with Scotty. How I threatened to come back and take care of him once and for all.

"And I think that blabbermouth was you!" he added, flexing his massive biceps.

By now he was so close I could look up into his nose hairs.

"I can assure you it wasn't me," I said, my voice quivering like the lily-livered weakling I am.

"You were there the day I attacked him."

"I wasn't the only one who saw you. The way gossip travels on your block, I'm sure all the neighbors knew about it the next day."

"Yeah, but you're the only one who's been snooping around asking questions."

Down by his side, it looked like his bandaged fist was squaring off to deliver a knuckleburger.

"I'd mind my own business if I were you," he growled, his breath—none too savory—blasting down on me. "You wouldn't want to wind up sharing space in the morgue with Scotty, would you?"

Call me wacky, but I if wasn't mistaken, it looked like I'd just received a death threat.

I was standing there, shaking in my shoes, tensing for the impact of a knuckleburger, when Marlon turned on his heels and stomped off to a nearby monster SUV.

As he sped off in his van, I somehow managed to gather my wits and did what any sensible person would do after receiving a death threat.

I went back to the market for another pint of Chunky Monkey.

Okay, two pints.

Chapter 22

I woke up the next morning, deep in the throes of a Chunky Monkey hangover—tummy aching, head throbbing, my breath reeking of chocolate and bananas.

As I sat up in bed, checking for chocolate stains on my pillowcase, I felt a sharp stab in my shoulder. And suddenly the memory of my meetup with Marlon came rushing back into my consciousness.

Good heavens. The man had threatened to kill me!

I needed to call Lt. Muntner and tell him about Marlon's death threat. It took several phone calls to track down the detective, but when I finally did, I was shunted to his voice mail. After leaving an urgent message for him to call me, I hung up, resolving to put all thoughts of Marlon aside and get on with my day.

Normally at this point I'd be padding downstairs for breakfast. But that morning—Ripley's, take note—I actually had no appetite.

Instead I decided to go for a brisk walk, hoping the exercise would clear the cobwebs from my brain and the Chunky Monkey from my thighs.

Throwing on some capris and a tee, I started down the stairs. At the sound of Lance rattling around the kitchen, I snuck out the front door, unwilling to face a lecture about the evils of Chunky Monkey binges.

I set off, determined to walk for a full hour. Needless to say, after twenty minutes I was wheezing like an old jalopy. So I threw in the towel and turned around to go back home, fantasizing about a cinnamon raisin bagel slathered with butter and strawberry jam.

I'd just about staggered back to Casa Van Hooten when I noticed a sprawling Spanish hacienda with a FOR SALE sign out front. The listing agent, I saw, was Bitsy Clayton—the same agent who'd called Elise the day I stopped by to visit.

Even though Marlon was now the front-runner in my suspect sweepstakes, I couldn't afford to rule anyone out. I still hadn't forgotten my theory that Elise may have discovered Scotty's will while she was raiding his office on Christmas Eve, giving her ample motive to bump him off. Nor had I forgotten those rubber gloves I'd seen on her dinette table, the gloves she may have worn while wielding the murder weapon.

On an impulse, I took out my cell phone and called Bitsy, pretending to be a prospective buyer, and made an appointment to see the Spanish hacienda later that morning.

It was a long shot, but I was hoping Bitsy might help me figure out exactly when Elise had learned of her inheritance.

Back at Casa Van H, Lance was unfortunately still in the kitchen, sipping his ghastly grass smoothie. Somehow I managed to tune out his binge eating lecture as I scarfed down my cinnamon raisin bagel.

Then I headed upstairs to my heavenly rain forest shower, luxuriating under its tingling jets of hot water. Getting out of the shower, however, I was alarmed to see an ugly red bruise on my shoulder. A memento from my meet-up with Marlon. And that was just from his grip. I shuddered to think what he might have done if he'd actually landed a jab.

For a minute I was tempted to heed Marlon's warning and give up my investigation.

But only for a minute. I refused to let the big lug intimidate me. We Austens are made of sterner stuff. I would be strong. I would be courageous. Most important, I would be ratting him out to the cops the minute Lt. Muntner returned my call.

In the meanwhile, it was time to spiff myself up for my appointment with Bitsy Clayton.

I wore the same outfit I wore on my disastrous date with Ryan Gosling II—silk blouse, skinny jeans, blazer, and Manolos. The look, I fervently hoped, of a gal who could maybe possibly in her wildest dreams afford to buy a house in Bel Air.

After scrunching my curls and slapping on some lipstick, I flipped open my laptop and checked out

Bitsy's website. It was really quite impressive, loaded
with photos of fabulous homes she was represent-
ing, as well as pictures of megamansions she'd sold
in the past. Clearly, Bitsy was a mover and shaker in
the rarefied world of Bel Air real estate. Scrolling
through the photos of her past listings, I blinked
in recognition to see Connie's house in the photo
gallery. So Bitsy had been Connie's broker. A fun
factoid that was about to come in quite handy.

As it happened, my outfit was not quite good
enough for Bel Air. It might have passed muster in
Mar Vista or Cheviot Hills, but I could see by the
way Bitsy Clayton was looking me over that she had
her doubts about me as a prospective buyer. For
this kind of nabe, I should have been sporting
haut couture togs and rocks on my fingers the size
of Milk Duds.

"So nice to meet you," Bitsy said, with a dubious
smile.

A short, bouncy dame, a tad on the plump side,
she had the baby-faced looks of a menopausal kew-
pie doll.

She reached out to shake my hand, almost
blinding me in the process with an eye-popping di-
amond on one of her pudgy fingers.

Her smile, however, remained dubious.

And it was at this moment that I decided to play
the Connie card. After all, it had worked so well
with Mrs. Sinclair, I figured I'd give it another
shot.

Making use of the info I'd unearthed on Bitsy's

website, I said, "One of your former clients, Connie Van Hooten, has told me so many wonderful things about you."

"*You* know Connie?" Bitsy asked, with just a tad too much incredulity in her voice for my liking.

"Indeed, I do. We're both on the board at St. John's Hospital."

By now, I was beginning to believe it myself.

"Well, come on in," she said, her smile turning a lot more genuine. "Let me give you the tour."

And we were off and running. For the second time in two days I was getting a Bel Air house tour. One more house, and I'd be starring in my own episode of *House Hunters*.

Bitsy guided me through the charming Spanish beauty, pointing out its vaulted beamed ceilings, Moorish archways, and painstakingly preserved original tile.

Bitsy proved to be quite a Chatty Cathy, babbling on about the home's original features and modern conveniences, waxing euphoric about the state of the art media room and farmhouse kitchen sink.

As much as I tried, I simply could not stem the flow of her sales chatter and get the conversational ball bouncing over to Scotty's murder. But finally, in the kitchen, as Bitsy stopped to wipe a smudge off an otherwise spotless quartz counter, I got the opening I'd been waiting for.

"I suppose you've heard about the murder on the next block?" I said quickly, before she could resume her sales spiel.

"Yes, poor Scotty Parker," she tsked. "Such a lovely man."

Obviously, she hadn't known him very well.

"I hope it won't be affecting property values in the neighborhood," I said, my brow furrowed with fake concern.

"Of course not," she assured me with a wave of her bejeweled hand. "Bel Air property values never go down."

"Connie told me that Scotty's first wife, Elise, has inherited everything," I tossed out casually, pretending to inspect the eight-burner stainless steel oven. "Including the house."

"I know!" Bitsy beamed. "I'm her broker."

"Wow. What a coincidence," I said, hoping she'd believe that's all it was. "From what I hear, poor Elise could really use the windfall. Connie said she called her with the good news on Christmas Day."

This, of course, was the feeble trap I was setting. If I could get Bitsy to say that Elise had called her on Christmas Day, the day before Elise got the official news she was inheriting everything, that would be proof that Elise had known about the will, giving her more than enough motive to kill Scotty.

"How odd," Bitsy replied. "I didn't hear from her until the day after Christmas. Elise told me she'd just then heard about Scotty's will."

So much for my trap.

It looked like Elise hadn't known about the will, or had been smart enough to keep quiet until the news of her inheritance was official.

I was just about to write off my little sleuthing excursion as a bust when Bitsy said:

"So gruesome the way poor Scotty was killed. Elise told me he was bludgeoned to death with a frozen Yule log. One he'd bought half price, because it had the inscription MERRY CHRISTMAS, AUNT HARRIET! written on it.

"Imagine!" she said, wrinkling her tiny nose in disapproval. "Buying secondhand pastry. Scotty always was a bit on the frugal side," she added, in the understatement of the millennium.

And suddenly alarm bells started clanging in my brain.

There'd been absolutely no mention of the murder weapon in the news. Of that, I was certain. I'd been following the story carefully. And there'd been no mention of dear Aunt Harriet, either.

How the heck had Elise known about the murder weapon—unless she'd been the one using it?

Chapter 23

With Elise back on top of my suspect list, I wasted no time zipping across town to her apartment in Hollywood.

It wasn't till I was standing at her intercom, however, that I realized there was no way she was going to buzz me in. Lest you forget, the last time I'd seen her, I'd been passing myself off as her attorney's fictional assistant.

So I spent the next fifteen minutes pretending to read the menu in the window of the kabob joint underneath her apartment, until someone finally came out of Elise's building. Quickly darting over, I managed to slip inside before the door slammed shut.

After which I rode the graffiti-encrusted elevator up to the second floor and made my way to Elise's apartment.

Girding my loins for battle, I knocked on her door.

"Who is it?" she called out from inside.

"Um . . . Special delivery," I replied, making sure to stand clear of her peephole.

When Elise opened the door, I almost gasped at the sight of her.

Gone was the frazzled gal I'd met with just two days ago. In her place stood a svelte woman in designer sweats, her blond hair shiny and freshly highlighted, her wrinkles Botoxed to oblivion.

It looked like someone had gotten an advance on her inheritance.

"You!" she cried, glaring at me.

Somehow I sensed she was not about to roll out the welcome mat.

"A small gift," I said, holding out a container I'd picked up at the kabob joint. "Some baba ganoush. To apologize for lying to you the other day."

"Who the hell are you, anyway?" she said, grabbing the baba ganoush without a syllable of thanks. "I called Scotty's attorney, and I know you don't work for him."

She stood there, arms clamped firmly across her chest, making no move to ask me in. For which I was actually grateful. Just in case she was the murderer, I was happy to be standing out in the hallway, with easy access to an escape route.

"I'm sorry I lied to you the other day. You wouldn't let me in and I had to think of an excuse to talk to you. I was at Scotty's house the morning he was murdered. I'm a suspect in the case, and I've been doing some investigating to clear my name."

"What's that got to do with me?" she snapped. "I

already told you I was here all morning long. I have no idea who killed Scotty. So I can't help you out."

Then the dawn came.

"Unless, of course, you think it was me."

A faint flush of irritation suffused her Botoxed cheeks.

"As a matter of fact," I said, "I happened to be speaking to Bitsy Clayton a little while ago and she mentioned that you knew all about the murder weapon—the frozen Yule log with MERRY CHRISTMAS, AUNT HARRIET!' written on it. I hope you won't take this the wrong way, but I can't help wondering how you knew about it, since there's been no mention of it whatsoever in the media."

I guess she did take it the wrong way, because the look she shot me could've punctured a tire.

"I'll tell you how I know about it, Sherlock. I called Missy to offer her my condolences. Not on losing Scotty, but on losing his fortune. And to congratulate her on getting out from under his thumb. I never resented Missy for her role in Scotty dumping me. I pitied her for what I knew she'd have to put up with. While we were on the phone, she told me about the murder, how she saw Scotty's body, and the murder weapon.

"So that's how I know about the Yule log with Aunt Harriet's name on it. Believe me. Or don't believe me. It's up to you. That's all I've got to say. In twenty minutes I've got to be in Beverly Hills to have my eyebrows shaped."

And without any further ado, she slammed the door in my face.

I rode down the creaky elevator, wondering

whether or not to believe her, and wishing I'd kept the baba ganoush.

I'd just pulled up to Casa Van Hooten and was getting out of my Corolla when I saw Lupe coming out of Scotty's house, a casserole dish in her hands.

"Guess what, Ms. Jaine!" she cried, hurrying to my side, her face wreathed in smiles. "I got the job with the nice family up the street! I'm starting next week."

"Congratulations, Lupe. That's wonderful!"

"I'm going to my sister's to celebrate with home-made tamales."

She held out the casserole dish and I took a sniff.

Yummy with a capital Yum.

"Here comes my nephew to pick me up."

Sure enough, the same young man with the sweet smile who'd picked up Lupe on Christmas Day pulled up in his blue Nissan.

"Hi, Aunt Lupe!" he said, getting out of the car and planting a kiss on her cheek. "Congratulations on your new job!

"I see this time you didn't forget the tamales," he added, taking the casserole dish.

"No," Lupe said. "Today I remembered."

Then, turning to me, she explained, "On Christmas Day I was in such a rush to get out of the house, I forgot the tamales I'd made."

"We had to turn around and come back to get them," her nephew added.

"Well, we'd better get going," Lupe said. "We've got a lot of partying to do!"

"Nice seeing you again," her nephew said, lobbing me his sweet smile.

"Have fun!" I called out as they got in the car.

It wasn't until they were halfway down the street that I realized what a bombshell had just exploded at my feet.

Lupe had returned to the house after I'd run into her on Christmas morning!

Which meant she could have made a detour to knock off her detested boss.

Maybe Scotty had caught her sneaking out of the house and forbade her to leave. Maybe he'd once again threatened to turn her family over to La Migra. Maybe, sick and tired of his threats, she'd grabbed the Yule log in a moment of rage and followed him to his office where she bonked him to an early grave.

I hated the idea of sweet little Lupe as a killer, but suspecting everybody and anybody comes with the territory when you're a hard-boiled, part-time, semiprofessional PI like *moi*.

I was standing there, trying not to think about Lupe stuck behind bars for twenty-five to life, when my cell phone rang.

At last. Lt. Muntner!

"What's up?" he asked.

"I have to talk to you about Scotty Parker's murder."

"Go ahead. Talk."

"No, I need to see you in person. There's something I've got to show you."

Namely, the blotchy red bruise on my shoulder. I wanted him to see what a violent nutcase Marlon Jenkins was.

"Okay, come on over."

He gave me his address, and soon I was back in my Corolla, tooling across town to Lt. Muntner's office at the LAPD's Wilshire Station, in a nuts and bolts blue collar neighborhood several light years away from the posh hills of Bel Air.

I told the officer at the front desk I was there to see Lt. Muntner, and minutes later, the stoop-shouldered cop came out to greet me in a wrinkled white shirt and loosened polyester tie. Nodding hello, he led me through the detectives' bullpen to his battered desk with a view of the parking lot.

But the only view I was interested in was the one of a spectacular pastrami sandwich sitting on his desk, a giant mound of meat crammed into two thick slices of rye, and bursting with Thousand Island dressing. Nearby were a kosher pickle and side of cole slaw.

It had been hours since my CRB, and I was a tad peckish.

"Have a seat," he said, pointing to a molded plastic chair within grabbing distance of the sandwich.

I guess he could tell by the way I was staring at his pastrami that I was lusting after it.

"Want some?" he asked, holding out half.

"Oh, no. I couldn't possibly."

Okay, so I took it. Scarfed it down in a record five bites.

And I ate his pickle, too, if you must know.

His heavy-lidded, seen-it-all eyes widened a tad in astonishment. Apparently, they hadn't seen everything.

"So how can I help you?" he asked, his fork hovering protectively over his side of cole slaw.

"I want to talk about Scotty's killer."

"And who might that be?"

Suddenly I started having doubts. This morning I was certain it was Marlon. But now, I wasn't so sure. What with Elise knowing all about the murder weapon, she'd become a very viable suspect. And I couldn't forget about Missy, the merry widow. And Dave, her besotted lover.

So I began rattling off my list of suspects, leaving out my suspicions about Lupe. (Just in case she wasn't the killer, I didn't want to get her family in trouble with the immigration authorities.)

I felt a tad guilty about ratting on Missy and Dave, after promising I wouldn't blab about their affair. But, as it turned out, I needn't have worried.

"Tell me something I don't already know," Lt. Muntner said after my recital. "What do you think we're doing here, Ms. Austen? Playing Parcheesi? We know all about Missy and Dave. And Marlon's fight with Scotty. And Elise Parker told us how she'd learned about the murder weapon from Missy."

"Well," I said, smiling weakly, "I'm glad we're on the same page."

"Do you have any actual evidence," the good detective wanted to know, "linking any of these people to the crime?"

This was it. The moment I'd been waiting for.

"As a matter of fact," I said, with no small amount of pride, "I have incontrovertible evidence that Marlon Jenkins is a very violent man. Last night he attacked me in the parking lot at Ralphs."

Lt. Muntner looked up from his pastrami sandwich. For the first time, he seemed interested in what I was saying.

"Marlon Jenkins attacked you?"

"Indeed he did. Just look at this."

With that, I took off my blazer, unbuttoned the top button of my blouse, and pulled it back to show him my bruised shoulder.

He blinked, puzzled.

"What's the damning evidence of Marlon's violence? Your bra strap?"

I looked down, and realized, much to my embarrassment, that the ugly splotch I'd seen in the bathroom that morning had faded away.

Oh, for crying out loud. How embarrassing. Here I was with my bra strap exposed in the middle of the Wilshire Station police department, a pastrami-gobbling shoulder flasher.

"It was red and bruised this morning," I insisted. "Honest."

"Would you care to press charges?" he asked. "Take out a restraining order? Call in the National Guard, perhaps?"

"That won't be necessary," I said, with as much dignity as I could muster under his barrage of sarcasm. "I guess it's time for me to be running along."

"Not so fast," he said, holding up a finger. "Before you go, there's one suspect we haven't discussed."

"And that would be . . . ?"

"You. The person found at the scene of the crime."

"You can't seriously think I killed Scotty. Don't tell me you actually dug up a plausible motive for me to murder him."

"No," he admitted. "Not yet."

I breathed a sigh of relief.

"But we have been informed that you've been running around town passing yourself off as a close friend of Constance Van Hooten and a legal assistant at the firm of Briskin, Todd, Washton, and Carmichael. Neither of which, I gather, is true."

"Okay, so I told a few fibs," I confessed. "I was just trying to gather some facts in an effort to clear my name."

"As I told you before, Ms. Austen," he said, "we here at the LAPD are trained professionals. We know what we're doing. Just leave the fact-gathering to us."

"Absolutely," I promised, fibbing yet again. "Will do."

And with that I got up and walked out of the bullpen, past all the detectives who'd no doubt been ogling my bra strap—my head held high, my spine erect, my tush stained with Thousand Island dressing.

* * *

Lance came storming home that night, his jaw clenched tight, his blond curls aquiver.

"Most annoying news," he snapped.

"What happened?" I asked. "They ran out of tuna niçoise at the cafeteria? Some other salesman stole one of your customers? Your tanning parlor got shut down by the vice squad again?"

"No, I got a phone call from Connie Van Hooten."

Oh, hell. I braced myself for what I knew was coming next.

"Apparently, you've been running around telling everyone you and she are BFFs."

"That's not true. I only told two people."

"Well, that's two people too many. Connie didn't like it. Not one bit."

"Gosh, Lance. I'm so sorry if I've done anything to compromise your relationship with her. I know what an important customer she is. Honestly, I feel awful. Just awful!"

"Can the drama," he said, waving aside my apologies. "Everything's okay. As usual, Uncle Lance saved the day. I told her you were bipolar and were having trouble with your meds."

"Bipolar??"

"And that you're under a lot of pressure because you'd recently lost both your parents in a parasailing accident."

"A parasailing accident??"

"And that you're a direct descendant of a relative of the real Jane Austen."

"A direct descendant of a relative of the real Jane Austen??"

"What—is there an echo in here? Why do you keep repeating everything I'm saying? The point is, I smoothed over troubled waters. All you have to do is send Connie an heirloom copy of *Pride and Prejudice* signed by the real Jane Austen."

"How the hell am I supposed to do that?"

"Just order an old copy on eBay, Google Jane Austen's signature, and trace it onto the book. She'll never know the difference.

"But really, Jaine," he added, without the faintest hint of irony, "you've got to stop telling such outrageous lies!"

YOU'VE GOT MAIL!

To: Jausten
From: Shoptillyoudrop
Subject: The Devil's Spawn

Hi, sweetheart!

Just back from an exciting morning in Grand Turk.
Saw the spot where John Glenn's space capsule
splashed back down to earth, toured a historic
lighthouse, and went shopping in a genuine salt
museum, where I bought the most divine bath
salts that smell just like the sea! Finally, we toured
Cockburn Town, a charming village loaded with
Victorian and early 20th-century architecture. Reminded me of our Scott and Zelda Fitzgerald New
Year's Eve costumes. How much fun it will be to
step back in time! Can't wait to see Daddy in his
puffy knickerbocker pants. I've been having the
most impossible time getting him to try them on,
but sooner or later, he's got to give in.

Back on board ship, we ate a late lunch at the buffet, where Daddy pointed out a redheaded little
boy, called him The Devil's Spawn. Honestly, I
don't know what gets into your father. The boy
looked perfectly innocent to me.

Off to another one of Lydia's fascinating lectures:
Christmas traditions in Norway!

XOXO,
Mom

To: Jausten
From: DaddyO
Subject: No Puffy Pants for the Iron Man!

Hi, Lambchop—
Stopped off at Grand Turk today. Saw a bunch of old houses and bought some salt.

Mom's been nagging me to try on my Scott Fitzgerald costume. I keep putting it off. Just the sight of those baggy pants makes me want to up-chuck. No way is Iron Man Hank Austen about to appear in public in puffy pants.

Great lunch at the buffet. Had an "everything" omelet (mushrooms, ham, tomatoes, bacon, and cheese), plus a chocolate éclair for dessert. The Brat was there, and wouldn't you know, with Mom at my side, he behaved like a perfect angel.

Mom's gone to hear Lydia blather on about Christmas in Norway, and I'm headed to the deck for a nice relaxing snooze.

Love 'n hugs from,
DaddyO

To: Jausten
From: DaddyO
Subject: Ultimate Revenge!

Well, Lambchop—I'm happy to report that The Brat finally got his comeuppance!

It all started as I was stretched out on a secluded deck chair, slipping off into a soothing doze. Then suddenly I was jolted awake by a loud banging noise on the wall right next to me.

Opening my eyes, I saw The Brat standing in front of me, holding a soccer ball. With a most aggravating smirk, he took the ball and bounced it against the wall, just inches from my head. Then he bounced it again. And again.

"Stop bouncing that ball," I said.

"What if I don't?" The Brat said, bouncing the ball.

By now, I'd had it up to my eyeballs with this kid.

"This is what happens if you don't!"

Like a shot I was up from my deck chair, snatching the ball from his grubby little hands.

"Hey!" he cried. "Gimme back my ball. It's a genuine Nike professional soccer ball. It cost my grandpa a hundred and fifty bucks."

"You want your ball?"

With that, I swung my arm back and tossed the damn thing clear overboard.

"Go get it!"

Needless to say, the kid was really steamed. Did my heart good to see his little face go purple with rage.

"Wait till I tell my grandpa. He's gonna get you for this."

I'd seen his grandfather today at lunch. A frail old guy with spindly legs and a thriving colony of liver spots.

I could take him on with one hand behind my back.

And so, leaving The Brat in major sulk mode, I headed over to the buffet, flush with victory.

Justice, at long last, has been served!!

Love 'n cuddles from,
Daddy
Aka The Avenger

To: Jausten
From: Shoptillyoudrop
Subject: Another Spellbinding Lecture!

Lydia's lecture was fascinating as usual. Did you
know that Norwegians hide their brooms at Christmas? I may try it next year, only I'll hide the vac-
uum. How relaxing that will be.

Meanwhile, Daddy's in a marvelous mood. I found
him at the buffet diving into a hot fudge sundae
and yapping about justice being served.

XOXO,
Mom

PS. Ever so excited about Isabel's 95th birthday
party. Can't wait to see the look on her face when
she gets a look at her new diamonette bracelet!!

Chapter 24

If only I were a true descendant of Jane Austen and my great-great-great-great-granny had snapped up Cousin Jane's book for a mere ninety pence. Do you know how much that darn thing would be worth today?

About a hundred and eighty thousand dollars! That's how much the last one raked in at auction.

Needless to say, I did not have a spare hundred and eighty thou to spring on a gift for Connie Van Hooten. So—after checking my emails and reading about Daddy's triumphant soccer ball coup—I spent the next morning on my laptop at the kitchen island scouring the Internet for a reasonably affordable first edition of *Pride and Prejudice*. Finally, I found a gilt-edged copy for eighty bucks.

Unfortunately, this first edition was published in 1980, a good hundred and sixty-three years after Jane's death. I only hoped Lance was right when he assured me that Connie never read anything

more challenging than *Vogue*, and that my little de-
ception would go undetected.

I'd just placed my order and was about to reward myself with an apple (okay, an apple Pop-
Tart) when I thought I heard a rustling sound
coming from the living room.

I put down my Pop-Tart and tiptoed to the
kitchen door, wondering if it had been my imagi-
nation. But, no. There it was again. That rustling
sound.

Omigod! Someone had broken into the house.

And right away, I thought of my hulking neme-
sis, Marlon Jenkins. What if he found out I'd rat-
ted him out to the police, and he'd come to exact
revenge?

I remembered his words to me in the parking
lot: *You wouldn't want to wind up sharing space in the
morgue with Scotty, would you?*

Grabbing a frying pan, I tiptoed out into the
hallway. Maybe I could catch Marlon unawares and
bop him over the head before he even saw me.

But when I peeked in the living room, I saw it
was a completely Marlon-free zone. No sign of the
Incredible Hulk anywhere.

The source of the rustling noise, I discovered,
was a squirrel—scampering down the fireplace.
Now he was squeezing past the fire screen and
making a beeline for the Christmas tree.

And then I realized what he was after: The
acorns on the acorn garlands!

No doubt he'd sniffed out the nuts and had
come for his midmorning snack.

I watched in horror as he leaped onto the tree,

bouncing from branch to branch, in search of the perfect acorn.

Oh, hell. With all that bouncing around, the tree was beginning to wobble.

Racing over, I managed to catch the tree before it fell, and stood there, propping it up. Meanwhile, Mini-Marlon, as I had come to think of my furry friend, had found the acorn of his dreams and, after biting off the cap, was nibbling away at the contents.

"Shoo!" I called out, but the squirrel glanced at me as if I was nothing more than an annoying aphid and went back to nibbling.

I couldn't stand there forever while the damn squirrel noshed at our Christmas tree.

"Beat it, buster!" I said, in my most authoritative voice, waving the frying pan at him.

The frying pan did the trick.

Mini-Marlon took one look at it and, reluctantly abandoning his acorn, skittered down off the tree.

I quickly tightened the screws at the base of the tree, securing it place. Thank heavens I'd averted disaster.

No, wait. I hadn't averted disaster. Not yet. Those of you paying close attention will no doubt realize there was still a squirrel roaming free in the Van Hooten manse.

Somehow I had to get rid of him.

I raced to the front door and opened it to give Mini-Marlon an easy exit. After which, I frantically started running around searching for him.

I finally found him in the dining room just about to leap onto Mrs. Van H's silk damask drapes. Oh, gaak! I could just picture his paw prints up and down that two-hundred-dollar-a-yard fabric.

"No!" I screeched, waving my frying pan.

At the sight of the pan, Mini-Marlon abandoned the drapes and was off and running. He led me on a merry chase through the dining room, the sun room (where he stopped for a beat to admire the view of the swimming pool), then into the kitchen, where he leaped onto the kitchen island and, much to my consternation, started nibbling on my Pop-Tart.

The nerve of some squirrels!

He then took a quick sniff of Lance's smoothie glass and had the good sense to run away from it as fast as his furry little legs could carry him. And before I knew it, we were back in the living room where Mini-Marlon once again made a beeline for the Christmas tree.

But I beat him to it, standing in front of the tree, warding him off with my trusty frying pan.

I was congratulating myself on yet another heroic rescue of the tree when Mini-Marlon suddenly scuttled across the room and made a flying leap onto Mrs. Van H's étagère.

The same étagère with about a gazillion dollars' worth of museum-quality bibelots! Perched next to the highly breakable Ming vase, he was eyeing a nearby Fabergé egg with interest. He probably thought it was something to eat.

Sure enough, he scooted past the Ming vase, miraculously not toppling it, and reached out to grab the Fabergé egg.

"No! No! No!" I shouted, visions of priceless collectibles plummeting to the hardwood floor below.

And then, like an angel from on high, my salvation arrived.

"Hello?" I heard someone calling out from the front door. "Is everything okay?"

The next thing I knew, Graham the mailman came walking in the living room.

"Graham. Thank God you're here! That damn squirrel broke into the house looking for acorns on our Christmas tree and now he's about to bite into Mrs. Van Hooten's Fabergé egg. One false move, and the Ming vase next to him is history!"

Graham looked over and saw Mini-Marlon, who was now standing stock still, perhaps realizing he was outnumbered two to one.

Graham, not missing a beat, went over to the Christmas tree and pulled off an acorn garland.

"Hey, fella," he called out in a voice as soft as velvet. "Look what I've got for you."

He held out the acorns in the palm of his hand.

Mini-Marlon blinked, then looked at Graham's hand, no doubt remembering why he'd broken into Casa Van Hooten in the first place.

His nose twitched with interest.

Graham took a step closer.

I squeezed my eyes shut, waiting for Mini-Marlon to take off in terror, breaking several thousand dollars' worth of doodads en route. But when I opened my eyes, I saw he hadn't moved an inch. He sat stock still, staring at the acorns in Graham's hand.

"C'mon, little guy," Graham cooed, crouching down on his knees. "I won't hurt you. I promise."

His voice was soft and soothing, Valium to Mini-Marlon's ears.

Much to my amazement, the squirrel jumped down off the étagère and slowly approached Graham. As Mini-Marlon moved forward, Graham, still crouched over, gradually eased backward, out of the room and into the hallway. Mini-Marlon followed, mesmerized—by the acorns, or Graham, I couldn't tell which.

At last they were at the threshold of the front door. Graham backed outside, and to my everlasting relief, Mini-Marlon followed him.

Graham continued retreating until they were safe on the front lawn.

But instead of just tossing the acorns for Mini-Marlon to eat, Graham kept holding out his hand.

And in a moment I'll never forget, Mini-Marlon scooted over to Graham and grabbed one of the acorns. While Mini-Marlon was nibbling to his heart's content, Graham actually reached over and petted him.

Even more miraculous, Mini-Marlon actually let him.

I stared at Graham in awe.

"Omigosh!" I cried. "You're a regular Squirrel Whisperer!"

"I guess I do have a way with animals," he said, with a modest shrug.

What a sweetheart! For once, Lance had latched on to a keeper.

Of course, if there's one thing I've learned in life, it's never interfere in other people's love lives.

If something goes wrong, you're the one they're sure to blame. Absolutely never ever get involved.

A rule I promptly proceeded to ignore.

"You know," I said, taking one of Cupid's arrows and aiming it straight at Graham. "Lance really likes you."

"I like him, too," Graham replied. "He's a great guy."

"Then how come you haven't made any moves to see him again? According to my calculations, he's probably sent you about two hundred forty-six texts."

"I know," Graham smiled. "He's quite the communicator. I've been wanting to ask him out, but I'm having a hard time getting over the death of my last love. It's been several years and I still haven't let go."

"Don't you think it's time you did? Sorry if I'm speaking out of turn, but a man as kind to squirrels as you are deserves a chance at love again."

By now Mini-Marlon was practically sitting in his lap.

"You're right," Graham said, with a decisive nod. "I've got to start putting myself out there. In the meanwhile, though, I'm afraid I've got mail to deliver."

He pointed to his mail cart down on the sidewalk.

"Omigosh! I'm so sorry I've kept you all this time. Thanks so much for coming to my rescue!"

"Thank *you*," he said, "for some very sound advice. I'll be in touch with Lance soon."

Yay, me! Maybe this matchmaker thing wasn't such a bad idea, after all.

"Lance is such an interesting guy," Graham was saying. "General manager of Neiman's. Former commando with the Navy Seals. And Calvin Klein underwear model."

Oh, Lordy. Can you believe the whoppers Lance had pawned off on Graham?

I'd just set up the world's sweetest squirrel whisperer with the Lyin' King.

So much for my gig as Cupid in elastic waist pants.

The phone was ringing when I got back in the house.

It was Lance, in advanced panic mode.

"Major emergency!" he cried. "I just realized I left my cell phone home! I've been busy all morning with a sale on Ferragamos. By the way, they've got the cutest strappy sandals for only two hundred thirty dollars that would be perfect for your Internet dates."

Yeah, right. The day I spend $230 on a pair of sandals is the day I drink one of Lance's grass smoothies.

"Anyhow," he blathered on, "I borrowed a customer's phone to call you—Thank you so much, Mrs. Otis. You've got the most beautiful instep of any woman I know!"

Then, turning off his gush-o-meter, he switched back to me, all business: "I think my phone's upstairs in my bathroom. You've got to get it and bring it over to me at Neiman's. What if Graham calls and I miss him?"

I considered telling him about my recent chat with his postal heartthrob, but decided against it. Why get his hopes up, in case Graham flaked out?

"Okay, I'll bring it over."

"Make it snappy! No dawdling!"

"You're welcome, Mein Führer."

I trotted upstairs and found his phone on his bathroom counter, crammed between his deep pore cleanser and his volumizing hair mousse. Snatching it up, I then followed Lance's strict orders and dashed downstairs and out to my Corolla.

Okay, so I dashed downstairs and nuked myself another Pop-Tart. But right after that I dashed out to my Corolla.

As I headed down the front path, I glanced next door and saw Dave Kellogg, carrying an armful of law books, waving good-bye to Missy.

"Just need to spend a few hours at the UCLA law library," he called out to her, tossing his books in the backseat of a bright red VW Beetle, "and then I'll be home."

Trying not to upchuck at the sight of him blowing Missy a batch of nauseating baby kisses, I got in my car and followed Dave as he drove down to Sunset Boulevard.

Then something very strange happened.

If Dave were going to UCLA, as he'd just told Missy, he'd be making a right turn on Sunset.

But instead, he turned left.

My curiosity piqued, I followed him, careful to stay several car lengths behind him. A handy technique I've honed in my years as a part-time, semi-professional PI and dedicated viewer of *Magnum, PI* reruns.

I tailed Dave south on Beverly Glen to Santa Monica Boulevard, not far from the Century City shopping center. For a minute, I thought maybe he was going to stop off to do an errand, but no, he kept driving until he got to a tree-lined street in the Rancho Park area of Los Angeles.

Stopping several houses away, I watched Dave pull into the driveway of a cute yellow cottage, with a white picket fence and a magnolia tree in the front yard.

He got out of his VW, leaving his books in the car, and sauntered up a brick path to the front door. And then, without a missing beat, he reached into his pocket, pulled out some keys and let himself in!

Whoa, Nelly! What the heck was going on?

Why did Dave need to rent a room from Scotty if he had a home of his own?

I was sitting in my Corolla, trying to make sense of it all, when I saw a mail carrier approach Dave's house and deposit some mail in the mailbox at the front of the picket fence.

I waited for Dave to come out to get it, but when several minutes passed and he still hadn't retrieved it, I took a chance and dashed over to do some snooping.

Hurriedly, I flipped open the door to the mailbox and pulled out its contents.

Riffling through his mail, I blinked in surprise to see that all the letters were addressed, not to

Dave Kellogg—but to someone named Dave Chambers.

Whaddya know? It looked like the love-struck law student had been living a double life. First, Dave Kellogg. Now, Dave Chambers.

Which one was the real Dave? And why the grand charade?

Yet another mystery to be solved in this dratted murder.

Chapter 25

"Thank heavens you're here!" Lance cried when I showed up at Neiman's, yanking his cell phone from my hand like an addict in desperate need of a fix.

"Omigosh!" he said, checking his messages. "Here's one from Graham!"

"Really?" I asked, in fake surprise.

"The best news ever!" He beamed from ear to ear. "He's invited me over to his apartment on New Year's Eve!"

Yay! My pep talk had worked!

Then his face clouded over.

"Hell, no!" he moaned.

"What's wrong?"

"He's invited you, too."

"What a catastrophe. Having to spend New Year's Eve with me."

"Jaine, sweetie. You know I adore you, and if I had to spend New Year's Eve with anyone without an Adam's apple, it would be you. But I can't possibly make progress with Graham with you on the scene. Promise you won't stay long? You'll make up an excuse and pretend you have a party to go to?"

"I promise I won't stay long."

"Thank you, hon," he said, throwing his arms around me in gratitude. "And who knows? Maybe, thanks to Smatch, you'll have a date of your own for New Year's Eve."

"Don't bet your Ferragamos on it."

"In the meanwhile," he said, "you simply must go upstairs and check out the sale they're having on cashmere sweaters. They're practically giving them away. If you find anything you like, I'll get it for you with my employee discount."

I sincerely doubted that Neiman's was practically giving anything away—least of all cashmere sweaters. But I took the elevator upstairs and wandered around, lost in a sea of three and four-figure price tags, grateful that my I COULD GIVE UP CHOCOLATE, BUT I'M NOT A QUITTER T-shirt was hidden under my blazer.

The cashmere sweaters were half-off, which was still triple what I'd pay for one, but just for kicks, I decided to try on a cute jewel-neck number with a row of delicate ruffles at the hem.

Major mistake.

Putting ruffles on my hips is like putting frosting on a BLT. Simply too much! Those damn ruffles made my hips look like the SS *Jaine Austen*.

I quickly whipped off the sweater, vowing to go on a strict diet.

A vow that came to an abrupt halt about three

minutes later when I was strolling past one of Neiman's restaurants. I'd eaten lunch with Lance at Neiman's a couple of times and ordered their burger, which was absolutely yummy. Gosh, I thought, a burger sure would hit the spot right about then.

Yes, I know I'd just vowed to go on a diet and it was utterly disgraceful of me to be even thinking of food, but I needed sustenance to help me get over the memory of those damn ruffles.

But then I saw something that sent all thoughts of ruffles shooting off into the stratosphere. There, seated at a cozy table for two, was Mrs. Sinclair, the chisel-cheekboned aristo.

And she was not alone.

Seated across from her was the bald guy from the Mercedes, the one on Scotty's security tape. The man Mrs. Sinclair had claimed was her brother.

At first glance, they looked perfectly innocent, smiling and chatting like two loving siblings.

But then I looked down and saw that Mrs. Sinclair had kicked off one of her heels and was rubbing the bald guy's calves with her toes. Definitely not a sisterly move.

Wow. What an Academy Award–winning performance she'd given the other day, when she'd hovered over her husband as if he were the love of her life.

Now the bald guy, his eyes glazed over with either lust or cataracts, took Mrs. Sinclair's perfectly manicured hand in his, and began kissing her fingertips.

Right there in the middle of the ladies who lunched!

No way was this guy her brother. Mrs. Sinclair was having an affair, all right. And Scotty had been about to blackmail her.

A perfect motive for murder.

"May I help you?"

I looked up to see a gazelle-like hostess standing before me, her white-blond hair swept up in a sleek chignon, menus cradled in her arms.

And with a sinking sensation, I realized she wasn't the only one who'd noticed me standing at the entrance to the restaurant.

Over at the Sinclair love nest, Mrs. Sinclair had torn her gaze from her inamorata and was now glaring at me with a look so icy, it could freeze a Jacuzzi.

I knew she was cheating on her husband.

And now she knew I knew.

The question was: What did she intend to do about it?

One thing for sure: I wasn't about to stick around and find out.

Chapter 26

Needless to say, I came to my senses and forgot about stuffing my face with a Neiman's burger. Instead I scooted over to the nearest Mickey D's and stuffed my face with a Quarter Pounder and fries.

Back at Casa Van Hooten, I somehow managed to shake off the haunting image of Mrs. Sinclair's death ray glare. True, she'd catapulted to the top of my suspect list. But I hadn't forgotten about a very important runner-up. Namely, Dave Kellogg—aka Chambers—and his cozy cottage in Rancho Park.

What was that all about?

Soon I was nestled on the living room couch with my laptop, Googling "Dave Chambers."

The results came up instantly. It turned out that Dave Chambers of Rancho Park, California, was a certified CPA. I clicked on his website, and sure enough, there was Dave's clean cut face smiling out at me.

If Dave was a CPA, why was he pretending to be a law student?

As my good buddy L. G. Carroll would say, this whole thing was getting curiouser and curiouser.

But I didn't have time to ponder the matter further. Not right then, anyway.

As it happened, I had to gussy myself up for another Smatch date.

I haven't told you because I didn't want to get your hopes up, but in spite of my last disastrous date with Phil, the white-collar crook, I'd decided to give Coon another Smatch date.

Clearly living with Lance had turned me into a dating daredevil.

I'd exchanged a few messages with *Mr. Write*, a very attractive screenwriter, into Scrabble, crossword puzzles, *Frasier* reruns, and cross-country skiing.

Except for that cross-county skiing thing, we were practically soulmates.

We'd agreed to meet for coffee that afternoon. So I hurried upstairs and slipped into what I was beginning to think of as my Smatch dating outfit: skinny jeans, blazer, and silk blouse.

Hopping in my Corolla, I drove over to where I was meeting *Mr. Write*—Los Angeles's original Farmers Market, a hodgepodge of produce stands and food stalls, with patio areas set among the stalls for al fresco dining.

I decided to park next door at the upscale Grove shopping center to take advantage of their first hour of free parking. After spiraling up what seemed like the Mt. Kilimanjaro of parking lots, I finally found a space and then rode the elevator back down to the ground floor.

There I hurried past shoppers busy returning unwanted Christmas gifts, and tourists riding the bright green trolley that wended its way along the main street of the mall.

Arriving at the decidedly less glitzy Farmers Market, I made my way to the West Patio where *Mr. Write*—whose real name was Duane—and I were to meet.

I scanned the tables for my future significant other. Finally I spotted a very handsome guy with a shock of tawny brown hair. He didn't look much like the picture I'd seen on Smatch, so at first I wasn't sure it was him. But then he looked up, shot me a big smile, and waved.

Yes! It *was* him! Yahoo! What a cutie!

I only hoped he wasn't going to turn out to be another royal waste of my time.

And good news: He wasn't about to waste my time at all. Because just then I turned around and saw he wasn't waving at me, but at a gorgeous young thing behind me, who went flitting over to his table and slapped him with a big wet smacker.

At that same moment, I heard someone calling my name.

"Yoo-hoo! Jaine!"

I turned to where the voice was coming from, but all I saw was a nanny with a toddler and an old man with a bad toupee. A very bad toupee. Honest. It looked like a live hamster on his head. I was surprised it didn't come with a running wheel.

"Jaine! Over here!"

The old man with the hamster toupee was waving me to his table.

Yikes! Don't tell me *he* was my date! The man was older than my dad! Heck, the guy was probably fraternity brothers with Methuselah.

As I walked over to his table, I could see a faint resemblance to the picture he'd posted on his profile. Only that picture must have been taken decades ago, when he had real hair on his head and not a napping hamster.

"Jaine, my dear," he said, reaching out to shake my hand. "So nice to meet you!"

Then he flashed me a gleaming smile, baring a set of teeth that, I am fairly certain, had been ordered online.

"Pardon me for not getting up," he said, "but my hip's a little out of whack. A recent skiing accident."

Yeah, right. The last time this guy had gone skiing Herbert Hoover was president.

"Do sit down!" he said, with a flash of his store-bought teeth.

"Sorry, Duane. But I can tell right now this will never work."

Oh, how I wish I'd had the nerve to actually say that. Instead, like the spineless wonder I am, I sat down across from him.

"I brought my own hot cocoa and peanut butter and jelly sandwich," Duane said, pointing to a thermos and wax-paper wrapped sandwich on the table. "But feel free to order anything you want. My treat."

With a flourish, he reached into his wallet, and handed me a dollar bill.

In a trance-like state, I got up and wandered over to the food stalls.

Now, you'd think I'd head straight for a pizza stand or a frozen yogurt joint, right?

Wrong.

The only thing that was going to get me through this encounter was my good buddy, Mr. Chardonnay.

So I headed to a booth that sold beer and wine.

For a fleeting instant I thought about asking the bartender if there was a back entrance to his booth, so I could slip out into an alley and make a run for it. But then I looked over at Duane, un-wrapping his PBJ, his hamster toupee slightly askew on his head.

I couldn't desert him. He was just too darn pathetic.

So I ordered a glass of wine, making up my mind to stick it out for a half hour, after which I would pretend to feel my phone vibrating with an emergency call that would send me scooting off to freedom.

Chardonnay in hand, I put on a brave smile and returned to the table, where I was greeted by Duane, dentures gleaming, holding out his hand.

Wait. Didn't we already shake hands?

Oh, well. At his age, maybe he forgot. I reached out to shake it again, but he just looked at me and said:

"Where's my change?"

Oh, Lordy. Obviously, the guy hadn't bought any booze since his hair fell out.

"I'm afraid the wine costs more than a dollar."

"Highway robbery," he tsked in disapproval.

"So," he said, as I reluctantly lowered my fanny into the chair across from him, "tell me all about yourself."

"Well," I began, "I'm a writer—"

And that's as far as I got.

I didn't know it, but the Duane Express was about to take off.

"I know!" he exclaimed, taking a big bite of his sandwich and treating me to a most unappetizing view of its contents as he chewed. "That's why I wrote you. I'm a writer, too. I just finished my latest screenplay."

Duane reached down into a frayed shopping bag and pulled out a dog-eared copy of a script.

The title page read:

Ricky
By Duane L. Forrester

"Want me to tell you the story line?"

God, no!

But before I could even open my mouth, he was off and running, reciting in excruciating detail what seemed like every beat of his story about a small-time boxer, a self-proclaimed "bum" from the wrong side of the tracks who gets a chance to take on the world's reigning heavyweight champion. How the fighter trains with a former bantamweight boxer and falls in love with the wallflower sister of his buddy and how, after much blood, sweat, and testosterone, he "goes the distance" against the champ, making it through the fight without getting knocked out—something no fighter has ever done before—proving to himself that he's not the bum he thought he was, and winning the hand of his true love.

In spite of Duane's excruciating delivery, I liked the story line a lot. I always had, ever since I'd first seen it on the screen as the Academy Award winning movie *Rocky*.

"Well? What do you think?" he asked when he'd finally finished his recital.

"It's great."

"I know," he beamed. "That's what everyone tells me."

"But isn't it an awful lot like *Rocky*?"

A look of annoyance flashed in his rheumy eyes.

"What do you mean? It's nothing like *Rocky*. First of all, my character is named Ricky. And the story isn't set in Philadelphia, it's in Pittsburgh. And he doesn't run up the stairs to the Philadelphia Museum of Art. He runs up the steps of a StairMaster.

"It's not the least bit like *Rocky*!" he shouted, banging his fist on the table.

Nearby the nanny looked over at us, alarmed.

"Right," I murmured, eager to placate him. "Not the least bit like *Rocky*."

"For your information, William Morris of the William Morris Agency is reading it right now!"

I didn't have the heart to tell him that the real William Morris died in the 1930s, sometime around Duane's last ski trip.

Having polished off the last of my chardonnay,

I'd had more than my fill of Duane L. Forrester. I was just about to pretend to hear my phone vibrating with a fake emergency phone call when Duane checked his watch and said:

"Well, Jaine. I hate to rush you out of here, but I'm expecting my next date any minute."

"Your next date?"

"Yes. I lined up five of 'em today. Plan to narrow it down to two lucky ladies. Sorry to say, you didn't make the cut."

What? The old geezer was rejecting *me*?

"You need to go before"—he looked down to consult a list on the back page of *Ricky*—"Kimberly shows up."

What nerve! Making me sit through his endless plagiarized saga, and then rejecting me!

If only I hadn't finished my wine, how I would have loved to toss it in his face.

I got up to go, fury oozing from every pore.

"One more thing," Duane said. "Seeing as things didn't work out between us, would you mind giving me back my dollar?"

By now I was surprised actual steam wasn't puffing out of my ears.

I'd used up his crappy dollar to buy my drink. The smallest bill I had was a five.

"Here you go," I said, slamming it down on the table. "Use it to buy yourself a new toupee. And this time, make sure it's dead before you put it on your head."

And yes, I really did say that. With the greatest of pleasure.

* * *

No doubt about it. I was through with Smatch.com. Done. Finito. Hasta la vista.

I stormed out of the Farmers Market and onto the streets of The Grove, still fuming over duplicitous Duane, or as I preferred to think of him, Hamsterhead.

The monumental gall of that guy! Posting a Smatch photo that had to be at least forty years old. Boring me senseless with his plagiarized screenplay. And that ghastly piece of animal fur on his head. I wouldn't have been the least bit surprised if the darn thing had fleas.

I was just about to cross The Grove's main street when I heard the clang of the trolley. I turned and saw the bright green tram approaching, filled with happy passengers, laughing and chattering, full of joie de vivre and enviably Duane-free.

And then, as I stood there, waiting for the trolley to pass, out of nowhere, I felt someone shove me from behind. A powerful shove that sent me sprawling onto the trolley tracks.

When I looked up, I shuddered to see the trolley barreling right at me.

I struggled to get to my feet, but my legs were like jelly, and I kept floundering on the tracks.

Any second now, that big hunk of steel was going to ram right into me!

Just as I was certain I was headed for that great Shopping Mall in the Sky, I heard the earsplitting sound of brakes squealing.

The trolley had come to a halt just inches from my nose.

The driver, a gangly guy in an old-fashioned train conductor's uniform, jumped down from his seat and came racing to my side.

"Are you okay?" he asked, brow furrowed in concern, visions of lawsuits no doubt dancing in his head.

"I'm fine."

And I was. Aside from a small scrape on my elbow, I hadn't been hurt.

(One of the advantages, I might point out, of having well-padded hips and thighs. I sent up a silent prayer of thanks to my guardian angels, Ben and Jerry.)

"Are you sure you're okay?" the trolley driver asked. "Nothing broken?"

"Really," I assured him. "I'm fine."

By now we were surrounded by a crowd of curious onlookers.

"But somebody pushed me."

"What?" The trolley driver blinked in disbelief.

"It's true. Someone shoved me onto the tracks." I turned to the crowd. "Did any of you see someone shove me?"

They all shook their heads *no.*

How very annoying. Where were all the people shooting cell phone videos when you needed them?

Then an elderly woman with a Nordstrom shopping bag and a headful of permed curls spoke up.

"I didn't see anyone push you," she said, "but I did notice someone running away as soon as you hit the tracks."

At last! Someone with powers of observation.

"Was it a man?" I asked eagerly. "Or a woman?"

"It all happened so fast, I couldn't tell. All I know is that the person was wearing a blue ski cap."

"A blue ski cap, huh?" I filed that tidbit away for future reference.

Assured that my bones were all in working order, the trolley driver escorted me across the tracks. After which, he resumed his seat on the trolley and continued on his route. The crowd dispersed and life at The Grove continued as usual.

I made my way to the parking lot and up Mt. Kilimanjaro to my car, my knees still weak, my heart pounding.

Someone in a blue ski cap had pushed me onto those tracks.

And that someone, I was certain, was Scotty's killer.

Chapter 27

I drove home in a daze, trying to figure out who'd given me that fateful shove.

My first thoughts flew to Marlon. Whoever shoved me was strong. And Marlon was nothing if not a bastion of strength.

But then I remembered Mrs. Sinclair and the death ray glare she'd beamed at me at Neiman's. It's quite possible she'd come home from her lovers' lunch, seen me leaving the house, hopped in her car, and followed me over to The Grove.

And what about Dave? Had he spotted me riffling through his mail? Having killed Scotty to clear the way to Missy, was he now prepared to do me in so I wouldn't go ratting on him to the police? And there was always Missy. True, she didn't seem like a killer, but anything was possible in the wacky world of homicide.

And finally, I couldn't forget about Elise, the now wealthy ex-wife. She'd known about the inscription on the murder weapon even though she'd claimed to be nowhere near the scene of the crime.

All these suspects were swirling in my brain like chocolate in a quart of fudge ripple. By the time I reached Casa Van Hooten, I was more confused than ever. All I wanted was a comforting cuddle with Pro and a nice hot bath to soak my frustrations away.

But, wait. There would be no comforting cuddle with Pro.

The little rat had tossed me aside like an empty can of minced mackerel guts.

It was with heavy heart that I climbed out of my Corolla—only to see my cheating angel nestled in the arms of Missy as they made their way up the front path to the former House of Scrooge.

"Hi, Jaine!" Missy called out, spotting me as I got out of the Corolla. "Guess where Scarlett and I just came from? The groomer's."

"And you lived to tell about it?"

Let's just say Prozac doesn't care for people coming at her with any kind of implements, unless said implements contain food.

"She was a perfect angel. Look! Isn't she the cutest thing you've ever seen?"

I gawked at the sight of Prozac, sporting a bright pink-bowed headband. This was almost as bad as her ridiculous mistletoe hat. And her reindeer antlers. Never in her old life would Prozac have put up with such a humiliating piece of headgear.

But now, she was actually preening.

Pretty in pink. That's moi!

"I wanted her to look extra nice before she goes back home with you," Missy said. Then, lobbing me a pleading look, she added, "I don't suppose you'd let her stay on with me? We've grown so very close."

"I'm afraid not."

In Missy's arms, Prozac looked up, alarmed.

Hey, what's all this talk about me moving back with whatshername?

"Just a few more days," Missy cooed, "and then you have to go back home, pumpkin face."

If I'd called her "pumpkin face," I would've lost an ear.

But Pro just purred like a buzzsaw.

"Ciao for now!" Missy said with a jaunty wave, skipping into the house, my former significant other practically glued to her arms.

I'd been so appalled at the sight of Prozac with that moronic bow in her hair I hadn't noticed a pile of trash waiting to be picked up by the garbage men.

Now I saw, spread out at the curb, Scotty's creaky office swivel chair, a carton full of notes for *The Return of Tiny Tim*, and the framed poster of Scotty's long-ago version of *A Christmas Carol*.

So much for keeping Scotty's memory alive.

I gazed at the faded poster of Scotty as a child, fresh-faced and, if not exactly innocent, at least not yet the jaded misanthrope he was destined to become.

I was checking out the names of the other cast members when suddenly I saw it. A name that sent my brain cells whirring:

Everett Chambers.

I flashed back to Christmas Eve, watching *A Christmas Carol* with Scotty as he trashed all the other actors, aiming most of his barbs at the man who played Bob Cratchit—Everett Chambers!

Everett Chambers! he'd said. *I've seen better acting from a ventriloquist's dummy!*

Was it possible that Dave Chambers was somehow related to Everett?

I'd been meaning to head straight for the tub when I got back to Casa Van Hooten. Instead, I made a beeline for my laptop and my good buddies at Google.

Before long I was reading all about Everett Chambers—his bio, his screen credits, and most important, his obituary.

Apparently the actor who'd played Bob Cratchit opposite Scotty's Tiny Tim had died two weeks after shooting wrapped on the movie. His wife was quoted as blaming her husband's death on the stress of working on the movie. In particular, working with young Scotty Parker, who, in the words of Mrs. Chambers, had been "quite a handful."

According to the obituary, in addition to his wife, Audrey, Mr. Chambers was survived by one son.

A boy named David.

Holy Moly. So Dave was Everett Chambers's son! And Scotty's bad behavior had driven his father to an early grave.

Had Dave Kellogg aka Chambers shown up at the House of Scrooge, not to rent a room, but to avenge the death of his father?

It sure looked that way to me.

Chapter 28

I slept poorly that night, tossing and turning on Connie Van Hooten's ultra-plush mattress. I dreamed I was sprawled out on the trolley tracks, frozen, unable to move, watching in terror as a ginormous trolley came charging at me, certain that the driver was Scotty's killer. But when his face came into view I saw it was Duane L. Forrester, grinning maniacally, his stupid hamster toupee askew on his head.

I bolted awake in a cold sweat, wondering which would be worse: coming face-to-face with Scotty's killer, or going on another date with Hamsterhead.

It was a close call.

Feeling like I'd been asleep for all of two minutes, I staggered down to the kitchen where Lance began chattering about our New Year's Eve date with Graham—trying to decide what to wear (Hugo Boss vs. Armani) and reminding me to make my excuses and leave as early as possible.

"Ten minutes would be optimal. Just enough to say hi and good-bye."

"Why not cut it down to thirty seconds? I could just drive by and wave."

"Would you?" he asked, hopefully.

"No, Lance. I'm not going to drive by and wave. I'm going to stop in for a drink and an hors d'oeuvre or three. And then I'll leave. I promise I'll be gone in time for you two to fall in love and live happily ever after."

An indignant sniff from His Royal Chatterbox.

"It looks like somebody woke up on the grouchy side of the bed this morning. Here. Have a lemongrass smoothie. You'll feel better in no time."

"You offer me one of your lawn mower smoothies one more time, Lance, and I'm going to park my fanny at Graham's all night long."

"Okay, okay! No smoothie," he said, glugging his down with gusto.

I proceeded to nuke myself a cup of strong black coffee—and another—and another—until at last I'd rejoined the land of the living and began functioning.

First thing on my agenda: Confront Dave Kellogg about his alter ego Dave Chambers.

I showered and dressed and headed next door, where Missy greeted me in a pink velour jog suit, grinning from ear to ear.

"Guess where Dave's taking me for New Year's Eve!" she said, eyes bright with anticipation. "Dancing at the Bel Air Hotel."

Whoa. That must have cost him at least six months of tax returns.

"And look what he bought me," she cried, skipping into the living room and holding up a giant gray stuffed elephant. "I'm calling him Ashley Wilkes. Isn't he the cutest thing you've ever seen?"

"Adorable." I nodded weakly.

"Elephants are supposed to bring good luck. And it certainly seems to be working. Dave says he's already got a new place lined up for us to live."

I just bet he did—a cozy little cottage in Rancho Park.

"Not only that, he says he's already saved up enough money so I don't have to go back to work!"

Clearly Dave hadn't clued her in on his life as a CPA.

"Speaking of Dave," I said as casually as possible, "is he around? I sort of wanted to talk to him."

"Oh?" she said, a questioning look in her eyes.

I couldn't very well tell her I suspected her beloved of being a killer, so I came up with the following fib:

"My cousin is thinking of applying to UCLA law school, and she had a couple of questions she wanted me to ask him."

That seemed to satisfy her.

"He's at the law library now, but he should be back later this afternoon. I'll tell him you stopped by."

"Thanks," I said, certain that the "law library" would turn out to be Dave's house in Rancho Park.

"Want to hear the love poem Dave left on my pillow this morning?" she asked, taking out a folded slip of paper from her bra.

Not if I wanted to keep down the CRB I'd scarfed down for breakfast, I didn't.

"I'd love to, but I've really got to go. Lots of errands to run."

"Okay, later then."

"Sure. Right. Absolutely."

With that I beat a hasty retreat, eager to hustle on over to Rancho Park and have it out with Dave Kellogg aka Chambers.

Zipping off in my Corolla, I was confident I would be able to remember the route I took to Dave's yesterday.

But I was wrong. Way wrong.

I spent at least twenty minutes circling the streets of Rancho Park, desperately searching for Dave's house, and cursing myself for not writing down his address.

Just when I was about to give up hope, I stumbled upon the yellow cottage with the white picket fence and the magnolia tree out front. Seconds later, I was making my way up the front path and ringing the bell.

Dave came to the door in khakis and blue oxford shirt, a pair of techno-nerd horn-rimmed glasses perched on his nose.

"Jaine." He gulped at the sight of me. "What are you doing here?"

"I could pretend I was here to have my taxes done by a certified CPA, but that would be a lie. Sort of like the life you're leading with Missy. May I come in, Mr. Chambers?"

He nodded, dazed, and led me into a cozy living room with a brick fireplace, hardwood floors, and beamed ceiling. The walls were lined with movie posters—all featuring Everett Chambers. And those were not the only testaments to Dave's father. The fireplace mantel, along with several end tables, were jammed with framed photos of the long-dead actor.

"Can I get you something to drink?" Dave asked.

"Thanks, I'm fine," I said, those three cups of coffee still sloshing around inside me.

"Well, I'm not. I need a scotch. Be right back.

"Make yourself at home," he added as he left the room, waving to a sofa in front of a bay window.

But I didn't sit down. Instead I did what I always do when I get the chance:

I snooped around, looking at the pictures on Dave's mantel and end tables. Mostly of Everett Chambers—some publicity stills, and plenty of candid shots with his wife and toddler Dave. All smiling radiantly into the camera.

Dave returned with a few inches of scotch in a highball glass. He plopped down into an armchair with a sigh, and I took a seat across from him on the sofa.

"Chocolate?" he offered, pointing to a box of Godiva truffles on the coffee table between us.

"I really shouldn't," I said, popping one in my mouth.

"Eat as many as you want. I'm allergic. One of my clients gave them to me as a Christmas gift."

"No, no. One is plenty," I said, reaching for another.

"So how did you discover the truth about me?"

"I followed you here the other day and checked the mail in your mailbox. All addressed to Dave Chambers. Then I saw your dad's name on Scotty's *Christmas Carol* poster and put two and two together."

"Yes," he said, taking another slug of his scotch, "I'm Everett Chambers's son. And just for the record, Scotty Parker killed my father. Not outright murder. But he killed him nonetheless. Scotty looked young for his age; he was actually thirteen when he played Tiny Tim. I guess he was going through an early teenage rebellion, because he was a real wiseacre, giving everybody lip, holding up production, making everyone's lives miserable. My dad had a bad heart. And after months of stress putting up with Scotty, his heart gave out. I was just a toddler when my dad died, but I have vivid memories of him. He was a wonderful man and didn't deserve to go the way he did.

"My mom never recovered from his death," he sighed, staring down into his highball glass. "She spent the rest of her life lonely and depressed."

Then he looked up, eyes burning with a long-nursed grudge.

"Scotty ruined our family and I never forgave him. I Googled him periodically to see what he was up to, like picking at a sore tooth. I even hired a detective to keep tabs on him. Then one day the detective told me Scotty, rich as Croesus, was actually renting out a room in his house. The monumental cheapskate wanted even more income.

"I paid a fortune for a fake ID and took the room, pretending to be a law student on a tight budget. I was hoping to get a look at his account books, find some financial hanky panky, and send him to jail for tax fraud."

Then his expression softened.

"What I didn't expect to find was Missy. The minute I saw her, I fell head over heels in love. Suddenly getting even with Scotty didn't seem so important. All the anger drained out of me. All I wanted was Missy.

"I came to Scotty's house to destroy him, but I swear, I didn't kill him."

He looked so sincere in his nerdy horn-rimmed glasses, I couldn't help but believe him.

"That's it," he said, swigging down the last of his scotch. "That's my story. Anything else you need?"

As a matter of fact, after all those coffees I'd sloshed down that morning, I desperately needed to take a tinkle.

"Would it be all right if I used your rest room?" I asked.

"No problem. I've only got one," he said, pointing down a hallway, "and I'm afraid it's not as tidy as it could be. But there's a clean guest towel on the rack."

"Thanks so much."

I trotted down the hallway to Dave's bathroom.

He did not lie. The bathroom was a mess. Wet towels lay on the floor. Globs of dried toothpaste dotted the sink.

I wondered if Missy realized what a slob she'd fallen in love with.

I was just wiping my hands on the guest towel when I glanced down at a filled-to-overflowing hamper and saw the sleeve of a blue oxford shirt popping out from under the lid.

The elbow of the shirt, I noticed, was stained with something dark.

And at that moment, my part-time, semiprofessional PI antennae sprang to life. I bent over and took a whiff.

Just as I'd thought: Chocolate.

When it comes to sniffing out the stuff, I'm a regular bloodhound.

But, wait. Hadn't Dave just told me he was allergic to chocolate? If so, what was he doing with it on the sleeve of his shirt? Was it possible, I wondered, that he got it while whacking Scotty with a Yule log?

Suddenly, instead of coffee, fear was now sloshing in my innards.

What if I was alone in the house with a killer?

I told myself I was being crazy. If the chocolate on Dave's sleeve was from the scene of the crime, wouldn't he have washed it out long ago?

Not if he was confident the cops had no clue to his double life.

No, I chided myself, I was overreacting. There had to be a thousand ways Dave could've gotten chocolate on his sleeve, and nine hundred and ninety-nine of them didn't involve a lethal Yule log.

I headed back to the living room to say good-bye and found Dave at the fireplace mantel, staring at a wedding photo of his parents, his eyes misted over with tears.

See? I was being nuts. Anyone this sensitive couldn't possibly be a killer.

I was standing there next to him when my eyes wandered over to a loose photo lying on the mantel—of Dave in a Santa sweatshirt.

But it wasn't the sweatshirt that caught my eye.

It was the hat on Dave's head:

A blue ski cap.

Just like the one worn by the guy who pushed me on the trolley tracks.

The fear in my innards started sloshing again.

First the chocolate on his shirt. Now the blue ski cap. Two strikes, and Dave was out.

I didn't care how innocent he looked in his nerd glasses.

Something told me I'd just been scarfing down Godiva truffles with Scotty's killer.

I shot out of that house like a highly caffeinated rocket, eager to get back to Casa Van Hooten and put in a call to Lt. Muntner.

Unfortunately, he wasn't at his desk when I called, so I was shunted to his voicemail, where I left a rather breathless message about Dave, his dual lives, and his very compelling motive for killing Scotty—filling him in on my harrowing incident on the Grove trolley tracks and my discovery of Dave's chocolate-stained shirt and incriminating blue ski cap.

I urged him to call me back ASAP, and hung up with a sense of accomplishment, waiting for the wheels of justice to spring into action.

In the meanwhile, I sat back, relaxed, and chowed down on a Godiva truffle I'd popped in my purse when Dave wasn't looking.

YOU'VE GOT MAIL!

CRUISE NEWS, SS **CARIBBEAN QUEEN**

> *The captain wishes to assure all passengers that the man they may have seen running through the ship last night clad in nothing but a loincloth and fright wig was not part of a terrorist attack, but merely a passenger in a most ill-advised New Year's Eve costume.*
>
> *Said passenger was held in the brig for two hours before being released in his wife's custody.*

To: Jausten
From: Shoptillyoudrop
Subject: I'm So Mad I Could Spit!

Never in my life have I been so humiliated! Poor Isabel Norton's birthday party was ruined—absolutely ruined! And it's all Daddy's fault!

The evening was a disaster from the get-go. It all started when I tried on my dress for Isabel's party and realized it was too tight. It's so darn unfair! Daddy's been stuffing his face at the buffet for the entire cruise and hasn't gained an ounce! But I, who have been nibbling on only the tiniest of cookies, managed to gain *five* pounds! I had to positively cram myself into that dress.

When I was finally ready to go, Daddy claimed he had a headache and would join me in a little while. But I knew what was really going on. He just wanted an excuse to get out of listening to Lydia's birthday tribute to Isabel.

I didn't care. I'd rather have him back in the cabin than at the dinner table, making wisecracks through Lydia's speech. So, in haste —and running late because I'd spent so much time agonizing over those dratted extra pounds—I grabbed Isabel's gift and hurried to the party.

From the minute I left the cabin, I had a feeling something wasn't right, but I couldn't put my finger on it. I just assumed the icky feeling in my tummy was the waistband of my dress digging into my gut.

It wasn't until Lydia had finally finished her tribute to Isabel (I must admit, it ran on quite a while) and Isabel was about to open her gift, that I looked at the box and realized what was bothering me. I'd grabbed the wrong box! The box with the diamonette bracelet was smaller than the one in Isabel's hands. I suddenly remembered that Daddy had gift-wrapped those dratted clacking false teeth in the same wrapping paper I'd used for Isabel's gift.

Oh, no! I grabbed the wrong gift by mistake! I watched in horror as sweet, darling Isabel opened her ninety-fifth birthday gift, only to find a pair of clacking false teeth inside. She smiled gamely, which made it all the worse, given that her teeth are clearly dentures.

I swear, I wanted to fall through a hole in the floor.

And just when I thought things couldn't possibly get any worse—Daddy came bursting into the dining room wearing nothing but a loincloth and fright wig!

I may never talk to him again.

XOXO,
Mom

To: Jausten
From: DaddyO
Subject: I Can Explain Everything!

I suppose Mom told you about my grand entrance at Isabel's party night. I know it looks bad, Lambchop, but honestly, I can explain everything.

First of all, it's not my fault that your mom grabbed those clacking false teeth to bring to the party. I think she needs to take the heat for that one.

As for my appearance in the loincloth and fright wig, here's how it happened:

I'd made up my mind to show up late for the party, refusing to sit through what was sure to be The Gasbag's endless tribute to Isabel. Taking advantage of Mom's absence, I decided to try on my costume for the New Year's Eve party, just to make sure everything was fitting properly. I had no sooner slipped into my loincloth and fright wig (which, by the way, were a terrific combo!) when there was a knock on our cabin door.

I opened it to find The Brat. How he found our cabin I'll never know. The little sneak had probably been tailing me ever since the soccer ball incident.

"My grandpa's coming to beat you up," he said with a smug smile.

"Your grandpa? The skinny guy with the knobby knees and liver spots?"

"No, not that grandpa. My other grandpa. Mr. Senior Universe."

I stepped out into the hallway and got the shock of my life.

There, thundering down the hallway, was a human boulder. A lumbering giant with muscles the size of rump roasts.

I consider myself a brave man, Lambchop, but I have to confess I was a wee bit terrified. And wouldn't you know, The Brat had taken advantage of my momentary shock to slam my cabin door shut. I was locked out. Nowhere to hide!

I could either stand up like a man and face the enemy. Or run for my life.

Needless to say, I started running.

Lucky for me, I ran track in high school. I thought for sure I could easily outrun The Boulder, but he was surprisingly speedy for a man of his bulk.

I raced down the corridor and considered buzzing for the elevator, but couldn't risk the chance that The Boulder would catch up with me. So up I ran, three flights of stairs, through the lobby, past the Christmas tree, the gift shops, and clusters of shocked passengers. It's not every day they saw a man in a loincloth and fright wig running through the Lido deck.

By this point, I was exhausted. The Boulder was gaining on me. Any minute now I would be pounded to smithereens.

But then, in a stroke of luck, I turned a corner and spotted a small door that I assumed was some sort of utility closet. Praying that the door wasn't locked, I turned the handle.

Hallelujah, it opened!

I dashed inside, certain I'd found refuge—only to realize I was in the middle of Isabel Norton's ninety-fifth birthday party. Mom was staring at me, aghast, as were all the other Tampa Vista-ites.

For a brief second, the only sound in the room was the castanet clacking of those Yakity Yak false teeth.

Ship security soon showed up and hauled me off to the brig. For which I was, to be honest, sort of grateful. At least they'd saved me from the clutches of The Boulder.

Mom insists I ruined Isabel's party. But I got a look at the roast beef they were serving. Looked darned good to me.

Mom had to bail me out of the brig, and pay $150 for the soccer ball I threw overboard. She says she's never speaking to me again.

Oh, well. Time to bite the bullet and make amends.

Love 'n smooches from,
Your DaddyO
(In the doghouse again!)

Chapter 29

I must admit I was rather annoyed the next morning when I still hadn't heard from Lt. Muntner.

Clearly he wasn't taking me very seriously.

I put in another call to him, once again getting shunted to his voice mail, and urged him to get back to me ipso pronto.

All thoughts of the murder were put on hold, however, when I read the latest emails from my parents.

Can you believe Daddy—racing through the *Caribbean Queen* wearing nothing but a loincloth and fright wig? And poor Isabel. Opening her birthday present, only to find those clacking false teeth!

Yet another disaster in Daddyland.

I was just about to log out of my email and leave my parents adrift in the Caribbean when I saw I had a message from someone at Smatch.

Memories of my recent encounter with Hamsterhead still etched in my cranium, I was all set to delete it. Especially since my correspondent, *Love in Venice*, didn't have a photo posted. Usually, when I came across a man without a photo, I zapped the guy to oblivion. But something, call it fate, made me read what *Love in Venice* had to say:

Warm, empathetic graphic illustrator, living in Venice, CA, with a view of the Pacific from my balcony. Seeking unpretentious woman. Someone who eats Chunky Monkey for breakfast. Does crossword puzzles in the tub. Enjoys wine at sunset and romantic walks to the refrigerator.
If you're a writer, that's a big plus.

PS. Must love cats!

Omigosh, the man had practically described me to a tee. And he didn't sound too shabby, either. I've always had a thing for artists. And one with a view of the Pacific from his balcony sounded particularly appealing.

He'd written me a note, saying:

I think we'd really hit it off. Care to meet up and find out?
Yes! Yes! A thousand times yes!!! were the words I was tempted to write in reply. Instead I went with the far more restrained: I would indeed.

A few more volleys and we'd set up a date to meet the next day.

Yes, I know I'd sworn off Smatch for all eternity, but this guy seemed special. I'd go on the date and hope for the best, fully realizing it could all blow up in my face. I just prayed this time there would be no bad toupees or arrest records involved.

In the meanwhile, my mind lingered on the final words of *Love in Venice*'s profile:

Must love cats!

I really had to do something to repair my shattered relationship with Prozac. I prayed that once we were back home, she'd forget about her insane crush on Missy.

But why wait till we got home? Why not spend New Year's Eve with her like I always did, cuddled together, watching TV and eating Chinese takeout? Lance wouldn't care. The minute I left Graham's place, he and Graham would be sailing off on the Love Boat together.

Eager to reunite with my pampered princess, I popped next door to tell Missy of my New Year's Eve plans.

Lupe let me in, in jeans and a sweatshirt, her hair swept up in a sloppy ponytail.

"Ms. Jaine! Excuse the way I look. I'm right in the middle of packing. Tomorrow I leave for my new job."

"That's wonderful!" I said, relieved Lupe wasn't the killer, that her return trip to The House of Scrooge on Christmas morning did not involve bonking her employer to death.

"Is Missy around?" I asked.

"Upstairs, getting dressed. Mr. Dave is taking her out on a special New Year's Eve date."

I hurried upstairs where I found Missy checking herself out in a full-length mirror, modeling a bling-studded evening dress so skimpy, it was practically a bikini.

"Oh, hi, Jaine," she said. "I was just trying to decide what to wear tonight.

"What do you think?" she asked, modeling her Band Aid-sized hoochfest. "Is it okay for the Bel Air Hotel?"

Only if they allowed hookers at the bar.

"You think it's too much?"

"Maybe just a tad," I said, at my diplomatic best. "You might want to go for something a bit more modest."

"You're right," she said. "Isn't she, Ashley-Washley? Mommy needs to wear something more modest."

I looked over at Missy's bed and realized for the first time that Prozac was no longer in her place of honor on Missy's faux mink throw. She had been displaced by Ashley Wilkes, the gray stuffed elephant. Missy was clearly gaga over her fuzzy gift from Dave.

And Pro was none too happy about it.

I knew Prozac's snit fits when I saw one, and right then, she was in major snit fit mode, sitting at the corner of Missy's bed, her tail thumping like a bass drum, her eyes narrowed into angry slits.

"Isn't Ashley the most adorable thing ever?" Missy was cooing. "Aren't you, sweetums?" she said, nuzzling the elephant's trunk.

From the corner of the bed, another angry thump of Prozac's tail.

My God! The woman's a moron. Talking to a lump of stuffing! What did I ever see in her? She has the IQ of a radish.

When I reached down to pick her up, Prozac practically leaped into my arms.

Thank goodness you're here!

Then she gazed up at me lovingly, the kind of look I sometimes get after a marathon belly rub.

Can you ever forgive me for abandoning you? I must have been blinded by human tuna.

"How about this one?" Missy was saying, back at her closet, holding out a silky black number. "What do you think?"

"It's great," I said, barely looking at it, clutching Prozac close to my heart, right where she belonged.

Reunited at last.

Missy was delighted when I told her of my plans to spend New Year's Eve with Prozac.

"What a wonderful idea! I hate the thought of Scarlett, Rhett, and Ashley Wilkes being alone on this special night! What an angel you are to keep them company. Isn't she, Ashley?" she added, kissing her stuffed elephant on the trunk.

At which point, Prozac practically rolled her eyes in disgust.

I left Pro sulking on Missy's bed, and headed over to Hop Li Chinese restaurant in Westwood to pick up our New Year's Eve feast: spring rolls, steamed dumplings, and—Prozac's favorite—shrimp with lobster sauce.

Lance was upstairs in his room when I returned to the casa, his bed littered with enough outfits to stock the men's department at Bloomie's.

"Oh, good! You're home!" he cried when he saw me. "I desperately need your advice. I've narrowed it down to two choices to wow Graham tonight: Blue cashmere sweater and khaki slacks. Or jeans and turtleneck?"

I looked over his choices and came to a decision.

"Blue cashmere and khaki."

"Okay, then. Jeans and turtleneck it is!"

Lance always does this. For some reason he is convinced that I have no fashion sense whatsoever, that moths come to my closet to commit suicide.

After all these years, I don't even bother to get insulted anymore.

"Well, time for my bath!" he chirped. "And to work my magic on my bod!"

Then off Lance trotted to his bathroom, where he spent the next several hours doing heaven knows what to his body. I suspect waxing, self-tanning, and deep pore cleansing were involved.

I spent the afternoon in my bedroom, forcing myself to work on an online mailer to generate business in the new year. I'd been away from work long enough. It was time to start hustling.

But I was having a hard time concentrating, wondering why I hadn't heard from Lt. Muntner, and spending far too much time daydreaming about my upcoming date with *Love in Venice*.

I was right in the middle of a most enjoyable fantasy where my online Romeo—who bore a striking resemblance to Jude Law—and I were sipping wine at sunset on his balcony overlooking the Pacific, when I was jolted back to reality by the terrifying appearance of Lance skipping into my bedroom, his face covered in the most appalling mask of blue goo.

"Yuck! What's that disgusting glop on your face?"

"A detoxifying, hydrating antioxidant gluten-free facial mask. Guaranteed to remove any and all impurities. You really ought to try it, hon," he said, holding out a jar of the stuff. "It'll do wonders for those enlarged pores of yours."

"Thanks ever so, but I'll pass."

"Don't you want to look good for tonight?"

"Tonight? I'm only staying at Graham's for fifteen minutes, remember?"

"I know, sweetheart, but you never know who you'll bump into in the freezer aisle on your run for Chunky Monkey."

"For your information," I huffed, "I won't be going on any Chunky Monkey runs tonight."

Which was true. I'd already stopped off for a pint on my way home from my trip to the Chinese restaurant.

"Suit yourself," he shrugged. "But you're making a big mistake. You never know what life has in store for you, a chance encounter when you least expect it. Just like with me and Graham. I happened to run into him one day when I was picking up Connie's mail, and the next thing I knew he was asking me out for New Year's Eve."

I blinked in disbelief.

"Are you insane? You chased down that guy like a fox during hunting season. You sent him enough texts to fill the Gutenberg Bible."

"I may have written him a few notes," Lance sniffed, "but it was fate that brought us together."

Oh, brother. How delusional could one man be?

He left the jar of goo on my night table, just in case I wanted to go around looking like an extra from *Revenge of the Slime People*, and trotted off to get dressed.

After a few more stabs at trying to get some work done on my mailer, I gave up and flipped on the TV to while away the time until we left for Graham's.

I'd just zapped past some "diamonette" earrings on the Home Shopping Club and reached a local news station when I saw something that made me jolt up in Connie Van Hooten's Queen Anne chair.

There on the screen behind a surgically enhanced anchor was a photo of Dave Kellogg aka Chambers, who, according to the anchor, had just been brought down to police headquarters for questioning in the murder of former child actor, Scotty Parker.

So Lt. Muntner got my message after all!

It sure would've been nice of him to let me know.

Chapter 30

Lance was a happy camper as he drove over to Graham's apartment in Burbank, checking his curls in the rearview mirror every two minutes.

He'd seen Dave being hauled away on the news, and was quite impressed when I told him how I'd tipped off the police.

"Honestly, hon," he said. "You deserve a medal or something."

Indeed I did. And a cash reward wouldn't hurt either.

Holiday traffic on the freeways was sluggish that night, but Lance was totally unfazed, planning his first weekend getaway with Graham, conducting a one-man debate between the mountains vs. the beach, the beach winning out in the end because of the chance to see Graham in a pair of Speedos.

At last we arrived at Graham's apartment, a squat stucco building with azaleas out front and Christmas lights strung along the balconies.

"Now remember," Lance said as we headed up to the front entrance. "Fifteen minutes, and you're gone."

"Yes, Lance," I sighed. "I remember."

"You can take my car, and I'll Uber it home. With any luck," he winked, "tomorrow morning."

Graham buzzed us into the building and we made our way down a long corridor to his apartment.

After a final fluff of his curls, Lance rang the bell, and Graham came to the door, looking *très* hunky in a skin-tight tuxedo T-shirt and Bermuda shorts.

"Hey, guys," Graham grinned. "Great to see you!"

"You, too!" Lance gulped, eyeing Graham's abs with more than a tad of prurient interest.

Graham took our jackets and hung them on a coatrack in the entranceway, then led us into the living room—very tastefully decorated with black leather furniture, steamer trunk coffee table, Christmas tree in the corner, and gas flames flickering in a phony fireplace.

"Sit down, guys." Graham gestured to his sofa. "Make yourselves comfy."

"Jaine can't stay long," Lance said before my fanny had even hit the cushion. "She's got a party to go to. She'll only be here about fifteen minutes or so. Isn't that right, Jaine?"

"Ow!" I cried, in response to the kick he'd just given me behind the steamer trunk.

"That's too bad," Graham said, easing his bod into a chair across from us. "Are you sure you can't stay a little longer?"

"Maybe I will stay a little longer," I said, smiling sweetly at Lance, payback for that kick.

"I just love what you've done with your place, Graham!" Lance gushed, after another quick jab at my ankles. "It's so *you*!"

I, on the other hand, was not focused on the décor but rather on the plate of rather yummy looking mini-quiches Graham had set out on the coffee table.

"Help yourself to an hors d'oeuvre," Graham said, no doubt seeing the food lust in my eyes.

He didn't have to ask twice.

I was just about to bite into an eggy beauty when I happened to notice a pair of bright pink eyes staring up at me from the front of the fireplace. Holy mackerel. It was a rabbit! For a minute I thought it was going to hop on my lap and nab my quiche. Then I realized it wasn't alive—but dead and stuffed.

A chill ran down my spine.

"That's Peter," Graham said. "He passed away a few years ago. He loved to sit in front of the fireplace."

Lance blinked, confused.

"You mean like Peter, your old boyfriend, who also died a few years ago?"

Graham smiled a wistful smile.

"No, you must have misunderstood. The Peter I told you about was my rabbit. We were very close. Rabbits are really quite underrated as pets. They can be amazingly affectionate. At least, my Peter was." His eyes misted over. "Truth be told, I'm still not quite over his loss."

Lance told me Graham kept calling Peter his "honeybunny." Now I knew why.

"Well, I don't want to bring the party down—" Graham said.

Too late for that.

"—so I'll just zip into the kitchen for some champagne."

"My God," I whispered to Lance the minute he was gone. "The guy is in love with his dead stuffed rabbit!"

"Okay, so he's a little quirky," Lance said. "I like quirky."

Talk about being blinded by lust.

A cork popped in the kitchen, and seconds later Graham came bounding back into the living room with a bottle of champagne and three glasses on a tray.

"Here's the bubbly!" he announced, the model of a gracious host.

He poured us all champagne, and I took a healthy slug of mine, trying not to look at Peter's eyes staring up at me from in front of the fireplace.

I decided right then and there to make an early exit, after all. In fact, I wasn't even sure I was going to last fifteen minutes.

While I sat there, counting down the seconds till my getaway, Lance was babbling up a storm, gushing about how he'd always been fascinated by the US Postal Service.

"So many people have such awful handwriting; it's amazing anyone gets any mail at all! And I just love how you carry on through rain and snow and sleet and hail! Not that we have any sleet or snow or hail in L.A., but still. All that walking! No wonder you're in such fab shape!"

Oh, for crying out loud. Why didn't he just go sit in the guy's lap?

After Lance finished waxing euphoric about Graham's life as a mail carrier, he leaned forward, chin in hand, in prime time interview mode.

"So tell me. However did you get started in such a fascinating career?"

"I didn't always want to be a mail carrier," Graham said.

"Oh?" Lance blinked, all agog, as if he was about to hear Al Einstein explain his theory of relativity.

"No, when I first came to L.A., like every other guy who played the lead in his high school drama club, my dream was to break into show biz."

He got up and brought back a framed picture of himself from a nearby bookshelf—a professional head shot, taken sometime in his twenties. And indeed, he'd been an utter knockout.

"But you were so handsome!" Lance gushed. "And you still are! I'm surprised you're not a big star today."

I have to confess, I was a bit surprised, too. If Graham could act half as well as he looked, he seemed destined for some sort of career in the business.

"I took a job at the post office to make ends meet and was actually starting to make some progress, going to auditions after work and on my days off. I even got a few commercials and some small parts in TV shows.

"But then," he sighed, "it all came to an end."

"Why?" Lance asked, breathless, in his own special brand of hammy overacting. "What on earth happened?"

"My agent had lined up an important audition for me in an A-list movie. But in a bit of horrible luck, the night before the audition, I ate some stale cherry-filled chocolates, not realizing that the cherry filling had gone bad. I wound up with a virulent case of food poisoning.

"I wanted the job so badly, I decided to go to the audition anyway. It was the opportunity of a lifetime. Besides, I figured the worst of the food poisoning had passed.

"But I was wrong. The worst hadn't passed. I wound up throwing up on the Italian leather loafers of one of Hollywood's biggest directors," he said, shuddering at the memory, "all of which was captured on someone's phone. The video went viral, and overnight, I became an untouchable, my show biz career dead and buried."

"That's so unfair!" Lance cried, thoroughly outraged, no doubt ready to picket the Academy of Motion Picture Arts and Sciences on Graham's behalf.

It really was a painful story, though—Graham's career crashing down in shambles all because of some stale chocolates.

And then suddenly something in Graham's tale of woe rang a bell. *The stale chocolates!* I remembered Graham telling me about the horrible Christmas gifts he'd gotten from Scotty—used socks, recycled toothbrushes—and stale chocolates!

What if the chocolates Graham had eaten before that fateful audition had been a gift from Scotty?

What if Scotty's crappy Christmas gift had ruined Graham's dreams of stardom? What if Graham never forgot—or forgave—and was bent on revenge?

How easy it would have been for him to gain access to the house on Christmas Day. All the windows were open. He could've climbed right in, seen the Yule log on the kitchen counter, and killed the man who'd ruined his career.

What if I'd been wrong about Dave and Graham was the real killer? Had I just sent an innocent man to jail?

After all, the blue ski cap I'd seen Dave wearing in that photo was a fairly common item. I bet there were scads of them floating around the city. And who knew where that chocolate stain on his shirt had come from? Maybe he'd bumped into someone eating a chocolate-frosted cupcake. Or maybe my nose had been wrong. Maybe it wasn't even chocolate. Maybe it had been carob or some other chocolate substitute. Or even common garden dirt.

Just then a timer dinged in the kitchen.

"My stuffed mushrooms!" Graham said, jumping up. "Be right back."

He scooted off to the kitchen, and the minute he was gone, Lance whirled on me.

"Will you stop eating all the hors d'oeuvres? You're like a human dustbuster."

I looked down at the plate of mini-quiches and saw there were just a paltry few left.

Traumatized by the thought that I'd possibly sent the wrong man to prison, I must have gone into one of my eating trances, where calories find their way unbidden into my body and I barely remember a single bite.

"Lance, you know how I eat when I'm stressed."

"And when you're happy, sad, anxious, exhilarated, sleepy—"

"Enough! You've made your point. Listen to me. I think Graham may be the one who killed Scotty."

"Don't be ridiculous. No one that adorable could possibly be a killer."

"Graham just told us his career was ruined because he ate stale chocolates. And guess who gave him stale chocolates for Christmas once? Scotty Parker! I think Graham has been nursing a grudge all these years and finally took his revenge."

"That's the silliest thing I ever heard!"

"The guy is clearly nuts, carrying a torch for a dead rabbit he's got stuffed in front of his fireplace."

"This is all conjecture on your part, Jaine. You have no proof the poisoned chocolates Graham ate that day came from Scotty, or that Graham was anywhere near Scotty's house the day he was killed."

"I don't care. As soon as I leave, I'm calling the cops."

"Right. Just like you called the cops about Dave."

He had me there. Maybe Lance was right. Maybe I was jumping to conclusions again. This whole case had my mind in a spin. But then, just as I was beginning to doubt myself, I glanced over at the coatrack where Graham had hung our jackets.

There, hanging from one of the rungs, was a navy blue ski cap.

Why would he have it hanging on his coatrack in this unseasonably warm weather if he hadn't recently used it?

I'd rushed to judgment with Dave. But this time I was fairly certain that the ski cap hanging from Graham's coatrack was the one worn by the man who'd pushed me onto the trolley tracks—the same man who killed Scotty Parker.

"I'm sorry, Lance. I've made up my mind. The minute I get out of here, I'm calling the cops."

"That's what you think."

I looked up and saw Graham standing in the kitchen doorway, not with a plate of stuffed mushrooms—but wielding a most intimidating butcher knife.

"I've been listening to every word you said on Peter's baby monitor." He pointed to a white plastic speaker on the fireplace mantel. "No way are you calling the cops. You're not going anywhere. I killed that bastard Scotty for ruining my life. And I have no compunction whatsoever about killing you, too."

With that, he came charging at me, waving the butcher knife, Norman Bates come to life.

Hell, no! I couldn't die like this. Absolutely not. I refused to be Janet Leigh in the shower scene.

I looked around, desperate for a way to save myself. And then I saw it:

Peter Rabbit.

Snatching him up from the floor, I clutched the stuffed critter in front of my chest.

"If you kill me," I said, "you're going to have to go through Peter first."

Graham stopped, appalled at the thought of stabbing his true love.

At which point, Lance finally came to his senses and bonked Graham over the head with the champagne bottle.

"You know, I think you may be right about him being the killer," he finally conceded, staring at Graham's body sprawled out on the floor. "I'll just sit on his chest to make sure he doesn't go anywhere."

"He's unconscious, Lance."

"I know. But why take chances?"

I reached for my cell phone and called 911.

Soon the place was crawling with cops.

And after Lance was pried from Graham's now conscious body, Graham was hauled off to jail.

"TTYL!" Lance called out as they carted him away.

Some people never give up, do they?

We got home just in time to see Dave walking up the front path to The House of Scrooge.

If he had any idea I'd been the one responsible for having him brought in for questioning, he showed no signs of it. He was too busy kissing Missy to even notice me.

Back at Casa Van Hooten, I asked Lance if he wanted to spend the rest of the night with me and Pro, but he declined, saying he was way too depressed to celebrate.

"I was so deeply in love," he groaned. "I'll never get over Graham. Never!"

Which would have all been quite touching if he hadn't been on his laptop at the time, checking out hotties on Smatch.

I left him some shrimp with lobster sauce and headed next door with the rest of my Chinese chow (and a celebratory pint of Chunky Monkey).

I'm pleased to say I spent New Year's Eve right where I belonged, cuddled up on Missy's faux mink throw, poor Ashley Wilkes banished to an armchair, Prozac nestled on my chest.

"Happy New Year, sweetheart," I whispered in her fuzzy ear. "I've missed you so."

And she looked up at me in that precious way of hers that could mean only one thing:

Got any more spring rolls?

YOU'VE GOT MAIL!

**To: Jausten
From: Shoptillyoudrop
Subject: All Is Forgiven**

Well, sweetheart, I've forgiven Daddy.

He told me about those dreadful pranks that little boy played on him. Frankly, I would've thrown that soccer ball overboard, too.

Meanwhile, Daddy's been sweet as pie, bought me flowers and the most adorable *Caribbean Queen* earrings from the gift shop.

Most important, he promised to hang his new tiki mask in the garage when we get home.

PS. We had a marvelous time at the New Year's Eve cocktail party. Isabel was wearing her new diamonette bracelet. And Daddy looked simply divine as F. Scott Fitzgerald.

**To: Jausten
From: DaddyO
Subject: Tarzan Will Return!**

Dearest Lambchop—

I'm happy to report I'm back in your mom's good graces. It took a lot of groveling, not to mention a

pricey trip to the gift shop, but she's finally
forgiven me. Of course, I had to wear those silly
puffy pants to the New Year's Eve costume party.
Which actually didn't look so bad, after all. I think a
man of my inherent manliness can pull off the puffy
pant look.

I still haven't given up on my loincloth and fright
wig, though. Don't tell Mom, but I'm saving them
for next year's Tampa Vista's Halloween party.
Won't that be a hoot?

Off to the buffet, for one last éclair—

Love 'n snuggles from
DaddyO

To: Jausten
From: Shoptillyoudrop
Subject: Banned Forever

It turns out that dreadful little boy had been playing
pranks on lots of people on board. He's been
banned from all future travel on the *Caribbean
Queen*.

But then again, so has Daddy.

Epilogue

I trudged over to the Starbucks where I was meeting *Love in Venice* with all the enthusiasm of a condemned man heading off for the gas chamber.

Why, oh, why had I said yes to yet another Smatch date?

Suddenly it seemed like the worst idea ever.

Hadn't I learned my lesson after Duane "Hamster-head" Forrester?

Not only had I agreed to meet another disaster in the making, I'd agreed to meet him without even seeing his photo.

For all I knew I'd be hooking up with Shrek V.

I'd reached the door to Starbucks and could delay the inevitable no longer.

Taking a deep breath, I opened the door and stepped inside.

And then I saw him sitting at a table, nursing a coffee. Tall, lanky, with the soulful brown eyes of a medieval saint.

Instantly, before a word was spoken, I felt a jolt of yearning. The same jolt of yearning I'd felt many years ago when I'd first met him.

Because the man sitting before me was none other than my ex-husband, The Blob.

Could he possibly be *Love in Venice*?

Indeed he was.

"Jaine!" he cried, hurrying to my side. "I'm so happy you came!"

He took me by the hand, setting off a spark I hadn't felt in years, and led me to his table.

"I ordered you a Frappuccino. With extra whipped cream. Just the way you like it."

So boggled was I, I barely even noticed the mountain of calories on the table beside me.

"I put my profile on Smatch," he said, "hoping I'd find you. I've never stopped loving you."

His eyes shone with what I could've sworn was sincerity.

"I know I wasn't the best of husbands."

No kidding. The one year he remembered my birthday he bought me a tool belt. (Used.)

"But I swear I've changed."

He certainly looked it. The last time I saw him, he'd been a scruffy mess, from his greasy hair to his unwashed feet shuffling in their flip-flops.

But today his hair was shiny clean, cut short at the sides, long and slightly spiky on top, with sexy sun-bleached highlights. He wore a crisp white shirt with just-tight-enough jeans.

"You must believe me, Jaine. I've turned over a new leaf."

A line I'd heard many times before. The man

had turned over enough new leaves to start a bon-
fire.

"I gave up trying to be the next Picasso," he said
with a wry smile, "and got myself a steady job as a
graphic artist."

(For years, I'd been the breadwinner in our
household, while The Blob dedicated himself to
his "art," churning out a slow trickle of paintings
in between Netflix binges.)

Now he reached out and touched my cheek
with the tip of his fingers, and I felt an X-rated tin-
gle in my day-of-the-week panties.

"Please, Jaine," he whispered, his soulful eyes
shining. "Give me another chance."

God, he looked good. But I couldn't let some
spiky hair and tight jeans sway me. He'd made so
many promises to me in the past, promises he
never kept.

Inside my head a little voice was shouting, *Run!
He fooled you before. He'll fool you again!*

That little voice was right. I had to get out of
there. No way was I giving The Blob another
chance.

I told myself to turn around to make a break for
it. But instead, much to my amazement, I found
myself heading straight for his open arms.

And before I knew it, he had me swept up in a
blockbuster of a kiss.

Holy moly. I'd forgotten what a good kisser he
was.

By now the little voice in my head was shouting
at the top of its lungs for me to get out before it
was too late.

But then The Blob started nibbling on my ear-lobe, and I melted like the whipped cream on my Frappuccino.

I told the little voice in my head to mind its own beeswax, and puckered up for another liplock.

After a dry spell, freelance writer Jaine Austen's life is suddenly full of romance. For one thing, she's re-connected with her ex—though her cat, Prozac, isn't happy about it. And Jaine's also got a new ghost-writing gig, working on a steamy novel called Fifty Shades of Turquoise . . .

Daisy Kincaid is in her sixties and heiress to a fortune. Now she wants to make a name for herself as a romance author . . . with a little help from Jaine, that is. As Jaine labors away on love scenes, she gets to know the wealthy woman's gentleman friend, her household staff, and her social circle—every one of whom is horrified when Daisy falls under the spell of a much younger stud named Tommy, a rude, crude lothario who's made himself a fixture in Daisy's Bel Air mansion.

After Tommy and Daisy shock everyone by announcing their engagement, it doesn't take long for someone to stab him in the neck—with the solid gold Swiss Army knife that Daisy gave him as a gift. The challenging part is trying to narrow down the list of suspects. Jaine's going to have to put a bookmark in that love story and focus all her creative talent into untangling a tale of money and murder . . .

Please turn the page for an exciting sneak peek of Laura Levine's next Jaine Austen mystery DEATH OF A GIGOLO coming soon wherever print and e-books are sold!

Prologue

The Los Angeles morning fog was rolling in, thick as whipped cream on a Mocha Frappuccino. But inside my bedroom it was bright and sunny, a Technicolor world with Disney bluebirds chirping at my shoulders.

The reason for all this sunshine and light?

I'm thrilled to report that Cupid, who'd been snubbing me for years, had suddenly come flying into my life, pinging me with his arrow of love.

Thanks to the wonders of Internet dating, I'd reconnected with my ex-husband, formerly known as The Blob, now known as the Most Wonderful Man in the World. Or, as it appeared on his driver's license, Dickie Elliott.

True, our marriage had been a disaster—littered with forgotten birthdays, serial unemployment, and toenail clippings in the kitchen sink. (His, not mine.)

But over the years we'd been apart, Dickie had changed.

Gone was the slacker in flip-flops, rooted to the sofa watching *Beavis and Butt-Head* reruns. My former Dufus Royale now had a steady job as a graphic artist and a condo in Venice with a spectacular view of the Pacific.

I'd been seeing him for a while (six weeks, three days, and fourteen and a half hours—but who's counting?), and had rediscovered the sweet, sensitive artist I'd fallen in love with when I'd first met him.

Yes, Cupid was certainly zinging his arrow my way, and for that I was supremely grateful.

I was lying in bed that morning, Cinderella in a GOT CHOCOLATE? sleep tee, trying to ignore my cat, Prozac, clawing me for her breakfast, when my cell phone buzzed.

Eagerly, I reached for it.

"Morning, sweetie."

Do you hear angels singing? I did. It was *him*!

"See you tonight?" he asked, his voice like warm velvet.

"My place at seven," I managed to say after my heart stopped ricocheting in my chest.

"Miss you," he cooed.

"Miss you more."

"No, miss *you* more."

"No, miss *you* more."

"No, miss *you*—"

By now Prozac was thumping her tail in disgust.

Any more of this goo, I'm gonna hurl a hairball.

After a volley of kissy noises with Dickie, I hung up to face Prozac's wrath.

Sad to say, my kitty was not on board my love train. She sensed that this was something serious. And she didn't like it. Not one bit. No way was she about to relinquish her title as my Significant Other.

I'd tried my best to explain to her that there was plenty of room in my heart for her *and* Dickie, but she was having none of it. Every time he stopped by my apartment, she was a hissing, scratching bundle of hostility.

But I didn't have time to worry about Prozac. I had to shower and dress for a very important job interview.

Yes, it seemed that love had entered my life in more ways than one. That very morning I was headed off to apply for a job co-authoring a romance novel!

My neighbor, Lance Venable, who, as a shoe salesman at Neiman Marcus, fondles the tootsies of the one-percenters, had set me up with one of his mega-wealthy customers, a would-be romance novelist by the name of Daisy Kincaid.

Admittedly I had zero qualifications to write a romance novel, having spent the past several years writing ads for low-rent clients like Toiletmasters Plumbers (*In a Rush to Flush? Call Toiletmasters!*), Fiedler on the Roof roofers, and Tip Top Cleaners (*We Clean For You! We Press For You! We Even Dye For You!*).

But the recent reappearance of Cupid in my life had inspired me to take on the challenge. (Not to mention the $10,000 Daisy was paying.)

I'd sent her a writing sample, a seven-page mini-romance I'd managed to dash off about a man and a woman in the same apartment building who fall in love when they keep getting each other's mail by mistake.

It wasn't exactly *Wuthering Heights,* but I thought it was cute. I only hoped Daisy would like it and offer me the job.

Breakfast duly scarfed down, I was gazing at a framed photo of Dickie on my coffee table, day-dreaming about my possible new life as a romance novelist—and, not incidentally, the whipped cream on a Mocha Frappuccino—when I realized if I didn't hurry I'd be late for my interview.

After a quickie shower, I popped into my official job interview outfit—skinny jeans, silk blouse, and blazer—accessorized with silver hoop earrings and my one and only pair of Manolo Blahniks.

A dash of lipstick, a crunch of my curls, and I was set to go.

"Wish me luck," I called out to Prozac as I grabbed my car keys.

But she was too busy hissing at Dickie's picture to even glance my way.

Chapter 1

The first thing I noticed as I drove up to Daisy Kincaid's estate was a brass plaque at the foot of her driveway, engraved with the words *LA BELLE VIE*.

Thanks to Mrs. Wallis, my French teacher at Hermosa High (*Bonjour*, Mme. Wallis!), I knew that *la belle vie* meant "beautiful life."

No kidding, I thought, as I wended my way up to Daisy's villa—a castle-like affair with arched colonnades, enough balconies to house a troupe of Rapunzels, and a gurgling fountain out front.

Think Downton Abbey with palm trees.

I parked in the circular gravel driveway, and after a quick inspection of my curls in my rearview mirror, I trotted over to ring the doorbell.

Deep chimes reverberated within the house, and seconds later, the front door was opened by a svelte young blonde, her hair coiled in a chignon. So elegant did she look that for an instant I thought she was Daisy Kincaid. But then I realized she was wearing a crisp, white maid's uniform.

"Ms. Austen?" she asked.

"That's me."

"Come right in. Ms. Kincaid is expecting you."

I followed her through a foyer the size of a hotel lobby into a living room littered with priceless bibelots and centuries-old antiques.

"Have a seat," she said. "Ms. Kincaid will be right with you."

With that, she left me to marvel at the gewgaws strewn around me. I was looking at the painting hanging over the fireplace (signed by a fellow named Picasso) when I smelled a blast of tea rose perfume.

I turned to see a short marshmallow of a woman with a wide smile and neon red pixie hairdo. She floated toward me in a turquoise caftan—turquoise necklace nestled in her ample bosom, turquoise bracelets jangling from her arms, and a honker of a turquoise ring on her pinkie.

"Jaine, dear," she trilled, extending her bejeweled hand. "So lovely to meet you. Do have a seat."

I parked my fanny on a sofa no doubt once owned by Louis XIV as Daisy plunked herself down on an equally posh armchair.

"Lance has told me so much about you! I can't believe you're the one who wrote *In a rush to flush? Call Toiletmasters*! I see it on bus benches all over town."

I put on my best aw shucks smile.

"And to think! You're an Emmy-winning TV writer, too."

Darn that Lance. He's always making up the most outrageous lies. True, I once worked on a long-forgotten TV sitcom and had another gig on an equally forgettable reality show, but the closest I ever came to an Emmy was seeing one on TV.

"I'm afraid I didn't really win an Emmy," I admitted, hoping it wasn't going to cost me the job. "Lance must have gotten his facts mixed up."

"Oh well. No matter," Daisy replied with a sweep of her turquoise sleeve. "I was very impressed by the little story you wrote. *Romance at the Mailbox.* So precious."

"I'm glad you liked it."

"Liked it? I loved it! I just know we're going to make a terrific writing team."

"Does that mean I get the job?"

"Indeed you do!"

Yes! I got the job!

"Do you want to hear my story idea?" she asked, eyes twinkling with excitement.

"Absolutely!"

"I'm calling it *Fifty Shades of Turquoise!*"

Whoa, Nelly. Suddenly I saw a Cease & Desist order from E. L. James's attorneys winging our way.

"Are you sure you can use that name? It's awfully similar to *Fifty Shades of Grey.*"

"Oh, poo! Grey is so blah, and turquoise is so much more fun. I just adore the color!"

No surprise there, I thought, taking in her caftan, jewelry, and assorted turquoise throw pillows strewn among the antiques.

"Our book won't be at all like that dreary little grey series."

That only sold about a gazillion books.

"So what's the story line?" I asked, praying it didn't involve handcuffs and chains.

As luck would have it, it did not involve any handcuffs or chains.

In fact, it had no plot whatsoever.

"I haven't exactly worked out the details yet," Daisy confessed. "I thought you could do that. You'll sketch out the story, and I'll do the fine-tuning. All I know is that I want there to be a fifty-room mansion with every room painted a different shade of turquoise, and that somehow the heroine winds up making love to the hero in every one of those rooms."

Sex in fifty turquoise rooms? Suddenly my confidence as a romance writer plummeted. No way was I going to be able to write this bilge.

"So what do you think?" Daisy asked with an eager smile. "Are you on board?"

Absolutely not. I had to steer clear of this train wreck of a novel before it took off.

"As I told Lance," Daisy reminded me, "the salary will be ten thousand dollars."

"When do we start?"

What can I say? I've got the backbone of a Slurpee.

"Just sign right here," she said, whipping out a contract from the pocket of her caftan.

Thrilled to see all the zeroes on my salary, I signed on the dotted line.

"Let's start right now," Daisy said. "I hope you don't mind working here at the house. That way it will be easier for us to collaborate."

"I don't mind a bit," I assured her. Working there would be like working at the Four Seasons. Besides, I was getting tired of Prozac stomping on my keyboard in one of her anti-Dickie meltdowns.

Daisy led me to her office, a spacious room at the rear of the house—which I was relieved to see was not painted turquoise. Instead, it was bright white, with a wood beamed ceiling and French doors providing a breathtaking view of a pool and tennis court beyond.

One wall featured an ornately carved bookcase filled with thick, leather-bound volumes; another wall adorned with what looked like a genuine Renoir.

Two antique desks were face-to-face in the middle of the room, topped with twin laptops and Villeroy & Boch mugs filled to capacity with sharpened pencils. Seated at one of the desks was a sturdy thirtysomething gal with Harry Potter glasses and a mop of sandy hair even curlier than mine.

"Jaine, I'd like you to meet Kate, my personal assistant. You two will be sharing the office."

"Welcome aboard!" Kate said, shooting me a friendly smile.

"You can use my desk while you're working here," Daisy said. "And here's your laptop." She pointed to a shiny silver beauty on my desk. "I bought it especially for our little project."

Holy moly! The woman bought a brand-new computer for one file. I was in the land of the one-percenters, all right.

"I'd better scoot along now so you can get started."

And with a flash of her turquoise ring, Daisy waved good-bye and sailed out of the room.

The minute she was gone, Kate shot me a pitying gaze.

"So you're the poor soul who got saddled with *Fifty Shades of Turquoise*. What a clunker, huh?"

"It does seem a bit far-fetched," I said, trying to be tactful as I settled down at my desk.

"Oh, well. At least you're getting ten thousand bucks out of the deal."

I guess she could see the look of surprise on my face when she mentioned my salary, because she hastened to explain, "I do Daisy's books and keep track of all her expenses. So I pretty much know what she's paying for everything.

"Daisy's an utter doll to work for," she added, slinging her Nikes on her desk. "The pay is great, and rumor has it, she's left all her employees a generous chunk of change in her will."

Talk about your job perks.

"And as if all that weren't enough, the food's terrific, too. Raymond, her chef, used to work at some fancy French restaurant. And the freezer is stocked with Dove Bars, Eskimo Pies, and whatever flavor ice cream you like. My favorite is Chunky Monkey."

"You're kidding. So's mine!"

"It's a good thing I wear elastic waist pants," she said, "otherwise I'd never make it out of here alive."

"You wear elastic waist pants?"

Elastic waist pants just happen to be a staple of my wardrobe, second only to my CUCKOO FOR COCOA PUFFS T-shirts.

"Can't live without 'em."

"Me too!" I marveled. "It's unbelievable. Curly hair. Chunky Monkey. Elastic waist pants. I think we may have been separated at birth."

We spent the next several minutes chattling about curl definers, curl shapers, curl straighteners, and our mutual adulation of Ben & Jerry. I could've gone on yakking like this for hours, anything to avoid facing *Fifty Shades of Turquoise*, but Kate was made of sterner stuff.

"I'd better get back to work," she said. "Just ask if you need anything."

With no more diversionary tactics left, I opened a *Fifty Shades of Turquoise* file on Daisy's brand-new laptop and stared at the blank screen in front of me.

And kept on staring.

Not a single idea popped into my cranium.

Filled with a growing sense of panic, wondering how I was ever going to wrangle my heroine into fifty shades of turquoise lovemaking, my eyes wandered to a framed photo on my desk—of a middle-aged man in a business suit, with a toddler on his lap.

Kate looked up from her Excel spreadsheet and saw me staring at the photo.

"That's Daisy with her dad," she explained. "He died when Daisy was very young and left Daisy a fortune. From what I gather, her mom wasn't exactly a model parent, foisted her off on a bunch of nannies. When she was in her twenties, Daisy got married, but it was total bust, lasted less than a year. After that, she became a recluse."

"Daisy, a recluse?"

I couldn't picture the bubbly redhead I'd just met walled off from the world.

"I know. It's hard to believe, but for decades she lived with only a companion, dividing her time between her Connecticut mansion and her country home in Tuscany, never socializing and rarely leaving the house except for an occasional nature walk."

"What made her come out of her shell?" I asked, still boggled at this downer version of Daisy.

"A horrible accident." Kate grimaced. "On her last trip to Tuscany, her companion was killed while hiking. Fell off a cliff on a mountain trail. Daisy told me that was a turning point in her life. It made her realize how fleeting life is, and how she was throwing hers away. So she came back to the States, determined to live life to the fullest. Moved to Los Angeles, started making friends and wearing a lot of turquoise."

What a story! If only I could think of something half as interesting for the book.

After a few minutes staring outside at the pool and wishing I were lying on one of the chaises, sipping margaritas with Dickie, I forced myself to return to the task at hand.

By the time the maid arrived to summon us to lunch, you'll be proud to learn I did manage to write something down:

Note to self: Buy margarita mix.

Chapter 2

By now the morning fog had burned off and, what with the sun shining its little heart out, lunch was being served at the pool.

"Daisy always invites me to join her for meals," Kate said as we made our way outside. "Like I told you, she's a doll to work for. And wait till you taste Raymond's chow. Yum!"

Out on the patio, Daisy sat at a glass-topped wrought iron table with matching wrought iron chairs—cushioned in turquoise, of course.

Seated at her side was a silver-haired gent somewhere in his sixties, dressed in tennis whites, his pot belly not quite concealed under his polo, skinny legs popping out from white shorts.

"That's Clayton," Kate whispered as we approached the table. "Lives down the street. Daisy's gentleman caller. He's gaga over her."

Indeed, he seemed to be gazing at Daisy with the ardor of a geriatric Romeo.

"It was quite a match," he was saying. "I beat him all three sets. And he calls himself a tennis pro."

"Hello, girls!" Daisy said, catching sight of us. "Jaine, come meet my dear friend, Clayton Manning."

Clayton jumped up to take my hand, his face a deep (possibly carcinogenic) tan, etched with wrinkles, watery blue eyes startling against his leathery skin.

"A pleasure to meet you, my dear."

"Clayton was just telling me about his exploits on the tennis court," Daisy said as Kate and I took our seats. "He's such a good player."

"I'm always trying to get Daisy to hit a few balls, but I can't seem to talk her into it."

"It's a disgrace," Daisy said ruefully. "Here I've got a perfectly lovely tennis court"—she gestured to the court beyond the pool—"and I never use it. I much prefer my morning walks."

"That's how we met," Clayton said, beaming at the memory. "Daisy was out for her morning constitutional and I was getting my mail. I took one look at her and forgot all about the one million dollars I may or may not have won from Publishers Clearing House."

He shot Daisy another look of love, which she rewarded with a weak smile.

Somehow I got the impression that Daisy wasn't quite ready to play Juliet to Clayton's Romeo.

"Clayton, dear," she said, eager to steer the conversation away from love among the Aarpsters. "Jaine is helping me write my romance novel."

Helping her? What the what? I was writing the

darn thing. That is, I would've been writing it if I could think of a plot.

"So how are you coming along?" Daisy asked eagerly.

"Great," I lied.

"Wonderful! I'll stop by at the end of the day and see what you've got so far."

Oh, hell. I was going to have to come up with something by the end of the day.

I was quickly distracted from the image of my blank computer screen, however, when Daisy's beautiful blond maid showed up, elegant in her white uniform, wheeling a trolley with our lunches.

"Solange, honey," Daisy said. "I forgot to ask. How did your audition go?" Then, turning to me, she added, "Solange is an aspiring actress."

So that explained what this stunner was doing wheeling food trolleys.

"Ms. Kincaid is so kind," Solange said. "She lets me take time off to go to auditions."

"Did you get the part?" Daisy asked.

Solange shook her head wistfully.

"Don't give up," Daisy said, patting her arm. "I just know one day I'm going to see you up on the big screen, and I'll be able to say, 'She used to make my bed!' "

Solange grinned and, turning to the trolley, announced:

"Salmon *en croûte.*"

At first, I was disappointed. I'm not much of a fish fan. But this salmon, I saw, as Solange placed my plate in front of me, was wrapped in a flaky pastry shell. And as far as I'm concerned, anything with the word "pastry" can't be all bad.

I took a bite, and suddenly I was in fish heaven. The stuff was dee-lish.

Kate hadn't been exaggerating when she raved about Daisy's chef.

I was busy inhaling my salmon, Clayton in the middle of a highly dubious story about beating Andre Agassi in a charity tennis match, when a regal gal with salt-and-pepper hair came sweeping out onto the patio in billowy palazzo pants and a chiffon blouse. In her hand, she held a newspaper.

"That's Esme Larkin," Kate whispered to me. "Daisy's BFF."

Clayton, ever the gentleman, jumped up and pulled out a nearby chair for our new guest.

"Daisy, darling!" Esme said, bending down to air-kiss her buddy. "So wonderful to see you. And you, too, Clayton!"

Clearly not as egalitarian as Daisy, she lobbed a brisk nod at Kate and a questioning glance at me.

"Esme," Daisy said, leaping into the breach, "this is Jaine Austen."

Esme's stone-gray eyes swept over me, suddenly intrigued.

"Any relation to the world-renowned author?" she asked.

"Afraid not."

"Pity," she said, instantly dismissing me as an object of interest.

"Jaine's helping me write my book," Daisy explained.

"*Fifty Shades of Turquoise!*" Esme gushed. "Such a fabulous title. Absolutely delicious."

That last bit uttered while looking longingly at the salmon on our plates.

"Esme, hon," Daisy said, following her gaze, "have you eaten lunch?"

"Actually, no. I've had such a hectic morning."

"Let me get you some salmon."

"If it's not a bother."

"No bother at all."

Daisy pressed a button on an intercom at the table.

"One more salmon, please, Solange."

"Of course, ma'am." Solange's voice, laced with static, came out from the machine.

"I'm not really all that hungry," Esme said, "but I suppose I can force down a few bites. Meanwhile, darling, I've got wonderful news!"

With that, she waved the newspaper she'd been carrying, the *Bel Air Society News*, a glossy, tabloid-sized paper filled with pictures of rich people showing off their facelifts at charity galas.

"Here you are on the front page!" Esme squealed. "In an article about our benefit for the Animal Welfare League."

She held out the paper so we could all see it.

The headline read:

Daisy Kincaid Hosts Charity Fundraiser at La Belle Vie

And indeed, there was a picture of Daisy holding a champagne glass.

A frown marred Daisy's face.

"Oh, dear. You know how I hate publicity. It's so showy. My father always believed in giving anonymously. He disapproved of people who gave only to see their names in print. You promised you wouldn't have any photographers at the event."

"But I didn't, darling. I shot this photo myself on my iPhone and couldn't resist sending it to the paper. You're not miffed at me, are you?"

She arranged her chiseled features into a look of remorse.

"Of course not, hon," Daisy said, her smile back in action. "I could never be miffed at you.

"Esme is chairman of the Bel Air Animal Welfare League," Daisy explained to me, "and is a positive saint to all those poor abandoned cats and dogs."

Somehow it was hard to picture this granite-faced gal as a saint.

"We couldn't do our work without you, Daisy," Esme said. "We'd be positively lost without your generous donations."

In the middle of this mutual admiration praise-fest, Solange showed up with Esme's salmon.

She had no sooner put it down on the table than Esme swan dived into it. For someone who wasn't very hungry, she sure was packing it away.

Can't say as I blame her. I was practically licking my plate.

And dessert—a creamy chocolate mousse—was equally fabu-licious.

At the end of the meal, Daisy's chef, a lithe ponytailed guy, came out onto the patio in his white chef's jacket.

"Was everything to your liking, ma'am?" he asked Daisy.

"Oh, Raymond. It was divine, as usual. You are, without doubt, an absolute genius in the kitchen."

He glowed under her praise.

And I had to agree.

With meals like this, maybe writing *Fifty Shades of Turquoise* wouldn't be so bad, after all.

FIFTY SHADES OF TURQUOISE
Outline

Clarissa Weatherly, a raven-haired beauty with mesmerizing emerald eyes, is a spoiled socialite, living the high life in New York, dabbling at her job in an art gallery, engaged to be married to a dashing English nobleman. Then suddenly her world falls apart when she gets the tragic news that her father has died. Even more tragic, he's gambled away nearly all his fortune, leaving her penniless.

Clarissa is devastated, especially at the thought of losing Weatherly Manor, the fifty-room mansion where she grew up in Colorado. The home that stores so many precious memories is now in fore-closure. The only thing that remains of her father's estate is his turquoise mine, which is on the brink of shutting down.

More devastation is headed Clarissa's way when she tells her British nobleman fiancé that she is now penniless and he breaks off their engagement.

Blinded by tears, yet determined to save her childhood home, she returns to Colorado to take over the reins of the turquoise mine and turn it into a profit-making venture.

Back home at the mine, she discovers a crooked foreman, who has been robbing her father blind. She fires him on the spot. Knowing nothing about mining, she must rely on MAX LAREDO, a burly miner with abs of steel, to help her save her busi-

ness. Accustomed to being treated like a princess all her life, Clarissa is furious when Max bosses her around and barks orders at her. She absolutely hates this swaggering idiot! At least that's what she tells herself. Underneath his swagger, she senses a good man with a kind heart. Not to mention those abs of steel. As they work together, side by side, overcoming one obstacle after another, she finds herself growing more and more attracted to this rough-hewn rock of a man. Together, they continue to work tirelessly, and at last, they do it! They make enough money to buy back Clarissa's childhood mansion! Weatherly Manor is saved!

Not only that, the mine is soon making money hand over fist.

And before Clarissa knows it, Algernon, her former fiancé, shows up, begging her to take him back.

For a minute, she's tempted, but then she takes a good look at him and sees him for the moneygrubbing cad he is. She realizes at that moment that her true love is Max, the burly miner.

She finds him at the mine, and there among the turquoise stones, they fall into each other's arms. The first of many nights of bliss to come.

Clarissa marries Max and, after buying back her fifty-room mansion, she has each room painted a different shade of turquoise—and proceeds to make love in every one of them with her studly new hubby.

Okay, that's the bilge I dreamed up for Daisy. I gave it to her to read at the end of the day and headed home, praying she'd like it.

Chapter 3

Unlike Clarissa Weatherly's, my life was not a raging sex-a-thon.

Determined to play it safe and not rush into things, I'd put off having dipsy doodle with Dickie. Sure, we'd fooled around, but as yet, we hadn't gone the distance.

But tonight, I'd decided, was the night.

I'd invited Dickie over for a home cooked dinner (well, home cooked by my neighborhood Italian restaurant) of lasagna, antipasto salad, and tiramisu for dessert. Bolstered by a glass of Chianti or two, I planned on letting my reformed ex sweep me off to the bedroom to consummate our newly rekindled love.

After handing in my magnum opus to Daisy, I headed home to shower and dress—with a pit stop to pick up my Italian dinner.

Back at my apartment, I found Prozac sprawled

on the sofa, luxuriating in her umpteenth nap of the day.

"Hi, sweetpea," I said, scratching her behind her ears.

She gazed up at me with a loving expression that could mean only one thing:

I smell lasagna. When do we eat?

I'd cut my pampered princess the tiniest sliver of lasagna and was just putting the rest in the oven to keep warm when my neighbor Lance came banging at my front door.

Lance and I share a modest duplex on the fringes of Beverly Hills, light years away from the megamansions north of Wilshire.

"Hey, hon," he said, sailing into my apartment in cutoffs and T-shirt, his tight blond curls moussed to perfection. "Want to grab dinner and a movie?"

"Not tonight, Lance. I'm seeing Dickie."

A look of disapproval flitted across his face.

"Again?"

"Yes, again. I've been seeing Dickie for the past six weeks, three days, and twenty-two and a half hours, give or take a second or two. And I'm not about to stop now."

He shook his head, tsking in disapproval.

"Jaine, honey, I don't want to rain on your parade, but have you forgotten all the misery that guy put you through when you were married? The forgotten birthdays? The chronic unemployment? And what about the time he gave you those used flowers for your anniversary?"

It's true. On our fourth—and final—anniversary, Dickie had given me a bouquet he'd picked from

the neighbor's trash without even bothering to remove the accompanying card. (*Happy Bat Mitzvah,
Kimberly!*)

That, in fact, had been the last straw, the final
indignity that sent me scuttling off to see a divorce
attorney.

But that was a long time ago. Things were different now.

"Dickie's changed," I insisted. "He's not the
man he used to be."

"Nobody really changes, Jaine. Honestly," he
said, taking my hands in his. "I think you're making a big mistake. I only want what's best for you."

But did he really? I wondered.

Sure, on the surface, Lance believed he was
looking out for my best interests. But underneath
his concern, I detected a mother lode of jealousy.

For years Lance and I had been wading together through a swamp of losers, searching for
Mr. Right. Now I'd found my true love while he
was still stuck kissing frogs.

So far, I hadn't confronted him with my suspicions. And I wasn't about to do it then. I had to get
ready for my all-important date with Dickie.

"I know you care about me, Lance, but I
promise I'll be fine. Now you've got to scoot so I
can take a shower and get dressed."

"Okay," he said. "If you're sure you know what
you're doing . . ."

"Trust me, Lance. I know what I'm doing."

A skeptical meow from Prozac.

*She knows what she's doing like I know advanced cal-
culus.*

After gently shoving Lance out the door, I set the table (with actual cloth napkins instead of my usual stash of paper napkins from KFC) and raced off to prep for my night of passion.

In the shower, I loofahed my skin to a rosy glow. Thoroughly exfoliated, I slipped into a pair of skinny jeans; slouchy, pink V-neck sweater; and strappy leather sandals.

Then I slapped on some makeup and sprayed myself with some divine Jo Malone White Jasmine perfume I'd splurged on at Nordstrom. It had been worth the splurge. Dickie loved it and was always telling me how good I smelled.

Back in the living room, I twirled in front of Pro.

"How do I look?"

She gazed up at me through slitted eyes.

Like a woman about to cheat on her cat.

Was there no one in my life who supported me on this Dickie thing?

But I didn't have time to mope about my lack of moral support, because just then Dickie showed up on my doorstep, tall and lanky in tight jeans and a denim work shirt, highlights glistening in his sun-bleached hair, his soulful brown eyes burning with what I hoped was lust.

From her perch on the sofa, Prozac lobbed him a genial hiss.

"Hey there," he said, running his finger along my cheek. "You smell great."

Thank you, Jo Malone!

Then he pulled me into his arms for a steamroller of a kiss.

"Nice to see you, too," I managed to croak when we finally came up for air, my nether regions melting into a puddle of goo.

"I brought something for Prozac," he said.

Having been temporarily blinded by his tight jeans, I now realized he was carrying a squeaky toy mouse.

"Look what I got you, Prozac!" he said, tossing it to her.

She gazed at it disdainfully, then batted it away with the expertise of a World Series champ.

"Prozac!" I admonished her. "How could you?"

"No worries," Dickie said. "She'll get used to me in time."

An angry thump of Pro's tail.

Wanna bet?

After a few more steamy smooches, Dickie and I finally wrenched ourselves away from each other and settled down to dinner.

Normally, Pro shows up any time she's within pouncing distance of food. But that night she stayed firmly planted on the sofa, perfecting her hissing skills.

Aside from the hairball Dickie found in his napkin, dinner was dreamy.

I'd lowered the lights and lit candles to ramp up the romance.

And it was working.

Sipping our wine, we rubbed each other's arms and played footsie under the table, all the while chatting about our respective days.

Dickie told me about the project he was working on at his ad agency, and I told him about my new job with Daisy, confiding my fears about being able to write a romance novel.

That's the great thing about the new Dickie. The old Dickie would have jumped straight to "Jeez, I sure hope you don't get fired. We could use the money for a new power drill."

But the new Dickie—thanks to a guy named Hapi, a new age guru he'd been studying with—was bubbling with affirmations and positive energy.

"Don't worry, Jaine," he reassured me. "I'm sure you'll do great. Just think good thoughts. Every time I feel challenged, I tell myself, 'I always find a way out of any problem life throws in my path.'"

A disgusted hiss from the sofa.

If only you could find a way out of this apartment.

We continued to scarf down our chow, me making a conscious effort not to inhale mine at my usual speed of light. I was sitting there trying to figure out which was yummier, Dickie's bod or the lasagna (Dickie's bod the clear winner), and thinking about the tiramisu I'd picked up for dessert, when Dickie dropped his bombshell.

"This lasagna's super, hon. I'm so impressed that you had the time to roll out the pasta yourself."

Okay, so I'd fibbed a little.

"But I'm afraid it's the last time I'll be eating it. I've decided to follow in Hapi's footsteps and become a vegetarian."

"No biggie. We can always eat meatless lasagna."

"It's more than that. In addition to meat, I'm giving up fats, glutens, and sugars."

Holy mackerel? What was there left to eat? Oh, well. To each his own, right?

And that's when he lowered the boom.

"I was hoping you'd give it a try, too. If we're going to be together, I want you to be at your healthy best. So what do you say?"

Was he kidding? No pizza? No fried chicken? No Quarter Pounders? No way!

But then he took my hand in his, and I felt an electric charge in my Happy Place.

"Sure," I said, in a lovestruck daze. "Why not?"

Obviously my hormones had taken control of my vocal cords.

"Wonderful!" he grinned.

With that, he pulled me up from my seat and folded me in his arms for another round of high-voltage smooching.

"What do you say," he murmured in my ear, "we skip the tiramisu and have dessert in the bedroom?"

What?? No tiramisu??

But, my hormones still raging, I wound up saying, "Yes. The bedroom. Now!"

Clinging together, we stumbled into my bedroom, specially spruced up for the occasion and spritzed with White Jasmine.

We flopped onto the bed and began tearing off each other's clothes with the kind of abandon that comes after six weeks, three days, and twenty-three and a half hours of abstinence.

Our lustfest screeched to a halt, however, when a furry ball of yowling rage came burrowing between us like a nun at a high school dance.

What the heck do you two think you're doing?

Furious, I scooped her off the bed and frog-marched her back to the living room, where I plopped her on the sofa.

She gave me her patented Abandoned Orphan look, yowling at the top of her lungs.

Okay, go ahead. Break my heart! Desert me for that gluten-free gasbag! Leave me alone and lonely with nothing but your favorite throw pillow to claw to shreds—

I left her mid-yowl and raced back to the bedroom, shutting the door firmly behind me.

I was ready to hurl myself into Dickie's arms when I noticed an ugly scratch along one of them—a farewell gift from Prozac, no doubt.

"Omigosh. you're bleeding! Can I get you some Bactine?"

"No, no," he said, ignoring his arm and pulling me to him. "I'm fine. Now that you're here."

The flame of our lust, I must admit, had been slightly dampened by Prozac's dramatic entrance, but now we were building up another head of steam. Things were just about to shift into All Systems Go when we were assailed by a fresh batch of yowls from Pro, scratching wildly at the bedroom door.

Dickie sighed and rolled over onto his back.

"I don't think this is going to work, Jaine."

"You're telling me!"

That last bit of wisdom from Lance, who can hear everything through our paper-thin walls.

"Next time," Dickie said, "let's meet up at my place."

"Good idea."

Again, from Lance.

Dickie threw on his clothes and, after a quick peck on my cheek, made his way past a hissing Prozac out my front door.

"I may never speak to you again," I said to Prozac as I watched Dickie walk down the path to his car. "You're in big trouble, young lady. Big trouble."

She yawned in boredom.

Yeah, right. Whatever. Now let's have some tiramisu.

There was no denying it. My cat was spoiled rotten. If things were going to work with me and Dickie, I had to stop being such a patsy and show her who was boss.

From now on, things were going to be different. I was going to be a tough cookie, a stern taskmaster, a strict disciplinarian.

And my new Show Prozac Who's Boss regime would start that very night.

Right after I gave her just the teensiest slice of tiramisu.

YOU'VE GOT MAIL!

To: Jausten
From: Shoptillyoudrop
Subject: Exciting News!

Hi, sweetheart!

Hope all is well with you and your precious cat, Zoloft.

Exciting news here in Florida. Lydia Pinkus, beloved president of the Tampa Vistas Homeowners Association, is organizing a sculpture class—to be taught by a local sculptor and owner of one of Tampa's most prestigious art galleries. I'm always so impressed with the way Lydia finds such fascinating things for us to do.

I can't wait to broaden my artistic horizons with this fun and stimulating class!

I tried to talk Daddy into going, but he absolutely refuses.

XOXO,
Mom

To: Jausten
From: DaddyO
Subject: A Gift from the Gods

Dearest Lambchop—Your mom's been yammering all morning about some stupid sculpture class Lydia "The Battle-Ax" Pinkus is organizing.

That's one class I won't be going to. As I always say, a day without Lydia Pinkus is a gift from the gods.

Love 'n snuggles from,
DaddyO

PS. Guess what came in the mail? A discount coupon for a $5 haircut. Now *that's* something to get excited about! I think I'll give it a try.

To: Jausten
From: Shoptillyoudrop
Subject: Cheating on Harvy

Daddy just went off to get a discount haircut. I can't believe he's "cheating" on Harvy, the stylist who's been cutting our hair for the past fifteen years. Harvy always does such a lovely job. But you know Daddy. He can't resist a bargain.

XOXO,
Mom

PS. I only hope Harvy doesn't find out about Daddy's betrayal. I once went to Supercuts for an emergency trim while Harvy was on vacation, and it took him three months to forgive me. Every time I called for an appointment he claimed he was booked. It was sheer agony until he finally relented and agreed to see me.

To: Jausten
From: Shoptillyoudrop
Subject: The Worst Haircut Ever!

OMG! Daddy just came back from the discount hair salon with the worst haircut ever! Not only did they dye his hair an Eddie Munster jet black, they tortured the few remaining hairs on the top of his head so they're standing straight up. I swear, he looks like a balding porcupine.

Worst of all, the whole thing is glued together with a ghastly hair "wax" that smells like bad fish.

XOXO,
Mom

PS. Between the cut, the blowout, and the dye job, that $5 haircut wound up costing $125!

To: Jausten
From: DaddyO
Subject: The Best Haircut Ever!

Just got back from Big Al's discount hair salon with the best haircut ever. A Metrosexual Mohawk that takes at least ten years off my life. All the stylists at the salon said I look fantastic.

And you should've seen the looks I got on the way home. People couldn't take their eyes off me.

What's more, Big Al gave me a complimentary jar of his special styling wax. Mom says it smells like bad fish, but I don't know what she's talking about. It has a delightfully tangy aroma, very mild. In fact, I can hardly smell it.

Love 'n hugs,
From your very stylish
DaddyO

Connect with Us

Visit us online at
KensingtonBooks.com
to read more from your favorite authors, see books
by series, view reading group guides, and more.

Join us on social media

for sneak peeks, chances to win books and prize packs,
and to share your thoughts with other readers.

facebook.com/kensingtonpublishing
twitter.com/kensingtonbooks

Tell us what you think!

To share your thoughts, submit a review,
or sign up for our eNewsletters, please visit:
KensingtonBooks.com/TellUs.